DRAGONFLY

CARIN HART

For those of you who would watch as a distinguished mafia leader bloodied his hands in your honor—then immediately let him put them all over you...

FOREWORD

Thank you for checking out *Dragonfly*!

This is the third book in the ongoing **Deal with the Devil** series, and the first that features a member of the Libellula crime family. The hero in this book is the lead Dragonfly himself, Damien Libellula—forty years old, overprotective, and seemingly a gentleman... until you betray him or his Family and he can be *brutal*.

Savannah is the perfect heroine for him. A former goody-goody who came out of a four-year prison stint transformed, all she wants to do is see Damien dead. And when she tries, somehow she ends up standing in front of good old Judge Callihan as Damien decides that, instead of executing her, he'll *marry* her.

And since she goes along with it because she's sure she'll get the chance to finish the job, she becomes his wife—and the war between the manipulative mafia leader and the determined ex-con begins with a wedding night they'll both remember...

Dragonfly includes: murder; blackmail/forced marriage; forced proximity/captive romance; dubcon; prison/prison trauma (including SA in prison for the h); knives/stabbing/blood; knife play; unprotected sex; praise kink; spanking; guns; drugs; microchipping/tracking; counterfeiting; family abandonment; family planning (including a reversed vasectomy); prior suicidal ideation; questionable mental health; animal abuse (the kitty is okay, just sedated!); and the heroine stalking the hero for a change.

If all of that's something you feel comfortable reading, please enjoy!

xoxo,
Carin

Revenge List

PROLOGUE

GEORGIA

FIVE YEARS EARLIER

The bell over my shop's door tinkled, and my life as I knew it was over.

In Springfield, whether you live in the seedier parts of the city or the more suburban areas along the outer edge, you learn to be wary of a man in a suit—and not for the reason you might think. It's been a crime hotspot my entire life, and even if you do your best to avoid the gangs, the local mafias, the organized syndicates that rule the whole city, sometimes they find *you*.

These two don't give off the vibe that they're criminals. Still, something about how they move single-file down one of the narrow aisles that separate the cash wrap from the entrance has my greeting catching in my throat.

The one in front is a couple of inches taller than the other, and quite a few pounds heavier. He's light on his feet, though, and when he heads straight for me instead of looking around the store, any hope that he stopped by for a test booster or maybe a weight loss supplement dies a quick death.

Two years in business has trained me to offer any customer who walks into Healthy Habits by Georgia a customer service grin. Even if I stumble over my "what brings you in today" spiel, I can at least smile at him.

He doesn't smile back. Instead, pulling out a black wallet, flashing me a Springfield Police Department badge, he asks, "Miss Georgia Gayle?"

My heart just about stops beating.

Well, I wasn't wrong, was I? Cops. I've got *cops* in my store. Detectives, from the look of the suits, and they want *me*.

I'm not a fan of the police. Law enforcement makes me uncomfortable. With all the news stories about cops being just as bad as the gangsters that run Springfield—and about how crooked the SPD is in particular—whenever I see a uniform or a badge, I start convincing myself that I committed a shit ton of crimes and just conveniently forgot about them.

Why else would a pair of DTs be looking for me?

I could lie. I could pretend that—despite the name

on my sign—there's no Georgia here. Maybe I'd be better off acting like she's my boss and I'm some poor sales clerk who has no way of getting in contact with her.

I don't do any of that. Deep down, I'm a goody-goody. It's not that I want to help the SPD, but I hate getting into trouble. It goes back to being an anxious mess of an only child with a narc mother and a workaholic father who was rarely home, and with the misfortune to be born with this pathologic need not to piss people off.

You'd think that, at twenty-five and finally living happily on my own, I'd have gotten over that by now. Considering I gulp, struggling to keep my nervous smile in place as I nod, you'd be wrong.

"Hi. Yes. I'm Georgia. Can I help you?"

The taller detective glances at his partner. The second suit has straw-colored hair, mud-brown eyes, and a flat expression that only ramps up my anxiety.

Without a word, he reaches inside of his suit jacket. Pulling out a thick envelope, he passes it over to the taller—lead?—detective.

The taller detective has thinning brown hair, a dent in his chin, and a slight grin that might pass for friendly if he hadn't already stoically flashed his badge before. Rifling through the envelope in his hand, he pulls out a thin rectangular-shaped sheaf of paper.

"Yes, miss, you can. My name is Detective Chestnut.

This is Detective Lewis. We have a couple of questions for you. First, tell me... do you recognize this?"

He places it on my countertop, using his pointer finger to position it in front of me.

"Um. Yeah. This is one of my deposit slips."

"That's your signature, right?"

"Uh-huh."

"And this"—he turns the slip over—"you filled this out yourself?"

Chestnut taps the lines on the back of the deposit where I usually mark how many coins, how many singles, how many fives, tens, twenties, fifties, and hundreds I'd put into the deposit bag before I dropped it off inside of the Springfield Bank depository after closing.

I might own and run this business by myself, but I do my banking through the branch about two blocks away. All of the daily deposits go there, and I get any change I need for the drawer from one of the tellers.

"Yes. I'm the only employee here. I do everything myself."

The shorter detective—Lewis—nods as if that was all he needs to hear. Leaving the other cop at my cash wrap, he slips away.

Chestnut clears his throat, drawing my attention back to him. "Miss Gayle, are you aware that there is currently an outfit in Springfield that's pushing counterfeit bills through small, locally-owned businesses?"

"I... no. I had no idea."

The last lingering hint of his earlier smile fades. Dipping into the envelope again, he pulls out a stack of deposit slips at least half an inch thick. He plops them on top of the first one.

"Each deposit slip here has your account number and signature on it," he says needlessly before dropping the bomb on me: "And each one of these was marked as coming from a bag that contained at least one counterfeit bill."

Holy shit. There's gotta be at least fifty slips there. Even if they were each only representing a bad twenty, I'm looking at a good thousand dollars loss in front of me.

I feel queasy. Gripping the edge of the counter, I peer up at him. "My store was hit?"

"If it was only one or two deposits, I could believe it was just bad luck. But when our sting operation caught all of these"—Chestnut uses his thumb to fan out the stack of deposit slips—"in just one quarter, our task force came to a different conclusion."

And?

Seconds away from panicking, I wait for him to tell me what it is. Because, I'm sorry, I'm so confused. The suit made me nervous; the idea that my bank account is screwed-up has my stomach going tight.

No. There's gotta be some mistake. Something... something's wrong. I've done the training. I have the counterfeit pen right next to my register stand. When a customer gives me anything over a twenty for the drawer, I check all the markers to make sure it's real. And who even uses cash anymore? A good eighty percent of my sales are either debit or credit. This is impossible.

Seriously. There's no way he's telling me that I've been depositing fake money for *months*—

—only that's *exactly* what he's telling me, isn't it?

The bell over my shop's door tinkles again, and when Detective Lewis marches back into my store, he's not alone.

There are two more cops with him. One's a blonde woman with her hair pulled back in a low ponytail, the other a dark-haired man about my age with piercing blue eyes. In the back of my mind, I realize I've seen him patrolling on foot outside of my store more than a few times over the years.

There's something about being slapped in the face with a uniform that makes this seem so much more *real*. The suits had me nervous, but the uniforms... the badges pinned to their chests... the guns on their hips... holy shit. I think I'm going to pass out.

"Please, no," I say, my voice coming out strangled. "There has to be some mistake."

They don't seem to think so.

Detective Lewis nods at the male cop, gesturing toward me with a wag of his finger. The uniformed officer immediately eases around the side of the cash wrap, joining me behind the counter.

His nameplate says M. Burns. His undeniable smirk says that I'm in deep, deep shit.

A pair of handcuffs appear in his grip as if by magic. "Hands behind your back."

Even as I'm trying desperately to argue, to *understand*, I do what I'm told.

The bite of the metal around my wrist is a shock, but it only gets worse when Detective Lewis finally decides to speak up as Officer Burns starts maneuvering my stunned body away from the cash wrap.

"Georgia Gayle, you're under arrest for the charge of passing counterfeit currency. You have the right to remain silent. Anything you say can be used against you in a court of law..."

Revenge List

ONE
GHOST

SAVANNAH

I t took seven months for me to kill off Georgia
Gayle completely.

Georgia Gayle was an earnest twenty-five-
year-old brunette whose pride and joy was the vitamin
store she owned in downtown Springfield. She avoided
her parents the best she could, dreamed of going back
to school for a business degree, was between
boyfriends at the time, though she'd hoped the boy
who worked at the deli might ask her out for coffee.

Four years in the Madison Correctional Facility—
the minimum security prison I was trapped in until
they released me nine months ago—and the woman
who was marched into that hellhole was dead by the
time she was allowed out again.

Erasing my identity as best I could just made it so that the rest of the world knew she was long gone.

I changed my name. As a nod to who I was, I chose 'Savannah'. Trading my born-and-bred Springfield accent for a Southern drawl, I tacked on 'Montgomery' as my new last name when I got my first set of fake papers.

The brunette with hints of gold woven through her soft curls disappeared when I dyed my hair black. I tried out colored contacts, too, to really change my appearance, but like the nose job I couldn't afford, the dark brown contacts weren't worth the trouble. They dried the shit out of my eyes, and after two weeks of struggling with them and the stupid eye drops I pocketed from the drugstore, I had to be satisfied with the lighter shade instead.

Make-up helps. A little bit of contour changed the whole shape of my face until it became *Savannah*'s face. I lost twenty pounds in prison. I thought I'd put them back on once I was on the outside again, but when the choice is between paying rent in my shitty apartment or eating more than one quick meal a day, a roof over my head wins. Now my cheeks are sunken in instead of rosy and round, giving me a fittingly fox-like look.

After all, I lost everything when I got arrested. My store. My home. My *future...*

Georgia was already a ghost. Her parents disowned

her long before she was sentenced. Her friends? Gone. Her reputation? Shattered.

Her sanity?

Nonexistent.

Because of one man, I lost four fucking years of my life, plus any bit of *good* that was left in goody-goody Georgia Gayle.

Oh. Supposedly, I got lucky. That's what the judge told me. I didn't have any priors, and part of what makes counterfeiting a crime is the intent. The prosecutors needed to prove that I accepted those hundred dollar bills gleefully from the real crooks, putting them into my deposits so that they could circulate through the bank.

They couldn't. That's because I was a naive fucking idiot who never thought twice about the repeat meathead customers I'd get in my store, two, maybe three times a week for each of them, paying for their five-pound tubs of protein powder with cash that my counterfeit pen never flagged as fake. Just grateful to get the sale each time, it never dawned on me that they were giving me funny money—or that my shop was being used to funnel counterfeit bills for the Libellula Family.

Because that was precisely what was happening. Worse, it seems like I was the sacrificial lamb. One of the most powerful local mafias, the Libellula Family was untouchable—but I wasn't. For all the fake bills they passed then (and still do now), *I* was the one who got snagged because one bank clerk tried to be a hero and brought it to the higher-ups at the SPD.

Snitch. Even I knew better than to go up against the local mafias so it was no surprise to me that he was conveniently missing by the time I was being prosecuted. Once I heard the name Libellula getting thrown around, I kinda accepted he had to be dead for trying to rat out the counterfeiting ring.

Just like I was bound to be after my stint in prison.

I was looking at a possible twenty-year sentence. That's not even counting the fines. The ten grand they slapped me with is just more salt in the wound when you think about it, but considering some fines can go upward of a quarter-million dollars, it could've been so much worse.

Tell that to the new world I had to navigate in prison. The guards who looked the other way when it came to mistreatment and unfairness. The fellow inmates who sniffed out weakness like a great white tracking blood in the water. The depersonalization—the *dehumanization*—that happened inside...

I never expected to survive a prison stint. A minimum security prison—Club fucking Fed—might be for non-violent offenders or white collar criminals, but once it's lights out, a prison is a goddamn prison, and Georgia Gayle wasn't made for prison.

But Savannah Montgomery could be. And once I realized that I had to get through my sentence if only so that someone else could pay for crimes that were never mine, I would do it.

I made my revenge list my first year inside. The paper is worn now, with the same two bullet points on it, and I only recently got to put a check next to the first one.

Kill Georgia Gayle.

She's gone, and she's not coming back.

And if Savannah Montgomery has her way, it'll be the same for the second name on my list…

Because there was only one thought that kept me going during the four years after I got arrested, plus the months I've been out: get the man who ruined my life.

He has no idea who I am. He's not the one who came into my store to pass his gang's counterfeit bills through me, but that doesn't matter. As the head of the Libellula Family, his criminal enterprise ruined my life.

And I'm going to take his.

I'm going to kill Damien Libellula.

Revenge List

TWO
GONE

SAVANNAH

How to kill one of the most powerful, infamous, *dangerous* men in the city?

That's the question that kept me up at nights while I was in prison.

Well, no. I had plenty of other reasons to be awake well after lights out—the whispers, the worry, the quiet, all while praying my cellmate would fall asleep first...—but I distracted myself from my nightmares by plotting Damien's downfall.

Damien... you'd think that I'd want to distance myself from the head of the Libellula Family by calling him by his last name. In the beginning, I did. Making him the target for my rage was inevitable since all I really *want* to do is take down the gang that cost

Georgia her life. I'd go for Libellula himself, and like a house of fucking cards, his Family would topple down.

I'd cut the head off that snake. It doesn't matter that he didn't personally target me. Oh, no. He gives the orders, he runs the counterfeiting operation that gives his syndicate all the power, and he's the one I'll use to get my revenge.

Will it be easy? No. But I need it. I crave vengeance more than my freedom, and while Georgia was no killer, Savannah would be.

Once out, I got to work—and almost immediately realized I underestimated how hard it would be. While the head Dragonfly himself isn't a bogeyman like the Devil of Springfield, spoken of in whispers without having a visible presence around the city, just because I could *see* Libellula, that didn't mean I could get close to him.

He has bodyguards. Plenty of 'soldiers' that seem to flock to him wherever he goes. Cronies. Occasionally a woman, too, and since it's always the same young blonde, I figure it has to be his trophy wife.

Figure because, for all of my research on the man, he's as much a ghost as I am now.

Any and all information beyond his name and age is wiped. Unless you're a Dragonfly yourself, involved with his tight-knit crime family, there's nothing to learn about the man through simple online research.

Nope. If I wanted to get to know him enough to

take him down, I had to do a little reconnaissance myself.

That was a little easier. Once the last of my assets were released to me, I used every single penny to get the ball rolling on my new identity. I might hate Portia for turning our cellie arrangement into something that benefited her and her sense of entitlement, but she did pass along some of her contacts to me on the outside as a 'thank you' for four years of being her bitch.

With the new identity and the last six hundred bucks I had, I bought the shittiest beater that still ran that I could before I managed to upgrade last month. The rideshare company wouldn't hire an ex-con—even if it was only a misdemeanor on my record—but *Savannah* has a clean slate. No convictions. No traffic violations. I got the job and have spent every free moment I have either driving customers around Springfield for a paycheck—or obsessively stalking Damien Libellula.

That's when I started to call him *Damien*. From the shadows, from across the street, from the coffee shop opposite one of the gang-owned restaurants on the East End of Springfield, I watched him. I learned everything I could. I *studied* this man, and I began to think I knew him.

But I couldn't get close enough. Instead, I had to satisfy my lust for his blood by promising myself *soon*.

Soon, I would take the gun I bought at the local pawn shop and aim it dead at him.

Soon, I would look him in his pale blue eyes and tell him that he deserves this for what he did to me.

Soon, I would make him realize that his fancy suits and his annoyingly distinguished features and handsome face won't do a single fucking thing to sway me from my plan.

From my *revenge*.

Soon, I would kill him—and then, maybe, I can finally move on.

I have to. When it seemed so much easier just to eat a bullet myself, I pushed past the darkness and went to the Springfield Animal Shelter. It might not seem fair to put the weight of my shattered mental health on the back of a three-year-old rescue cat named Orion, but I need something to live for that isn't just vengeance on a man who has no idea I ever existed.

Who still has no clue after four months of stalking him…

I refuse to hide in the shadows when I pull my trigger. I want him to know why I decided he was the one who needed to sacrifice his life for ruining mine. That's easier said than done, though, especially since he's always protected when he's moving around the city.

And when he isn't? Mr. Dragonfly is locked up tight in a large three-floor *manor* that sits in the middle of a street full of overcrowded apartment buildings that stretch high to the sky. A white building that stands out against the brick and the grime, I know it's on purpose, too. In the years I was in prison, he got even *more* powerful. Damien is untouchable and unrepentant, and the fact that he knocked down a complex that housed at least fifty families to build a manor for his own proves that.

It was also his way of taunting any law enforcement in the city that might still be on the straight and narrow. A true 'you can't fucking get me' gesture, and everything I'd discovered since I've been out only shows that, while he's cocky, he's also *right*.

And I hate that almost as much as I hate him.

I ALWAYS KNOW WHEN I'M PICKING UP A DRAGONFLY FOR a passenger.

It's not the fact that they're almost always these brash blowhards who think they can treat me like shit because I'm a woman, and because I'm their driver. That helps—as does the visible dragonfly tattoo that every single member of the Libellula Family has on their forearms—but so does the *vibe* they give off.

Plus, you know, the fact that I've started to catalogue the ones I see having business with Damien... I've got a folder in my phone with names, pictures, every sort of intel that might help me get closer to the mafia leader.

I've seen this one around a lot, usually a few steps behind Damien. He's big and beefy and *tall*, so tall that

I can feel his knees dig into the back of my seat after he maneuvers his muscular body into my car. His hair is cut short to his scalp in a buzz cut that makes him seem even more intimidating, though he has a deceptively gentle voice as he murmurs a greeting to me while he closes the door behind him.

His name is Vincent or Vinnie or something like that. I've overheard Damien calling him 'Vin', and if I had to guess, he's one of Damien's bodyguards.

Peering in my rearview mirror, I can catch a glimpse of the weapon on his hip as he adjusts his position, spreading his legs so that he's not kneeing me any longer.

I smile at him—because while my gun might be stowed in my purse, a smile is just as much a weapon for a woman like me—and confirm that the address that came through the app is correct.

It's not too far. Because I need to kill two birds with one stone by taking passengers and making money the same time as I search the streets of Springfield for some sign of Damien—either walking around like he owns the city, or driving around in this flashy red car of his—I keep my app set to rides on the East End. For the right price, I'll go anywhere, but when he nods that I did have the correct destination, I'm not surprised he's heading to an office building in the heart of Dragonfly territory.

Maybe I'll get lucky and he'll be going to meet Damien. I've already done twelve local rides this morning, and I was getting ready to break for some fast food when I decided to pick up this guy. I consider it a waste of a day if I don't see Damien at least once so this would make it worth it.

There's got to be a pattern. A method to his afternoons, a way to plot where he might be in the evening. Odds are I'll never find a way to get to him inside of his protected manor, and I don't want to risk gunning for him when he's out in the open. That would be a suicide mission, and no matter what, I'm going to be the one who survives our confrontation.

I have to. I've got a cat who needs me.

It's been days since I last set eyes on the sophisticated mobster. Saturday night, I watched him walk out of an upscale Italian restaurant, that petite blonde hanging off his arm. The man in my back seat was with them, a silent shadow who followed them all the way to the parked car. He started it first, making sure it was safe, then climbed out and stepped aside to let the other two in.

I was in my car, idling in a small parking lot next to the bakery. When Damien and his date pulled out, I slipped into traffic behind them, cursing when he brought her to his house.

I haven't seen him since. For all I know, they're still in there—and that doesn't help me at all, does it?

When I'm driving, I keep the radio tuned to a popular Top 40 station in Springfield. The volume's low so that I don't annoy my customers, but it's still enough background noise to drown out the thoughts bouncing around my brain.

Because it is low, though, I notice when one of my passengers is taking a call. Usually, I tune it out because it's not my business, but when it's a Dragonfly talking? I'm all-fucking-ears.

His voice is still way softer than I would expect as he talks into his phone.

"Hey, Lou. It's me. Yeah. I'm on my way. Yeah, I had to order a ride because the boss was busy." He pauses, and from the moment he says 'boss', I'm already way more invested than I should be. "My truck? Nah. I let Kieran borrow it a couple of days ago."

Kieran? Why does that name sound familiar? He's gotta be one of the gangsters that I've seen meeting with Damien.

The person on the other end of the phone must say something because it's about a minute or so before my passenger speaks up again.

"I don't fucking know what's going through that kid's head. I heard a rumor his ex is back in town and he's trying to make it work with her... right. Yeah. I remember how he got five leaves the summer she left him... yup. *Five.* I've told Damien he's too rabid to be let loose, but you know how the boss is. He likes his enforcers feral."

Leaves? Enforcers? I can only guess what they're talking about, but since I don't know for sure, that's just another reminder that no matter how long I've been stalking Damien Libellula, there's still so much I'm missing about his job and his life.

"Anyway," continues the passenger, "until he gives me my truck back, I've got to find a way to get where I'm going... yeah. I know I'm running late, but I'm not that far out and—*hey*!" He raises his voice, and I just know he's talking to me before he snaps, "Watch it!"

Huh?

Fuck!

I slam on my brakes just in time to miss smashing into the back of the car in front of me.

That was my fault. So distracted by the Dragonfly's conversation, I didn't notice that the light had turned red. The SUV in front of me had already stopped, and if it wasn't for my passenger shouting to catch my attention, I would've hit it.

Luckily, I don't, though my car jerks as I stop short. He curses under his breath as he pushes against his seatbelt before falling back in his seat. My own belt cuts into my neck. I hear a *thud* and know that my purse tipped behind me, falling from the center console where I had kept it and into the backseat, spilling half of its contents on the floor.

My heart fluttering in my chest, I turn my head in time to see that the big guy has bent over, already shoveling all my shit back into my purse.

"Oh my God. I'm so sorry."

"It's fine," he says gruffly. "No harm done."

Considering he's not my target, I'm glad. "Still. I

should probably get my brakes checked. They didn't respond the first time until I had to jam down on them."

It's a likely excuse. My car is at least twenty years old. It runs well enough to be a rideshare car, but it's obviously seen better days, and he agrees.

"Yeah. I noticed."

"You don't have to do that. I'll clean that up."

He pauses, glancing over at me. "You sure? I'm almost done."

Right, and if he keeps digging, odds are he might notice my gun sooner or later. "I'm sure. Thanks anyway. Besides, look. The light's green now and your destination is only two blocks away."

As I turn and start moving the car forward, he straightens up in his seat for a moment before I see him lean down again. Figuring he's the type of guy who can't leave well enough alone, he adjusts my purse so that it's not on its side anymore. Probably so nothing else falls out.

He never returns to his phone call. He must've disconnected it when I almost crashed, or maybe the other caller is just waiting for him to get back on the line. Either way, the rest of the car ride is silent until I pull up in front of his destination.

I'm not surprised when he climbs out of the car without even a 'take care'. Honestly, so long as he pays for the ride, it doesn't matter. I'm annoyed with myself for the near-accident, and even more frustrated when the big guy goes inside of the building with no sign that Damien Libellula is near.

Just in case, I decide to take a spin around the block. There's a parking lot behind the large building. Damien's flashy red car—with the vanity plate **DRGNFLY**—is unmistakable. I'll feel better if I check to see if it's there.

And if it is...

Once I've turned the first corner, giving me a line into the lot, I pull over again. Reaching into the back, I gather up my purse. Part of me wants to go through it just to organize it after my passenger threw everything back in, while the other part won't feel at ease until I know I have my gun in case the opportunity to take out Damien reveals itself.

I now own an inky-black Glock G43X. It's a subcompact gun, a real pocket pistol perfect for concealed carry. I don't have a permit, obviously, and I got it for two hundred bucks at a pawn shop that only cared if I had the cash for it. It weighs about a pound and a half loaded and usually sinks to the bottom of my purse.

That's why I'm not too worried when I don't see it right away. Beneath the mountain of receipts, scraps of paper with notes, my sunglasses, some tampons, my wallet, and the loose cough drops I keep in my bag, it could be buried all the way at the bottom. Only... it's not.

Panic wells up in me. Dumping every single thing

out of my purse onto the passenger seat, I go through it all, searching for the gun.

Nothing.

Okay. Calm down. My shit spilled. I almost rear-ended that SUV. Maybe my gun went under the seat. I unfasten the seatbelt before diving into the back, frantically shoving my hands under the passenger seat.

When I don't find it, I grab my phone. Using the flashlight, I hope it'll wink off the dark enclosure.

Still nothing, and I have to admit what I knew from the moment I emptied my bag.

My gun is *gone*.

Revenge List

THREE
MINE

DAMIEN

Something I've learned over the years is how easily a perfectly cooked rib-eye steak and a nice Malbec can blunt the murderous edges of even the most ruthless of gangsters.

My Family owns Il Sogno, an upscale ristorante in the heart of Dragonfly territory on the East End. Whenever I meet with the head of the Sinners Syndicate, we alternate between his turf and mine. Tonight it was my turn to host, and the staff didn't disappoint. Dinner was delicious as usual.

Company was better than I expected, too.

Lincoln leans back into his seat, legs spread as one hand sprawls out lazily on the tabletop. The other is hidden beneath it, no doubt on the Sig Sauer that is his constant companion. His dark eyes aren't as narrowed and suspicious as they usually are, though I'm not fooled. The Devil of Springfield will never be truly relaxed when he's the only Sinner visiting his old friend turned years-long rival.

Smart man.

Technically speaking, we have a truce. My counterpart on the West Side agreed to it last summer, nearly nine months ago, but we're both very aware that he was manipulated into giving me what I wanted.

Holding his beloved bride at gunpoint while I suggested the Sinners Syndicate join up with my Family might have been a little... much, but when the safety of my *family* is on the line, there isn't any length I won't go to to protect those I care about. Proving that my old friend still thought similarly enough to me, Lincoln gave me what I wanted in order to save his wife.

Ava Crewes was never in any danger. I might be jealous of what Lincoln found in his Saint Ava—the woman he was willing to sacrifice everything for—but she was just another pawn in the game of chess I've been playing for more than a decade now.

From the moment I formed the Libellula Family, marking the East End of this seedy city as our turf, there's only one thing I've ever wanted: security and safety for anyone who shares my surname. Money provided that. So did loyalty from every soul branded with a dragonfly. Joining up with Lincoln and his aptly named Sinners? To combine our might and block any threats to our power and control, I'd do worse than rekindle the friendship we once had.

So long as I never forget for a moment that he's visualizing hacking my head off the stump of my neck before twisting it with his bare hands the rest of the way as he's currently slicing into his steak with a flat expression, that is... and since it's been nine months and Lincoln isn't any closer to forgiving me for using his wife as leverage to get what I wanted, I *haven't*.

Still, we fake it. Because if I'm fanatical about protecting those under my care, that's at least one thing I still have in common with Lincoln. Especially now that Ava is only months away from giving birth to Lincoln's child, nothing will keep him from stamping out any and all threats. If he really thought I'd go after *his* family, I'd be eating his Sig Sauer right now instead of dipping my spoon into the tiramisu in front of me while Lincoln watches me enjoy my dessert.

He snorts. "Any day now, Damien. I get why you insist on these monthly meets to check in, but I'd like to get back home to my wife before my kid's in fucking college."

Considering his wife is still pregnant, that would be quite a feat if I kept him that long. Point taken all the same.

"I thought bad news might be easier to swallow with something sweet," I tell him. "Not my fault you passed on dessert."

His brow furrows. "The fuck you mean, bad news?

Don't tell me you made me sit through a whole meal talking bullshit about numbers and how the Breeze business in the Playground is doing only for you to drop this on me now." A rough sigh as he shifts in his seat. "Lay it on me. Is it Eclipse? Because I told you last month, I can handle Breeze as long as the cops keep their noses out of my business. But that newer shit is killing kids. I won't have that in my club."

Breeze started out as a hopped-up version of E, but some of our suppliers discovered that if you cut it with some other pharmaceuticals, it turns into a newer, stronger formula we call Eclipse. It's a moneymaker— and a recent problem.

I lower my spoon, letting it clink against the bottom of the glass bowl holding my dessert. "Our Eclipse is clean."

"Tell that to the three DBs Rolls and his guys have had to do clean-up duty on since the new year started."

I didn't say that there hasn't been a problem with somebody's supply. I said that *our* Eclipse is clean. It has to be. A dead body can't buy more drugs or line my pockets with their money.

As ever, I want addicts, not corpses.

I don't waste my breath explaining that to Lincoln. One of the reasons we went our separate ways all those years ago was because we couldn't agree on how to make crime pay for us. Back then, he was a brawler who fought for money, and I started out as a dealer for the guy who ran our gang. He went guns. I went drugs.

We've both branched out since then, but even now, I'm sure he thinks I only wanted a truce so I could push my product on his turf.

And while, yes, of course that's true... there's more to it than that.

I want the security having more men at my back can provide, and if that means certain... concessions, I'll do what I have to.

Lifting my hand, I snap my finger. Waiting for the signal, Christopher rises up from his table, striding over to mine while carrying the small briefcase he'd kept on the floor beneath his seat.

Lincoln doesn't blink as Christopher appears. Truce or no truce, he has to know that I have a handful of my men nearby to serve as any backup I might need—

—just like I spotted at least four Sinners conveniently positioned around the restaurant as I joined Lincoln at the table about an hour ago, barely touching their meals now.

Christopher is a loyal soldier. Too gangly and thin to be muscle, and too sensitive to do any wet work, I only took him on because he's Genevieve's closest friend. Honestly, he's her *only* friend. They met when they were eight in one of Gen's ballet classes, and my sister earned his loyalty for life when she started to beat the shit out of anyone who made fun of him for wanting to be a dancer like her. By the time he was eighteen, he could do fouetté turns like a beast, organize distribution, and even handle my calendar all while keeping a surreptitious eye on Gen for me.

I might not have wanted to hire him, but for the last seven years, he's made my life easier. I have plenty of enforcers. I only have one Christopher, and my assistant hands me the briefcase before vanishing into the shadows of the restaurant.

Flipping open the case, I remove the black gun.

Guns are Lincoln's specialty. He's instantly alert.

"Where did you get this?"

I could answer him. Lincoln wouldn't bat an eye if I mentioned that one of my enforcers had lent his truck to another, had to order a ride on his phone two nights ago, and he just so happened to notice the gun when it fell out of the young driver's purse. That he took it because the mark on the bottom caught his eye, but that he specifically chose her to be his driver because I asked him to...because I know exactly who she is even if I had no idea that she had an illegal gun on her—or *why* she would.

I could answer Lincoln...

I don't.

"It doesn't matter," is what I say instead.

"Fuck that, Damien. You can't insist on this Goddamn truce, drop this in my lap, then clam up when I ask you a question."

I can't?

Without a word, I purposely glance down at Lincoln's arm. With the heat in the restaurant cranked up high, he removed his suit jacket, tossing it on the back of the seat behind him. Sometime between the salads being served and the steaks being brought out, he rolled up the sleeves of his dress shirt, leaving the inked rosary wrapping his meaty forearm on display.

When I first met Lincoln Crewes fifteen years ago, the kid was a devout Catholic. That lasted until about the time he killed Skittery after the old junkie threatened Ava, but he didn't have that rosary back then. It's a more recent addition—he probably got it during the years following Heather Valiant's tragic death when Lincoln and his Sinners firmly became our rivals—and it's amused me since the moment I first saw it a few months ago.

A murderer who curses like a sailor, worships the woman he considers a saint, makes his money from selling death and women... and he wears a rosary on his arm as he blasphemes.

It's the small things in life that make me smile, and I would've if I wasn't holding a gun with an unfamiliar symbol on it.

Before I can show Lincoln that, he shrugs. "Maybe it's legit. Not every gun in Springfield has to come through me—"

Sighing, I angle the gun so that he can see what's been etched into the butt of the handle.

Every illegitimate gun that makes its way through Springfield has Devil's mark. Even if he buys from Valdez or Reno, once the serial numbers are filed off, the devil horns and tail are engraved somewhere on the weapon.

So why the fuck does this Glock have a *snowflake* etched instead?

I don't know, and I've spent more than a week searching for answers about this mark even before I found it on a confiscated weapon. Now that I've seen it on a gun, things have gotten a little more complicated —and it's Lincoln's turn to understand that.

His hand snatches out to grab it.

I disappear it back into the case before he can. "My enforcer found it. To show I'm not freezing you out, I'm letting you know, but it belongs to the Dragonflies now. Understand?"

A muscle tics in his jaw. "Keep the gun if that's what you want. I saw enough. A snowflake... who the fuck does *that* belong to?"

If I knew, I would've dealt with this situation myself before bringing it up to him. "I thought you could answer that for me. In the spirit of our truce. Remember, it's us against them now."

"Yeah? Well, that's nothing I've ever seen before—" He pauses, eyes flashing angrily. "Wait. What are you saying?" The hand on the table flexes, tugging on the tablecloth. "Is some other operation trying to move in our turf?"

Just for this meet, I placed the gun Vin took off the girl in the briefcase where I can keep tabs on it. As for what I have in the pocket of my suit jacket...

I reach inside, pulling out one of the baggies that's found its way through my properties. The Dragonflies might not have a trademark nightclub like the Devil's Playground on the West Side, but we own two concert halls, three clubs, countless restaurants, twelve bars, and more coffee shops than I can even think to number. That's not even mentioning all the businesses on our turf that we have a hand in, either.

If it was just some outside operation trying to give Lincoln and his boys a run for their money by bringing guns into Springfield, that would be fine. But once I discovered that someone else thinks they can cut into *my* business...

I show Lincoln the baggie full of white crystals, knowing he'd recognize it as the dirty Eclipse giving him trouble.

Tossing it onto the table, I tap the plastic, drawing his attention to the stamp on it.

It's a motherfucking snowflake.

Leaning back into my seat, I cross my arms over my chest, comforted by the weight of my stiletto's sheath and holster tucked beneath my pit.

Meeting the stunned look on Lincoln's face, I cock my head. "You tell me."

HE CAN'T, AND THAT PISSES ME OFF AS MUCH AS IT does him.

I don't like to get angry. Bad things happen when I lose my cool, but knowing that there's some upstart out there who thinks they can push their drugs through my city *and* run their guns past Lincoln? It's close.

We spend the rest of the meal trading intel. Lincoln vows that he'll have at least a name for the syndicate behind the snowflake within twenty-four hours; with his genius tech guy, Tanner, on the payroll, I don't doubt it. Then, when I can tell I've kept him from his pregnant wife long enough, we head out together as though half the restaurant didn't get up to leave when we did.

Lincoln has a personal driver. Years ago, Luca St. James was the getaway driver for a small-time burglary trio in Hamilton, the next state over. When their last job went south, he hopped in his car and headed right to Springfield, figuring he could get lost in the big city.

He didn't. He had a run-in with a couple of Sinners almost immediately, and while my intel is good, it's not infallible. I don't know how he managed to not only talk his way into joining Lincoln's syndicate, but also getting the gig of driving the Devil of Springfield around the city. He did, though, and he's been working for Lincoln ever since.

I can't do it. And maybe it's my control issues manifesting in a whole other way, but if I'm in a car? I'm going to be the one behind the wheel.

That doesn't mean I'm about to climb into my vehicle

without checking it over first. Vin is paranoid enough that he'll always hop in my car to see if it'll explode on me, but there's a difference between being paranoid and cautious. A cautious man who makes it to forty in a hard life knows precisely how to look for signs of tampering without having to open the car first—and that's exactly what I do.

Vin is at home with Genevieve tonight. I make sure Christopher leaves safely with his boyfriend du jour, then slip into my driver's seat. Only then, under the pretense of checking my rearview mirror, do I search for my shadow.

The ugly, banged-up, dark blue four-seater is parked along Verona Avenue, about six spots behind mine. Even though it's dusk, the setting sun playing tricks on me, I see the silhouette in the front seat and smile.

It's *her*.

How she thinks I don't notice that she's been following me around Springfield, I've got no clue. The ancient car might have been enough to escape my notice, but the first time I caught a glimpse of her out of the corner of my eye, I knew I'd never forget that face.

She's stunning. With hair as black as mine without any of the silver, and pretty light brown eyes that always seem to be watching me unblinkingly, she'd probably have an easier time passing as my sister than Genevieve does. My attraction to her, though... the way she has my cock twitching is nothing like the deep affection I have for Gen.

Her face is narrow and thin, her features sharp. I've seen her in a sundress, in jeans, in a pair of baggy sweatpants with her hair pulled on top of her head in a messy bun. She's worn a baseball cap, a floppy hat, and sunglasses that conceal her stare. It doesn't matter. I recognize her anywhere, and though I'm too busy for a relationship, the first time I saw her, I thought about taking her home for the night.

Then I realized she was stalking me and, instead of making a move on her, I've spent months waiting to see what it is she wants with me.

I'm used to women throwing themselves at my feet. In Springfield, the name Libellula means something—and I'm not referring to its literal translation of 'drag-onfly'. Women in this city think that, if they fuck me, they'll get a taste of my wealth.

My infamy.

My *power*.

Sorry, but no. If they fuck me, they get a night to remember, but that's about all. I haven't had a real rela-tionship in nearly four years, and even that only lasted eight months before she was pushing for a kid to tie me to her for life.

So I keep all my tête-à-têtes to one-night stands in a hotel my Family has a stake in, all the while ignoring how envious I am of Lincoln, who gets to return home to a wife who adores him every night.

I'm jealous, but realistic. Even I know that that kind of life isn't meant for me. At least I already have my Family.

Still, I can't deny that this woman has me intrigued, and even though I know I shouldn't pay her any mind, I didn't get to where I am by ignoring my instincts.

And when one of my soldiers lucked on ordering a ride last month and she was the driver, I figured it couldn't hurt to do just a little digging into who she might be.

The app gave the driver's name as Savannah Montgomery, but if that isn't the fakest shit I've ever heard, I don't know what is. She's good, though, I'll give her that. At first glance, the identity passes all tests.

But I've been in organized crime my whole life. First, when I watched my old man work for his crew before he was just another statistic. Then, when I followed in his shoes, working for Gunner while plotting my way into creating a Family of my own.

By the time I was thirty, I'd done just that. I'd taken over half of Springfield, creating a tight-knit group of men loyal to me. To the dragonfly. Whether they were soldiers, enforcers, underbosses, or lieutenants, they were *mine*. They do what they're told, and those who betray me, do so only once.

She's a mystery. An enigma. The shadow that I haven't been able to shake in months, though I can't say for sure that I've really tried.

But most of all? She'll be mine, too.
She just doesn't know it yet.

Revenge List

FOUR
REVENGE

SAVANNAH

I need a new weapon.

In Springfield, it's a lot easier to get your hands on a gun than it probably should be. That's what happens when one of the local mafias—in this case, the Sinners Syndicate—is known for gunrunning, and they want to make as much profit off of them as possible.

For the right price, you can buy one without jumping through the hoops of getting a permit, showing ID, and getting your fingerprints done. And when your cellmate tells you about a guy named Antonio who runs a pawn shop that's pretty reasonable, you can have it the same day.

Unless he's sold out.

Antonio switches the toothpick from one corner of

his mouth to the next. "Sorry, sweetheart. I've been cleaned out."

"What?" When I was here last, he had a whole back room full of guns for me to choose from. "All of them?"

"'Fraid so. I had a big buyer come through just the other day, and believe me when I say he ain't the kind of customer you refuse service to, if you get my drift."

Damien.

How much do you want to bet fucking *Damien* sent his guys around to buy up the guns? The Dragonflies don't deal in the gun trade, but it seems that every one of the gangsters I've seen has a gun on his hip.

Except for their leader, that is.

That makes sense. When he's surrounded by armed goons, he doesn't need to show off that he carries, too. Doesn't mean he's defenseless. Damien's preferred weapon is this thin knife he tucks inside of a leather holster hidden beneath his suit jacket.

I could get a knife, too. Antonio's got plenty. But when I need a little bit of space if I hope to survive our confrontation, I can't get close enough to stab him. I need the gun, but it looks like I'm shit out of luck for now.

Swallowing my frustration, I lean against the glass case. I use my arms to push up my tits, hoping that the free peek might be enough to jog his memory until he suddenly remembers he has a couple hidden behind his counter.

When all he does is stare down my shirt, I give him

a tiny smile. "So when should I come back, see if you got a shipment?"

He shrugs, eyes still glued to my chest. "Dunno. Week, maybe two. But if you're in a rush, you can always check out the West Side. Most guns come in through there."

Yeah. I guess I could. "Thanks."

"Don't mention it." Finally remembering there's more to me than a pair of boobs, Antonio glances up to meet my eyes and nods. "Watcha need it for anyway? Protection?"

"You could say that."

"Good girl like you, maybe Springfield's too hard of a place. Maybe you need to go back South."

Huh. It's nice to know that my affected drawl is still working.

"Maybe you're right," I lie. "But I came here because I have a job to do. I can't leave until I finish it."

"Yeah? Well, good luck."

I push away from the glass case. "Thanks."

I'll need it.

I DON'T HAVE A GUN, THOUGH I DO HAVE A NEW PICK-UP.

Who knows? Maybe luck's a little on my side tonight because, when I arrive to get my passenger, I see it's the same big guy who was in my ride when my gun went missing.

I want to ask him. I want to know if he saw the weapon, or if—like I suspect—he's responsible for it vanishing. I've gone through the whole vehicle at least four more times since the other day and it's nowhere to be found. Since I'm absolutely sure I had it in my purse before this Vin guy accepted my ride, it only makes sense that he has to know what happened to it.

I never get the chance. After he nods at me, as though he recognized me as the driver who had taken him to the office building the other day, he immediately takes out his phone. I just manage to confirm his destination is Il Sogno, one of the Dragonflies' properties, before he's got his phone to his ear.

"Hey. Yeah. I'm on my way." He pauses, then adds, "Yup. Kieran's still got my truck. Wait... what do you mean you saw it parked in front of the laundromat?" The big guy grumbles, and I'm glad I'm not the one he's making that noise out. "He said he had shit to do this week on the West Side. No, I don't know what it was, but if Kieran's back, I want my truck."

He lets the person on the other end of the phone speak some more, then says, "I'll let the boss know there's been a change of— what the fuck do you mean he knows?" He slaps the empty seat next to him. "Shit. I knew that kid was a loose cannon. Alright. You stay at the office. I'll see if I can catch up to Damien."

My ears perk up.

Damien.

My passenger finishes his call, then clears his

throat, trying to catch my attention despite the fact I've been listening intently to his entire conversation.

"Hey, uh... change of plans. Instead of Il Sogno, can you drop me off at Springfield Wash? The one on Main. I'll double your tip if you do."

Shit. To get a chance to see what Damien Libellula is up to right now, I'd wipe the ride clean. But since that might be pretty suspicious, I just say, "Sure," and update the address in my maps app.

The Springfield Wash off of Main is part of a strip mall with the row of businesses facing out and the parking lot built behind the strip. There's only one way in to the parking lot, but when I put my blinker on to turn into it, my passenger clears his throat again.

"The front's fine," he tells me, pointing at an empty spot in front of the parking meter. "You can let me out here."

Damn it. I was hoping to see if the flashy red car made it to the lot first or if we did.

"Sure thing," I answer, flicking the blinker off before pulling into the empty spot.

This time, I get a muttered 'thanks' as he climbs out of his car. I see him bee-line right for this pricy-looking truck that's a better fit for a man his size. He shakes his head, pats the bumper, then strides purposely toward the laundromat's front door.

Only after he slips inside do I kill the engine on my car. I figure I have five, ten minutes before some nosy meter maid comes by and sees that I didn't put any time into the parking meter. That should be more than enough time to go on foot, peeking around the edge of the last building near the entrance, searching for Damien.

And if I see him? I don't have a gun. I can't do shit about it.

But hell if I'm not curious to know about what's going down at Springfield Wash tonight.

THEY SAY CURIOSITY KILLED THE CAT, AND WHILE ORION is probably napping away peacefully in the fluffy cat bed I bought for him, I'm regretting tonight's snooping.

I knew that Damien is the head of the Libellula Family. I knew that he's a fucking mobster, and that the gangs in Springfield are a real threat. The guns aren't just fashion accessories. They're real, and these men are dangerous.

But what I saw...

Shit. I hope the girl's okay. That's all I can think about as I slide into my car, trying to calm my racing heart. I doubt she is. Even from the spot where I was standing near the entrance, I could see the way her head lolled, the blood covering her face, and now I knew something bad had gone down in the backroom of the laundromat.

I hadn't expected to walk in on that. I didn't even see the girl or the handsome blond man clutching her tightly to his chest at first. My attention was focused solely on Damien, but only when he started to talk to the other man did I realize he was waiting for them just outside the back door.

I'm pretty sure he saw me, too. Damien, and the blond. My damn curiosity got the better of me, and instead of backtracking before I could be caught, I inched closer, glaring at Damien, hating him even more on behalf of the poor unconscious girl the other man was holding.

Something happened in there. Something bad.

And there I was, without my weapon, and the blond man glaring at me as if *I* was the one who hurt the woman in his arms...

This doesn't have anything to do with me. Considering Damien was waiting outside the exit when the man muscled his way out, a gun in his hand as though he was prepared to blow away anyone who tried to stop him, I'm not sure he does, either. But he sticks around, talking to the other guy, while I walk back over to my car.

Part of me wants to stick around. The other part wants to wash my hands of what I saw.

One thing for sure: I can't even imagine calling the cops about this. They fucked me over when I went to prison, and it's not like they'll give a shit when most of the police force is paid off by Damien.

Watching the entrance to the parking lot in my rearview mirror, I'm still thinking about what I should do when another car turns the corner. It's a long car, black and shiny, taking the turn so quickly and so tightly, it's like it's being driven by a Nascar driver or something.

If I thought I was curious before, that's nothing compared to now. Sinking down in my seat, I watch, and I wait to see what's going to happen next.

I'm actually quite surprised when, within minutes, it's Damien's flashy red car that turns out of the exit and onto Main Street.

My hand on the ignition, I'm prepared to follow behind him when the most unexpected thing happens.

The red car pulls up alongside me.

My head swivels before I can think better of it, and there's Damien, those pale blue eyes piercing right through to my fucking soul as he stares dead at me. His inky-black hair is combed over perfectly, that grey streak near the front enough to make him appear distinguished and sophisticated instead of the criminal I know he is. Even though I hate him, I can't deny he's attractive despite having that whole 'older' guy thing going on.

This close, he's even *more* attractive, damn it.

He doesn't roll down his window. Neither do I. His lips quirk just enough to make my heart skip a beat before his car disappears down the street.

I watch him go, curious and confused when he makes a sharp left, parking his car along the inside of a wide alley that exists between a gym and a bank, both closed for the evening.

I wait two minutes to see if he's going to back out and continue on his way. In my rearview mirror, I catch sight of that long black car from before leaving the back of the strip mall. Right behind that car, there's a plain, nondescript black one. They both slip into traffic and disappear without paying any attention to Damien's car.

But if he's not parked over there, waiting for one of those cars, then what the hell is he doing?

My hand lands on my inner door handle. It wouldn't hurt for me to take a walk over there and get a peek, right? In the name of knowing what Damien is up to at any given moment, I have to go look.

I don't know what it is exactly that I expect to find, but I can tell you one thing: it's not Damien Libellula standing outside of his car by himself, leaning against the hood, legs crossed at the ankle, arms crossed over his chest while showing off his lean, toned body.

I had only planned on inching up to the edge of the corner, spying where he couldn't see me—but that was before I realized that he'd angled himself so that he'd catch me doing just that.

I freeze, and before I can turn tail and dash back to my car, he nods at me.

"I've been waiting for you." He uses his head to gesture for me to come closer. "Step inside. Let's have a chat."

This is a bad idea. A bad, bad idea. I'm caught, and I need to put some distance between us before I do something I'll regret.

But, fuck. I've waited months to confront this man, to unload all of my grief and anger and anxiety, to let him know he's the only one to blame for ruining my life... and it might be a fucking awful idea, but that doesn't stop me from pushing off from the brick wall and, with my head held high instead of cowering in front of the mafia leader, stalking over to him.

He's pleased, and I have to resist the urge to claw my nails down his perfectly tanned face.

"I was wondering if you were going to finally approach me, Savannah. I'm so glad you have."

What the—

Forget the faux pleasantries this murderous bastard has going on.

My name. Well, my *new* name, but still. He knows my *name*.

How does he know my name?

Revenge List

FIVE
PROPOSAL

SAVANNAH

My hands flex on their own, and he notices. Something tells me that this man notices *everything*.

Before I can find the words to demand he tell me how he knows who the hell I am, Damien pulls out something from behind him, lifting it up so I can see it as he says, "Wishing you had this?"

Screw knowing my name. I can deal with that. But when I see him holding my *Glock*...

"How did you get that?"

"No, my dear. The question is where did *you* get this?"

For some reason, he taps the butt of the gun, drawing my attention to the white snowflake that's on the bottom, then shifts just enough to toss *my* gun through the open window of his car.

No.

Well, he's not going to give me it back. That much is clear. So is the fact that this wasn't coincidental at all. He drove down this alley, setting the perfect trap for me, and now he's confronting me.

Good luck. He wants to know where I got my gun from?

I jut out my chin. "Screw you."

Amusement dances in his pale blue eyes. "Very well. I have men working on tracing it. You could've helped me out, but I'm not going to force you to do anything you don't want to." He chuckles softly. "Though if you're offering, I'd be happy to oblige."

My snort comes out before I can swallow it back. Pointedly ignoring his come-on, I scoff as I say, "Yeah, right. You? Forcing people to do shit... isn't that, like, your whole thing?"

He tilts his head toward me as if conceding my point. "True enough. In that case, I assume you know who I am."

Mr. Hotshot in Springfield... doesn't everyone?

Still, I could lie. I could tell him I have no idea that he's one of the most powerful men in Springfield. But if he's figured out who my new identity is *and* somehow knows that that gun used to be mine, what else does he know?

Pick your battles, Savannah. Don't give away any more than you have to... but give away just enough.

"Damien Libellula," I admit. "A Dragonfly."

"*The* Dragonfly," he corrects. "And the man you've been watching for months now."

Shit. He *knows*.

I don't deny it. I don't tell him he's right, either. I just stare at him, folding my arms under my tits like I did at the pawn shop.

And just like Antonio, Damien's gaze flickers over my cleavage.

Fucking *men.*

He recovers quicker, though. I'll give him that. He forces his eyes to meet mine, a tiny crooked smile playing on his thin lips. "You want to tell me why?" He pauses for a moment. "Did one of my rivals put you up to it?"

"I have my own reasons," I retort, and if it comes out shorter than I meant it to, I can't help it. I've imagined this confrontation with Damien a thousand times, and I've had the upper hand in all of them because he had no idea who I was or that I was stalking him.

But he does, and that throws me off.

He cocks his head. "So you have been watching me. Interesting."

I shrug.

"I'm a very busy man, Savannah. I don't have time to play these games, and even if I did, I'm too old to waste that time. So why don't you just tell me what it is that you want from me, and we can both go on our merry ways since I'm sure you're not actually interested in screwing me after all. Hmm? What do you say?"

This fucking prick. He's *dismissing* me.

Oh, no. He's not getting rid of me that easily.

Looking him over, too angry to think straight, I don't see any gun on him. That doesn't mean I'm naive enough to believe that he isn't armed. I've watched him enough to know that he always is. A gun's not his first weapon of choice, though. Oh, no. Not Damien. He has—

—*his knife*.

He's right-handed so the holster he wears is on his left side. Everything I've learned about this man says he doesn't go anywhere without it.

And, suddenly, I know what I'm going to do.

"Give me my gun back," I purr, taking a step closer to him.

He arches an eyebrow. "Maybe I was wrong before. Alright. I'll bite. What will you give me if I do?"

A bullet to the skull.

I smile.

See, no one else is around. This area of Springfield closes early, while the nightlife will start picking up once the sun goes down. This... this might be the only chance I have.

And I'm going to take it.

"Whatever you want," I murmur huskily.

"Is that so?"

I move into him. So close, my breasts bump his chest. He doesn't step back. Almost as if on instinct, his hand snakes around my waist, landing on the small of my back.

His lips part.

My hand lands on his hip, stealing whatever it is he was about to say next. Slowly, as he dips his head, I trail my finger up his side. I make sure I reach beneath his suit jacket as I do, touching his dress shirt instead as his mouth brushes against my neck.

"I thought you'd make me work a little harder than this, Savannah," he murmurs—and that does it. The absolute smugness mixed with his almost *disappointment* that I would trade sex for my gun flips the switch inside of me, letting me know that I have the right idea about what I'm going to do next.

I wasn't trying to convince him to give me a gun I no longer needed. I just wanted Damien to let me close enough that I could do *this*.

I find the hilt of his knife. Before he can stop me, I yank it out of his holster while stepping back, putting enough space between us that I can swing my arm and stab him in the first spot I can reach.

It's not as easy as I'd hoped it would be. Either I didn't put enough force into it, or the material of his thick suit jacket blunted the knife's edge, because it doesn't go in smoothly. I have to force it, and by the time I've gotten it most of the way in, it dawns on me what I just did.

I *stabbed* Damien Libellula. Not in the heart, either, or the chest where I might've actually accomplished what I set out to do. Oh, no. In my rage-fueled impulsiveness, I got him in the side, and apart from hissing out a curse, he doesn't fucking react at all.

I sure the hell do.

I thought I could do this. To get my revenge... I thought I could kill him. Maybe if I had my gun, I could've, but the way the knife *squelched* as I stabbed him... I think I'm going to hurl. I'm probably going to die. I always knew that, if I fucked up my one chance to get to him, I had to do the job right.

But I didn't. Damien is bowed over, staring at the knife in his side, but he doesn't drop. He didn't even scream. He's just sighing now, and I take that as my cue to get the fuck out of here.

I'm in over my head. I know it, and there's nothing I can do but hope like hell I can get to my car, get my cat, and get the hell out of Springfield while I can.

It's a plan. A good plan. My revenge can wait, but only if I can get out of this mess—

I slam into as hard as a brick wall with only the tiniest bit of give to it. I'd barely even torn out of the alley, running blindly toward where I left my car, but my forehead hits something first, then my nose, and as I try to stumble back and away from whatever it is, a rough hand closes around my upper arm.

My eyes are watering, but even through the tears, I can see a brawny chest in front of me. Tilting my head back, I take in a pair of piercing blue eyes, a buzz cut, plus an undeniably murderous expression— and now I immediately recognize the wall I ran into.

Damien's bodyguard.

Damn it. *Damn it*. I thought we were alone. I thought no one was watching. I'd completely forgotten the big guy had been dropped off at the laundromat, that he was near. Was it a coincidence that I ran into him—or was he posted out there just in case I tried to run?

When he squeezes my arm before dragging me back into the alley, shifting me so that I have no choice but to look at Damien, I'm pretty sure I have my answer.

"Got her, boss."

"Good job, Vin. Oh, Savannah… there are much better ways to get my attention, my dear."

My head shoots over to him. Even through the tears, the smirk on his face has me wishing I'd been brave enough to yank that knife out and plunge it into his heart.

Only I didn't—and the knife is still sticking out of his side.

He flicks his fingers at the giant behind me.

Next thing I know, I'm hoisted up. Vin has one big arm around my throat, the other around my waist. He lifts me a good foot off the ground, leaving my legs dangling as he tightens his hold on my throat.

Damien sucks in a breath, shifting his weight so

that he can lean with his good hip against his car as he studies me.

He could shoot me in the middle of the East End with my own gun—and nobody would even look twice. This man has the cops in his pocket and my weapon within reach.

Vin squeezes. "I got her."

"You're also choking her."

"You want I should just snap her neck?"

I close my eyes.

This is it. I *failed*.

I knew I needed to take my time. To learn everything I could about him, maybe find a way to infiltrate his life, get close to him somehow... but no. I let the memories make me mindless, and now I'm going to pay the price for my recklessness.

Poor Orion. He deserved a better owner than me. I just hope he finds a way to escape my apartment before it's too late—

"No. Let her go."

They snap open.

Without a word, Vin drops me. I don't land on my ass, though it's close, and it takes me a second to remember how to breathe while the black spots that surround the edge of my vision finally fade.

"I can... I can go?"

"No. Sorry. That was my mistake. I wasn't clear. I don't want my associate here to harm you, but that doesn't mean I'm just going to let you go. Let you get away with this."

My shoulders slump as Vin's massive hand closes around my bicep, tethering me to him again.

Damien nods in approval. "I do, however, have a… proposition to make to you. As a way for you to make up for what you've just done."

"Boss—"

He ignores Vin, and so do I. "What do you mean?"

"I want you to marry me. Become my bride."

My stomach lurches. He has to be fucking with me.

In case he's not, I gasp out, "That's not a proposition. That's a fucking proposal!"

"Hmm. I guess it is."

I'm a shit stalker. How did I spend months studying Damien only to just now realize that he's *nuts*? Fucking insane. He has that knife still sticking out of his side, the area around the tear darkening with blood, and instead of wanting me dead, his bright idea for revenge is to *propose*.

Even worse, he looks *amused* that I corrected his madness.

"Think of it this way," he continues when it's clear he's stunned me speechless, "regardless of the type of business I run, I *am* a businessman. Right now, Savannah, I'm giving you an opportunity. Consider it a business arrangement, if you will. Marry me, and we can pretend this"—his waves at the knife that's still sticking out of his side—"can be like water under the bridge. We forget all about it."

"And if I don't? If I don't marry you?"

I *can't* marry him?

"There are some other options we can come up with, I'm sure. Prison, for one. I know quite a few police officers. Attempted murder is a felony. You'll go away for a long, long time—"

I'm already shaking my head. It's a visceral reaction. I barely survived four years in a minimum security prison on a trumped-up misdemeanor charge. A felony? Maximum security as a violent offender? No. *No.*

"I could always let you go, but once my men learn you tried to kill me, I'd say you have... twenty-four hours before the bounty on your head means one of my Dragonflies is bringing it to me." Conversational as ever, he glances at the other man. "What do you say, Vin? Over? Under?"

"Under," Vin responds in a flat voice from behind me. "Give her a five-minute head start, boss, and I'll still have her delivered to you in ten."

"And that's why you have more leaves than anyone, and more sense in your head than Kieran who's currently rotting beneath the laundromat right now."

"Yeah, but he got killed by a Sinner for going after the wrong woman. And you want to marry the one who just tried to kill *you*?"

His icy gaze roves over my face as his upper lip curls. "*Yes.*"

At least I have some idea about what happened to that poor blonde woman I saw. Thanks to Vin here, I've heard the name Kieran multiple times this week. If he's the one who worked that girl over, I'm glad to hear he's dead.

Just... just not so happy that, if I don't marry the man I've spent months plotting to kill, I'm *next*.

What else can I do, though? His bodyguard means it. Given the chance, he'd snap my neck right now. And though I have no fucking idea why Damien Libellula wants to torture me by forcing me to become his wife, it's my only shot at survival.

I can't do prison again. I don't want to spend the rest of my life looking over my shoulder for the Dragonflies. I sure as fuck don't want to tie myself to their leader... but maybe it won't be so bad.

Hey. I wanted to infiltrate his life. I wanted to find a way to get close to Damien... can I get any closer than being his bride?

And once I have... I failed to kill him once. The next time?

I *won't*.

But I can't agree so easily. He has to guess I'm already plotting. I mean, that knife is still there! I tried to kill him! He's not even asking me about that! And yet... he's waiting for me to give him an answer as though it really matters if I'll willingly agree to this insanity or not.

I swallow the lump lodged in my throat that quite possibly may be my heart. "What about him? What if—"

"Him?" Damien echoes, cutting me off. "You mean Vin?"

The man who's squeezing my arm so tightly, it feels like he's about to tear it off? "Uh-huh."

"Vin didn't see anything," he says calmly. "Did you, Vin?"

Too calmly for a man with a *knife* sticking out of his *side*.

Am I dead? Is that it? The big oaf snapped my neck without warning, and now this is some split-second dream before my brain gets the memo that I'm gone?

Maybe—

"Nothing, boss," he rumbles grumpily.

"See? You have nothing to worry about," Damien says, and that's a fucking lie if I've ever heard one. "If you say 'yes' and agree to be my *loyal* bride, the only ones who ever need to know how this happened are us three. Say 'no' and, well, there's only one sentence for betrayal in the Libellula family."

"Death."

"That's right, Vin. *Death*."

Ah. He couldn't make himself any clearer with that last statement. If anyone betrays him... by forcing me to marry him, he's giving me a second chance. He's basically buying that loyalty he mentioned, but it comes with a price for me. If I betray him, I'm dead.

If I go to prison, I'm dead.

If I agree to be his wife, I'm probably dead even so...

But no matter what it takes, I'm going to take this man with me.

This man—

"Yes."

—*my soon-to-be husband.*

Revenge List

SIX

NEEDLE AND THREAD

DAMIEN

Beneath the sophisticated veneer, I'm a stubborn, ruthless man. Always have been, and it's only become more noticeable with age. I need to be in control, too, and usually am.

Therefore, it should come as no surprise that—even with my stiletto sticking out of my side and the pain beginning to creep up the longer it's in there—I have every intention of driving myself to see Elizabeth.

I've been stabbed before. My blade is actually a memento from the first gangster who tried to gut me back when I was still running for Gunner. He wanted the cash I was carrying, but his aim was no better than Savannah's. Just like her, he barely got through my jacket and my shirt. No organs were nicked, just fat and muscle, and I yanked that sticker out before slicing the kid's throat with his own knife.

I didn't know better then and, even if he didn't do much damage with the point, I nearly bled out anyway. Fifteen years of experience later and, despite how much I want to grab that same knife out, I keep it where it is. Until I can get checked out by our doc, it'll act like a plug and keep me on my feet.

It hurts. It fucking *hurts*. Luckily for me, my pain tolerance is high enough to pretend like it doesn't. I want little Miss murderer here to be thrown off by my nonplussed reaction to her attempt, especially since I'm going to use it to my advantage.

She tried to kill me. Why? I don't know. I still haven't figured out why she's been following me, either... but I will.

I've spent my whole life abiding by the old adage: keep your friends close and your enemies closer. It's the reason I insist on frequent dinners with Lincoln. Why I handle every interaction with the vice mayor personally instead of passing it off to one of my lieutenants, or someone in my inner circle like Michael or Vin.

And it's why I'm going to take this woman, make her mine like she's been for months now, and bring her to her knees where she belongs.

If I have to break her, I will. I look forward to it, too. From the first moment I picked up on her following me, *stalking* me, I've been intrigued. I won't deny that.

Maybe even obsessed with the promise of what kind of woman she is.

She's nothing like I've ever had before. I'm used to women willing to throw themselves in my bed, and as much fun as that was, it's too easy. Nothing about Savannah Montgomery will be—and I like the idea of that more than I should.

I blame Lincoln for this. For fifteen years, he was a miserable bastard who obsessed over the one woman who got away. But then he blackmailed Ava Monroe into becoming Ava Crewes, and now he's a smug bastard with a devoted wife, a kid on the way, and a satisfied smirk every time I see him that says he found the secret to the pleasures in life after he said 'I do'.

For whatever reason, Savannah hates me enough that she was willing to attack me on my own turf with my own knife. Fine. I don't need her love to make her my bride. To own her. To *control* her. I just need her to go along with it, and if she knows what's good for her, she will.

Prison. Death. Marriage.

I gave her a choice. It's up to her to decide what her fate will be, and when she does nothing but grit out her answer—"*Yes*"—it's sealed.

Vin muscled her into the backseat of my Maserati. Once she agreed to my madness, I jerked my chin at the car. I'm sure my cousin also thinks that the stab wound has rendered me temporarily insane, but he didn't hesitate. Moving quicker than he should be able to for a man of his size, he has her tucked in the back in seconds while I double-check my injury, then move toward the driver's side.

There's blood. A good amount of it, too, staining my dress shirt. The adrenaline has worn off enough that each step is agony. I swallow the pain, too stubborn to let anyone see how much it still fucking hurts, but Vin meets me at the door before I can open it.

"I'll drive, boss."

"Over my dead body."

His jaw goes tight. "If you don't hurry up and get that checked out by Dr. Lizzie, that might just be the case. C'mon. You really want me to have to tell Genny that you got offed on my watch?"

Genevieve. My baby sister might not be a baby anymore, but I'll be damned if she needs to know just how dangerous the life is. I've spent years protecting her from the realities of running a mafia syndicate in a city like Springfield. She doesn't need to know about *any* of this for now.

Of course, Vincent is right. If I stubbornly bleed out on the street, she will know—and he'll have to be the one to break the news to her.

Even in the Family, *family* comes first, and I won't do that to my sister or my cousin.

"Fine," I concede. Careful not to jostle my wounded side, I pull out my phone from my jacket pocket and check the time. "Elizabeth should still be at the office. She can patch me up first."

Vin raises his eyebrows when he hears 'first', but he doesn't comment on it. He just waits for me to move away from the door so that he can take the driver's seat.

I don't let anyone drive my cars. I especially don't let anyone drive them when I'm still capable of taking the wheel. But if I'm going to take a page out of Lincoln's playbook, I need to move fast.

I want a wife. More than that, I want this feisty, murderous woman to be that wife.

And while Vin speeds toward the other side of the East End, I fire off message after message to make sure that she will be before she can change her mind and decide that she'd rather risk the wrath of my men.

Because one thing for sure? Now that I've seen this side of her and decided I wanted to keep her, I *won't* change mine.

DOCTOR ELIZABETH HARPER SPENDS MORE THAN seventy hours a week at the Springfield East Clinic. The only doctor on the staff, she accepts a small paycheck to take care of any patient in need that walks through her doors.

For a much, much larger one, Elizabeth—also known as Liz to some, or Dr. Lizzie to Vin—is the Dragonflies' resident fixer-upper. Like so many of the SPD, she's on my payroll. Any one of my men who gets shot, stabbed, assaulted... any of them who needs some patchwork, they just have to head to the clinic, flash their mark, and Liz will take care of it, no questions asked.

Unlike the cops on the force, I don't have to bribe her to keep her mouth shut. The money helps—and she's worth every penny—but I earned her loyalty years ago when I found out that one of my soldiers was hassling the clinic, demanding to be paid for protection.

To me, that was outsourcing. If I didn't give the okay for the soldier to roll a local business, he was betraying the Family. You betray the Family, you die. It's as simple as that. So I had the soldier taken care of, then visited the clinic myself to assure the overworked doctor that she didn't need to pay my men to watch over her. She's a do-gooder, and I've got a bit of a soft spot for those. I could've used a place like the free clinic when I was getting started in the life, and I threw a donation her way to make up for the trouble the dead soldier caused her.

Somehow, without even meaning to, I bought myself a doc. Further proof that I didn't need to plot and plan and manipulate things for them to fall into place, and as Savannah sits silently in the exam room while Liz examines my stab wound, I just know that my impulsive decision to keep this woman will work out just the same.

It fucking *has* to.

I don't know what surprised the good doctor more:

the way I strode into her office with the knife in my side, or the fact that Savannah was sandwiched between Vin and me. That was non-negotiable. One way or another, I won't let that woman out of my sight until I'm ready to. I also don't trust Vin not to finish her off before she can try to come after me again.

Has the blood loss gone to my head? Perhaps, because I almost look forward to her doing just that.

Liz is about my age, give or take a few years. She wears her hair pulled back and out of her face, a pencil stuck into the golden yellow bun. Her lips purse a little when she does a preliminary examination of my wound.

She doesn't ask how I ended up with my own knife in my side. She's too smart to ask questions she won't like the answer to.

Instead, she tuts as she moves away from my bloody shirt. "Sutures," she announces. "Let me gather up what I'm going to need, then... Vincent?"

Vin straightens up from his post beside Savannah. "Yeah, doc?"

"Would you brace Damien's shoulders for me, keep him steady? I'm going to remove the knife, but I don't want him jumping around in case I nick him on the exit."

And give my new fiancée the opportunity to bolt while we're all distracted?

"Stay where you are, Vin. I'll be fine."

Liz is used to my stubborn side. After all, this isn't

the first time I've been one of her patients. So when she says, "I'd really rather he help," and I just look at her, she sighs and goes to grab the sterilized needle, thread, and everything else she'll need to stitch me up.

Once she has it all on a tray, she grabs a wad of gauze in one hand. With the other, she takes a firm hold on the hilt of my knife.

I can tell she wishes I would reconsider, but all she says is, "Ready?"

If only to make Liz feel a little better about being the doc in charge at the clinic, I move over to the examination table. I brace my legs and grip the edge of the cushion. There. I should be steady enough.

"On three."

Turning to look over my shoulder, I lock eyes with Savannah. "Of course."

I know the old trick. The doctor will count to three, I'll be waiting for the third count, but she'll pull on the second before I can tense up and make it worse—

"*One*."

Pain blossoms behind my eyes as Liz doesn't even wait until *two*. I refuse to react, refuse to blink, watching the look on Savannah's face go from horrified to stunned to plainly disturbed as I remain standing still as the doctor removes the knife.

I have to bite the inside of my cheek to keep from cursing, but it's worth it for Savannah to watch Liz work on me while I act completely unfazed.

That's right, cara mia. It takes more than a single slice in my side to take me down.

Of course, the good doctor wants to ensure that. With one firm tug, she yanks the stiletto out of me at the same time as she shoves the wad of gauze against my side. She quickly applies pressure in case I start bleeding profusely, but after a few seconds, she checks and lets out a sigh of relief.

I don't blame her. She's probably worried that, if anything happens to me, her security at the clinic might be in jeopardy.

She doesn't have to be. While I've purposely kept Genevieve out of the family business, there is one more Libellula around. Vin is one of my enforcers, my most trusted bodyguard, and my cousin. He'll take over if I die first, and he'll protect his Dr. Lizzie as much as I have.

And if he dies first? Then I better not.

Luckily, I'm not dying tonight. As Liz cleans up my wound to prep for stitching, she remarks again how lucky I am that the angle of the knife tore through muscle instead of my intestines or one of my kidneys.

I haven't turned away from Savannah. Not as Liz examined the stab wound, or when she instructed me to remove my jacket and my bloody dress shirt so that she could access it.

The doc notices. As she dabs my skin with some sort of analgesic, she says, "I'm sorry that your date got cut short."

I raise my eyebrows at my soon-to-be wife.

Savannah chokes.

Liz threads the needle, unaware of just how wrong of an idea she has. "When I was married to my ex, the most exciting thing that happened to us was the waiter bringing out a free dessert because they thought it was one of our birthdays. But then I started to work for Damien here, and these boys getting into gunfights and knife fights and even fistfights during a night out seems to be a lot more common."

With his back leaning against the wall, booted foot blocking the door from opening inward, Vin shrugs. "That's 'cause you've never been out to dinner with me, Dr. Lizzie. If you don't start none, there won't be none. Right, Damien?"

I know exactly what my cousin is doing. In his way, he's letting me know that he disapproves of my temporary lapse of judgment. If Savannah hadn't stabbed me, we wouldn't be here right now.

Very true. And, yet, I can't bring myself to care.

Instead, I'm suddenly eager to have this finished so that I can move on to the rest of the night.

"How much longer?" I ask, trying to gauge the amount of stitches she still needs to make in order to close the gap. The single stab wound itself is about eight, nine centimeters. I'm looking at about fifteen to twenty stitches when she's done so maybe we're halfway there? "I have plans for the evening." A quick glance at Savannah. "Don't *we*, my dear?"

Savannah still hasn't said a word. At that, though, she sputters, and I raise my eyebrows, daring her to refuse.

Liz tugs on the thread. Thanks to the numbing agents in the analgesic she applied, it doesn't *hurt,* though the sensation is strange enough that I feel it. I turn back around, but she's already on the next suture as if she hadn't pulled so roughly on the last one.

It must've been an accident, especially since she peers up at me during the next stitch, an amused expression on her face. "Grab dinner, get stabbed, go back for dessert. I tell you... there's never a dull moment with a Dragonfly."

I wonder how Liz would react if she knew it wasn't dessert we were heading off to get once she covers up my stitches, but a rushed wedding license instead. To be fair, it's probably the same way the good doc would react if she knew that it was *Savannah* who stuck me with my own knife.

But the knife's out now, my side is stitched, and Liz is giving instructions to Vin about how to take care of the dissolvable sutures because even she knows that it would be a waste of breath for her to try and tell me. Savannah is rubbing her thumbnail over her bottom lip, gaze darting from each of the three of us to the closed door as though she's wondering if it would be worth it to try to run now.

She could try. If I didn't chase her, Vin would, and

she won't like what'll happen if my enforcer gets his hands on her again and I'm not there to stop him.

I think she knows it, too. At the very least, she's resigned enough not to try to break out of the clinic.

I'm sure she thinks she has more time to escape me. I decide to let her live in that fantasy world a little longer. She'll be thrust into *my* world before she knows it. The least I can do is let her have some hope before I steal the last of it away from her.

It's the least she deserves for ruining one of my favorite jackets.

Moving away from the examination table, I grab my dress shirt, shrugging it back on so that it's covering the large white bandage that Liz used to protect my stitches. I do up the buttons, then pull on my suit jacket.

My first instinct is to get rid of it. Even if I send it off to my tailor, it'll never be the same again. But since I don't want to waste time getting another one—and I didn't think about my ruined shirt and coat when I was making my arrangements earlier—I wear it regardless.

It's almost poetic, isn't it? She tried to kill me while I was wearing this jacket. Why shouldn't I keep it on as I force her into marrying me?

Because that's exactly what I'm going to do.

And, now that I'm all patched up, I'm going to be the one to drive us there.

Revenge List

SEVEN
WIFE

SAVANNAH

Up until the moment I'm standing in a stuffy study, staring down at the wedding license waiting for my signature, I really thought I'd get out of this.

In what world do you stab a guy, mess up trying to kill him, and instead of him ordering his goon to retaliate, he *proposes*?

Not like I can call it that. Not really. Proposing implies that I actually had a choice whether or not I actually *wanted* to marry him, and since the choice was Damien or death, it's a no-brainer to go with the wedding.

I just... I guess I never thought he'd expect me to marry him *tonight*.

But that's exactly what just happened. In front of a

grey-haired judge wearing his robes and a fearful expression as he goes through the motions of performing a civil union with Vin as our 'witness', all that's left for me to do now is sign my life away.

Because in what world will this crooked judge force me to marry a man I tried to kill maybe two hours ago? In the criminal underbelly of Springfield, where being the head of a gang of thugs means that he can snap his fingers and expect everyone to do his bidding—or else.

Or else...

He threatened me with going to the cops. I couldn't let him do that. I couldn't... I can't go back to prison again. I would've rather his big goon snap my neck over being behind bars again. I almost let that happen, too, until he gave me another way out.

Marry him. I guess I don't know him half as well as I thought I did because I was convinced he already had a wife; if not a wife, then a partner. Plus, Damien's reputation precedes him. He's a ruthless bastard who hides it behind his pleasant smile and his thousand-dollar suits. The gentleman gangster, I never would've thought he'd let me get away with stabbing him.

To make me his *bride*? I have no idea what he's thinking. Why he's doing this. Even after all of his comments while he made me stand in the doctor's office as he got patched up... I was desperate to find a way out of this because I never once doubted that he'd make me go through with this.

And he did. Dashing his slanted signature on the

wedding license, smirking to himself as he sets the pen down, he seems almost pleased with himself.

If some crazy chick tried to seduce me, then stabbed me in the side with my own knife, I'd think twice about letting her get close enough to do it again. So unless he plans on marrying me to fuck with me before inevitably retaliating, going along with this if only to get a second chance to try again is the one upside to this insanity.

Sure, Damien. Let me be Mrs. Libellula. Let me go home to my apartment, run my own life with this civil tie between us, and the next time we meet, I'll fix this problem by making myself a widow.

That's my plan. I cling to it desperately as he places his hand on the small of my back, giving me just hard enough of a push to have me stumbling in my sneakers toward the desk.

Because, yup, I'm still wearing the t-shirt, jeans, and sneakers I pulled on this morning when I was getting ready for work. After leaving the Springfield East Clinic, he drove me and Vin all the way to the other side of Springfield, straight to Judge Callihan's huge-ass mansion.

I didn't even feel worthy walking on his expensive floors in my cheap, ten-dollar sneakers. Damien and Vin at least had suits on, even if Damien's is obviously blood-stained in the right light, but I look like he just picked me off the street and dragged me in here.

Oh, wait.

He *did*.

Judge Callihan didn't even blink at my appearance after the fucking *butler*—whose sneer tells me that he definitely did notice—at the door let us in, leading us toward the judge's personal office. He had everything ready for us, and when he referred to the message he received from Damien, I suddenly understood why he seemed so busy on his phone when Vin was rushing him to the clinic earlier.

I thought he was planning his revenge on me.

Nope. He was planning our *marriage*.

Once I've shuffled my feet up to the desk, he lifts his hand. His fingers slide through my hair, settling on my shoulder as he looms behind me. "Sign the license, wife."

I grit my teeth. When all I want to do is snap at him for calling me that, it's a much safer option to just go along with what he said without arguing.

At least, not in front of witnesses.

I pick up the pen. Next to Damien's signature, there's a blank line for me. Printing beneath it, I see my 'name': **SAVANNAH MONTGOMERY**.

I see it, and for the first time all night, I have the urge to smile.

I'm not Savannah. Not *legally*. And if I sign this license with my fake name, doesn't that make this marriage illegitimate?

It's a loophole. A very small one, too, and I know I'm grasping at straws. My future husband is a *mafia leader*. Somehow, I doubt he really gives a shot over the legalities of things. As it is, I'm pretty damn sure he's only going through the motions—having the judge marry us in his private study after courtroom hours with a hastily printed wedding license—so that I *believe* that we're married.

Let him. He wants to play this game? I'll play.

I'm going to fucking win, too.

Picking up the pen, I meet his gaze. There's a dare written into every line of his face, almost as though he's waiting for me to back out. To beg forgiveness. To call his goddamn bluff.

I don't. He set these events in motion when he could've just had the decency to die. Now? He'll have to face the consequences same as me.

Without a word, I scrawl *Savannah Montgomery* on the line, then toss the pen down.

Behind us, Vin groans.

Sorry, big guy. He might've pushed his luck as far as it could go, nagging Damien the entire ride over to the judge's house to reconsider, but my new husband seemed insistent on seeing this through to the point that Vin just stopped talking.

He didn't answer me when I point-blank asked him if he's the one who snatched my gun out of my purse, either...

Ah, well. I'll have to figure out a way to get it back. No way in hell is Damien going to let me get close enough to go for his knife again—unless he's a fucking moron, and even if I don't understand what his motives are, at least I'm sure he's not a fucking moron—so I'll have to be a little more... creative.

There's no time to think about that now. Once the ink on the license is dry, I'm basically considered his wife, and now I have to find out what that means to Damien—

The judge clears his throat. "If you're anything like Lincoln and his bride, I'm sure you're quite eager to consummate your marriage with this, er, lovely young lady here."

Lovely? Maybe if I had a full face of make-up on and my hair wasn't a wind-blown mess. And *young*... with my thirtieth birthday coming up in June, I'm only ten years or so younger than Damien. The way Judge Callihan says that, you'd think he was accusing Damien of robbing the cradle in a roundabout way.

But none of that really bothers me. Oh, no. It's the part where the judge so matter-of-factly mentions *consummating* our marriage that has my heart jumping into my throat.

His wrinkled face gets a bit of a leer to it as he adds, "I have a bathroom down the hall you might like to use."

Damien snorts. "Thank you, but no. I like to think I have a little more class and patience than Devil does. I'm taking my wife home."

Holy shit.

I don't think he's a moron, but I just might be.

Despite the way he came on to me in the alley before I stabbed him, it never occurred to me that he might have some kind of sexual motivation behind this forced marriage. But when he says he's taking his wife home...

I gulp. He doesn't mean my apartment, does he?

HE DOESN'T.

It's a twenty-minute ride back across town, and I spent every single fucking one of them wondering if it would be worth it to open the backseat door and dive out in the road before we make it to Damien's manor.

I think he could tell. At the very least, he instructed Vincent to sit in the back with me while he drove, almost as if he expected me to make a break for it and knew the big guy would be up to the task of stopping me.

I'm even more confused about his motivations now. After seeing him with that blonde for so many months, I was convinced he was in a relationship. Even if he wasn't, his good looks, his money, and his power have got to be one hell of an aphrodisiac. I hate him for what his gang did to me, and even I can't help but be a little physically attracted to him.

Does that mean I want to marry him? That I want to *fuck* him?

Hell, no. But there's got to be countless women who

would. He doesn't need to blackmail a woman into marrying him just to get laid. Especially not one who is responsible for the hole in his side, but that doesn't change the fact that—according to Judge Callihan, at least—I'm not Damien Libellula's wife.

And now I'm pulling up to the house that, only this morning, I would've given *anything* to get inside...

I knew his house was big. Even after I saw Judge Callihan's ritzy home, it didn't compare to Damien's.

Now I can say that his house is even *more* massive up close.

Thanks to the locked gate that surrounds the entire place, I could never get near enough to really check it out. It's always reminded me of the White House because of the pristine paneling that covers it, plus the intimidating gate that kept the rest of Springfield out. Instead of being super wide, it's taller, though the buildings bracketing the outer reach of the fence dwarf it. It's set back a bit, too, almost like it's too good to be part of the city.

But that's the thing. The skyscrapers in this part of the East End have, like, thirty floors compared to Libellula's three. How many people make their homes in those apartment, crammed into tiny spaces like mine? And here's the head of the Dragonflies taking up all this space just for him.

As if I couldn't hate him and what he stands for any more, having his big brute of a bodyguard enter the alarm code—those broad shoulders blocking me from seeing what numbers he punched in—before driving us down the length of the circular drive that brings us to the front steps.

He parks, and Damien shakes his head just enough to be noticeable.

"Bring the car to the garage," he says. "I'll get my wife settled in."

My wife.

My wife.

My. Wife.

I'm seconds away from spiraling. The more he repeats that—*my wife*—the more it's beginning to sink in that I agreed to this. I *married* him. And now... now he plans on bringing me inside his house to... what?

I don't know, and I'm terrified to find out.

I won't let him see that, though. I won't let him see how much being near him gets to me. I won't give him the fucking satisfaction of seeing that he's rattled me...

Pull it together, Savannah. Remember who you're supposed to be. Keep the accent; don't act bothered at all. Don't give him any excuse to change his mind before you can find a way out of this...

Damien gets out of his side of the car, then turns and opens my door for me.

My stomach tightens. I know better than to think he's being a gentleman, holding up the door. This is a reminder that I fucked up, I *failed*, and until I can get my hands on a weapon again, I have to go through this farce.

So when Damien offers me his hand to help me scoot out of the backseat, I pretend not to notice.

He lets me, though when he grabs my elbow to lead me inside and I shake him off, he pauses, thins his lips, and takes it again.

He doesn't squeeze it. There's no warning gesture. He just lays his hand lightly on my arm and I know that, no matter how many times I try to shake him off, he will stubbornly take hold of me again and again.

It's not worth the fight. Not when I still don't have any idea what game he's trying to play.

Once he disarms the alarm and lets us into the house, it takes every ounce of resolve I have not to gape at my surroundings. The outside was magnificent on purpose—a statement to his power and his wealth— but if I thought the inside would be understated even a little, I'm fucking wrong.

I feel like I'm walking into a museum. It's quiet, with an open entryway, a spiral stair in front of me that leads up, and a pair of decorated halls that lead off to the rest of the house. The floor is expensive tile, perfectly shiny and clean, and as I take a deep breath, I catch the hint of disinfectant on the air.

It doesn't look lived-in at all. As he leads me toward the spiral stairway, I half expect a docent to come out and offer us a tour.

Don't need one. Damien knows exactly where he's going—and though the next floor up has another wide hall with divots that lead to large rooms, there's one in particular that he guides me toward.

It doesn't take seeing the massive king-sized bed to realize that he's taken me to his bedroom.

I mean, that helps. So do the stuffed armchairs in one corner, the antique wooden furniture—including a nightstand and a dresser—that matches the headboard of the bed, but more than anything, it's the spicy musk overlaying the 'clean' scent that makes me sure it belongs to Damien.

It smells like him, and I hate that I like it.

Once I'm inside, I try not to lose it when the first thing he does is close the door behind us.

This is it. He has me right where he wants me, and I'm not even a little surprised when the *second* thing he does is shrug off his ruined jacket before he waves at the bed.

"This is our room. Our marital bed. If we're going to make this marriage work, there won't be any of this trying-to-kill-me bullshit. Outside of this room, go for it. Don't be surprised if I don't stop Vincent next time, but knock yourself out. In this room? I'll stop you, and you might not like the way I do." He shrugs off his blood-stained dress shirt, letting it fall to the floor. "Though I pride myself that, when I'm done with you, Savannah, you *will*."

Once his bare chest is on display—and I have to look at the sculpted, hairless torso like I did back at the clinic and wonder how the hell he's still in this good of shape at *forty*—it takes everything I have not to store.

Half-naked Damien. A bed.

Consummate...

"Stay over there," I tell him, backing up so that there are a good ten feet separating us. "I don't know what you think you're going to do tonight, but it's not with me."

"You're my wife—"

"You say I am."

"Judge Callihan says you are. The wedding license says the same. By tomorrow, the city of Springfield will know that you're mine."

Oh my god. He sounds so certain—like he fucking *means* it.

His gaze narrows as he takes one step toward me, then another. "What's the matter, Savannah? Is there someone you *don't* want to know that you agreed to be my bride?"

Look who's talking. I'm not the one who goes out with the same blonde chick all the time...

"No."

Damien looks thoughtful as he continues to stalk me. Once he got close, I backed up again, only for him to continue following me around the room.

"You said that so quickly. Either you're lying—"

"I'm not," I drawl lazily, pouring the honey into the Southern accent as he continues to herd me back toward his bed.

That's what he was doing. I know it, and so does he. But when he senses a kernel of truth in my fake accent, he pauses. "Really? You have to have someone you care about."

Someone he can use against me?

"Not anymore," I tell him honestly.

"They're dead?"

As good as.

"My, my. Ragna mia, hm? A black widow, is that it? I'm not your first victim?"

He's being playful now. Who would've thought?

He's playful—and I hate that he's backed me into a corner as easily as he moved me so that the bed is right behind me now.

Glaring at the bandage covering his skin, I snap. "A victim would've bled out and saved me from all this trouble."

"I'm so sorry. The next time you attempt to assassinate me, I'll be more considerate."

He's fucking with me. I know that, but something in my face gives away my intentions before I can keep them back.

Damien *tsks*. "So there will be a next time."

He can't honestly be surprised.

"I didn't stab you on accident," I remind him.

"No. But you did a piss-poor job of it, wife."

Revenge List

EIGHT
INTERRUPTION

SAVANNAH

Wife...

"Are you calling me that because you know how much it bothers me?"

"Consider it a reminder."

"What about the other thing you called me?" With my fake Southern accent, I try to mimic the Italian lilt that finds its way to Damien's voice when he switches to that language. All that happens is that it comes out like, "Run-yah me-a?"

"Ragna," he corrects. "Think 'lasagna'. Ragna. It means 'spider' in my birth language. Ragna mia is 'my spider'."

I don't know what's worse: the mafia leader referring to me as his wife or a fucking arachnid.

"Why?"

I thought I had been doing a good job of distracting him. If we had to keep this conversation going back and forth all night to keep him from remembering what he brought me into this room to do, I would. Anything to prevent him from finding a way to get me in that bed with him.

I'll sleep on the fucking floor first.

Go on, Damien. Tell me about this ridiculous pet name you've given your attempted murderer. Black widow... spider. I'm all ears as long as I'm not all naked.

I'm not, but when his hand goes to the waist of his black suit pants—while also drawing attention to the bulge pushing against them—I know that I didn't do as good a job of distracting him as I thought.

My chest heaving angrily, my low-cut t-shirt beneath my sweatshirt hoodie showing off my tits probably didn't help...

Damien does something to the button on his pants. They flick open, and by the time the zipper being tugged downward echoes almost deafeningly around the room, I've run out of time.

"Come here, wife."

No.

"You've stalled long enough, and yes... I know that's what you've been doing. That was fun for a while, but if there's one thing you need to know about your new husband? It's that I consider a good back-and-forth as foreplay."

Then, as if to prove he means it, Damien dips his tanned hand inside of his pants, pulling out his cock.

The first thing I look at is the dragonfly tattoo inked on his forearm after he rests his arm at his side. It's large, intricately detailed in shades of purples, greens, and blues, and wraps around his arm. It's like the mother of all other dragonfly symbols you see in Springfield, and I've been avoiding looking at his.

But when the choice comes between reminding myself who he is and eyeing his erection? The dragonfly wins.

But not for long. When Damien clears his throat, my traitorous eyes move a few inches over until I can't help but ogle his dick.

Why couldn't he have, like, a mushroom down there? Why does it have to be a good-looking cock? Not too fat, the right length, and with just a hint of a curve, I know it would be magical to have that thing inside of me.

No. *No*.

I shake my head. "What if I don't want to?"

He shrugs one shoulder, drawing attention to his wound this time. "I have sixteen stitches that tell me I don't give a shit."

"You might rip them open."

Damien smirks. "That sure of yourself?"

It's my turn to shrug.

His eyes darken just enough to match his mostly inky-black hair. That single silver streak... I've always wondered if it would be softer than the rest of his mane, but I doubted I'd ever get the chance to find out.

I won't now, either.

He takes his dick in his hand, giving it one leisurely stroke. "Come here," he repeats. "I won't go to bed on my wedding night unsatisfied."

Is that all?

I give my head a small shake, helping my hair fall behind my shoulder instead of in front of it. I don't have a hair tie on me at the moment, but you gotta do what you gotta do...

Moving toward him until I'm about two feet away, I lower myself to my knees. "You won't have to."

I shocked him. Something tells me that this was a test. He wanted to see if I'd just fall back on his bed, shuck off my jeans and panties, spread my legs wide open, and tell him to have at it.

I didn't. I won't. But if he's so fucking insistent on being *satisfied*...

He arches one eyebrow at me, dipping his chin at the same time. "*That* you want to do?

Does it matter? I'm offering.

"You want to come, *husband*? I'll let you have my hand or my mouth. Your choice. But that's it. You'd have to force me to do anything else."

I wait for him to tell me that, as his wife, it wouldn't be force. Like marital rape isn't a thing even when one partner wasn't blackmailed into joining with the other. Surprisingly, he doesn't.

"Then stay on your knees, Savannah, and open wide."

Not Savannah, I think as I inch closer so enough that I can reach his bobbing erection. Or, really, I'm only Savannah because he made it impossible for me to be Georgia...

I lay my fingers along the side of his cock, watching so closely that I see his slight shudder upon contact.

If this is a test, I don't know if I'm failing it or not, but there's something about his reaction that has me double-checking that he's about to let the woman who tried to *kill* him earlier tonight put her mouth on his most sensitive part.

In a husky voice that accentuates the draw, I ask him softly, "You really want me to do this?"

Damien's own voice turns slightly throaty as he gestures at his erection. "What do you think?"

That hate sex with this man would probably be worth the regret tomorrow morning...

"Go on," he urges, spreading his legs a little wider so that he can brace them. "We've had a long day. If you want to go to bed with me and just sleep, give me what you offered. Unless you've changed your mind?"

Not a chance.

Look. I get it. I suck him off and he won't molest me in my sleep—*tonight.*

Well, if that's the best I can expect from this monster...

Fine. Besides, it's just a blow job. I had to feast on

pussy nearly nightly for two-and-a-half years in order for Portia to share all her perks in prison while also keeping some other inmates and the guard—the fucking guards—off my back. I still wouldn't consider myself bi or anything since I was never attracted to her. Like I said, do what you gotta do, right?

Close your eyes, lick, get the job done.

Close your eyes—

I meet Damien's stare. With a rueful smile, I take a hold of his cock and put the head to my lips.

"No teeth," he warns.

Shame. "The faster I get you off, the faster I can go to bed and pretend this nightmare is over. Right?"

"If that's how you want to look at it."

Good enough. Parting my lips, I take him inside my mouth.

I'm sure he thinks he's won this battle. I'm betting he can't believe that he got me to agree to give him a blowjob so easily, either. And for the first thirty seconds or so as I run my tongue down the underside of his shaft, he's stiff—and I'm not just referring to his dick. He seems to be waiting for me to try to chomp off the tip or something, and when all I do is suck on his skin, he finally begins to relax enough to seem to enjoy it.

Of course, that's when I tug him out of the warmth of my mouth as I innocently ask, "What about the blonde?"

He goes tense immediately.

Ah-ha. Bulls-eye, just like I thought.

She's important to him. I figured as much, but I never targeted her because what was the point? My revenge wasn't about ruining Damien's life. It was about *ending* it. I've never seen her before. As far as I was concerned, she had nothing to do with this.

But if that's a way to get to Damien...

"Excuse me?"

I have a flippant, 'you heard me', halfway to my lip before I see the change in his expression.

Whoa.

Up until this moment, he's been amused. *Charming.* But the second I mentioned the blonde? I can see just how Damien Libellula became the powerful bastard that he is. There's no mercy in those pale blue eyes.

"Be careful, Savannah." Not spider. Not wife. Cool. Cold. *Savannah.*

I take his dick between my lips again, hollowing my cheeks as I use as much suction as I can to trigger the nerves on the head. I swirl my tongue over it next, and just when he closes his eyes so that I don't have to see the threat in them, I let his cock slip out with a gentle *pop.*

Gripping him by the base, I twist my wrist, stroking him a few times before I ask him, "What's the matter? Feel guilty? You have me on my knees, but she probably wouldn't like that, would she?"

His eyes snap open. "You don't know what you're talking about."

Maybe not. "Is she going to find out about me? I hope so. I can't *wait* to meet her."

I know in an instant that I went too far. I might not have asked him if she has anyone he cares about after he asked me the same, but I have an answer to that when he removes his stiletto knife in one fluid machine before I can finish my latest stroke.

Crouching his legs just enough to put me in his reach, the point of his knife touches my throat.

"I went to a lot of trouble to marry you," he says in a conversational tone. "Don't make me a widower on my wedding night."

Regret is a bitch, because I'm already wishing I never brought up the blonde.

I swallow because I can't keep myself from doing it, all the while expecting to feel the sharp stiletto piercing me any second now. When it doesn't, I whisper softly, "You'd kill me? Right now? When I'm as vulnerable as I can be?"

When he said we would have a truce while in this room?

Fool me, I *believed* him, too.

Now I'm on my knees in front of the man I hate most in this world. His cock is in my hand, the taste of his skin is in my mouth, and his knife is millimeters away from slitting my throat.

"My devious bride... you might be sucking your husband's cock right now, but if I lose my grip on this blade for even a second, you'd kill me. Wouldn't you?"

I would—and I hope he knows it.

Damien shifts the knife, using the flat of the cool blade to trace the edge of my jaw. He's not cutting me, though, and as if it'll save me, I tighten my grip and pump him a little harder.

"That's what I thought. So maybe I put this away." He slips it back into the holster, high enough that it's out of my reach while I'm on the floor. "And you go back to satisfying your new husband. Yes?"

"You know that this will only make me want you dead more," I say, rubbing the head against my bottom lip before I dart out my tongue, swirling it around the tip.

Damien blows a breath of air through his nose. "Sì. Oh, yes. I know. But it'll be worth your wrath, ragna mia, to know I had you on your knees on our wedding night."

In that case...

I twist my wrist again, stroking Damien from root to tip before answering him by lowering my head and swallowing as much of his erection as I can.

He wants me to satisfy him? *Fine.*

I'm not above using sex to control this man if I have to. And whatever happens after this, I don't think he cares.

His hand goes the back of my head, guiding me to bob up and down on the length of his cock. If he started to piston his hips just a little, he'd be straight-up fucking my mouth. He doesn't do that, though. Oh, no. If he did, he couldn't convince himself that I *wanted* to blow him. The mafia leader is going to stand as still as he can, threading his fingers through my hair as I do my best to make him come.

I'm distracted. I'll admit it. So focused on making Damien lose control, I don't notice that someone has opened the door and walked into the room with us until I hear a female voice shriek, "Damien? Oh, God, *Damien*."

From my position, I can just about make out a blonde woman—*that* blonde woman—before she spins around and dashes out the door.

It slams shut behind her, and I immediately try to pull away from him.

His fingers are tangled in my hair, pinning me in place for a few seconds before he sighs and lets go of me.

Damien is still hard. His cock is engorged at the head, and I can tell from the way his upper body goes tight that he was seconds away from blowing his load when we were interrupted.

That makes me irrationally happy, even if I had to be caught in such a position first.

I swipe the corners of my mouth with the back of my hand as he paces a little, his dick still out. "Um. Who was that?"

He doesn't answer me.

I persist. "Your wife—"

He spins on his heel, cock leading the fucking way. "*You* are my wife, Savannah."

That's what he thinks. "But your... your girlfriend—"

"Not my girlfriend."

She's *something*.

"I've seen her before. She's—"

It's like a chill comes over him. The hint of temper recedes, and he's back to the faux charming bastard I've seen a million times before.

"Not anyone I'll ever be intimate with," he says, moving until he's back in front of me again. "And now that I've chosen *you* to be my bride, I won't be fucking anyone else ever again. Like I told you before, that makes it your responsibility to satisfy me tonight. So," he grips his slick cock by the base, angling it toward me, "I'd appreciate it if you'd get back to what you were doing."

Has he lost his mind?

"You sure she won't care?" If he's cheating on who ever she is... "She looked like she needed to talk to you before she realized you were busy."

"Don't you worry about that, wife."

Wife again.

"But—"

"How are you still talking?" he asks, a hint of impatience finding its way to his tone now. "If your mouth was full of my cock, you shouldn't be able to question me on this."

God, I could so kill him right now—

Too bad his knife is out of my reach, I can't get to my gun, and he seems to think I won't attack him while we're in this room...

Okay. Let's get this over with. Tomorrow is another day, and I'm not giving up on my revenge just because I failed once.

Remember. It's just a blow job. It could be worse...

That's what I tell myself as I go right back to it, sucking and teasing, stroking him roughly while nibbling along his shaft with the edge of my teeth. Only the memory of the stiletto's point against my skin keeps me from actually biting him, but the pressure of my teeth is enough to have him bucking his hips just enough to be noticeable.

Now he *is* fucking my mouth, and by the time he's grunting softly as the salty, warm spunk fills my mouth, I'm nothing more than a vessel to get him off.

Wife? What wife?

He jerks his hips again, his dick still in my mouth as he finishes coming. I'm sure my new *husband* would want his wife to swallow, though I'd bet he's expecting me to spit his semen on the floor. Nope. I'm not giving him any reason to threaten me again.

I swallow it, and though it's not my favorite thing in the world to do, I manage to get it down without making a face at all.

Until he strokes the underside of my chin and murmurs, "Good girl."

Then? Then I glare up at him.

"There," I snap. "Happy?"

"Yes," he says bluntly. Dick. "Probably happier than my sister is, I'm sure."

He's such a fucking dick—

Wait.

Sister?

That was his *sister?*

His *sister* walked in on me blowing Damien?

As he watches me closely, searching for a reaction, I wish I could pretend that I could give a shit about what she walked in on. If only. My cheeks heating up, I fall back a little, ass against my heels, as I have only one thought:

Welcome to the fucking family, Savannah.

Revenge List

NINE
WHAT HAPPENS NOW

DAMIEN

Leaving my wife on her own after she gave me head is the last thing I want to do. I wasn't kidding when I told her it's my expectation that, now that she's agreed to be my wife, she makes sure I go to bed satisfied. I'm more than looking forward to doing the same for her, and though I draw the line at taking anything from a woman that she's not willing to give, the way she sucked me off in between telling me she hated me only makes me want to dominate her *more*.

But I can't, and not only because she's glaring at me as she wipes the corner of her mouth with her hand. Like a good girl, she swallowed every fucking drop I gave her after I blew my load in her mouth, but the venomous expression on her gorgeous face warns me that she's already plotting how she's going to try to assassinate me next.

Good luck, my dear.

Tucking my cock back into my pants, I hurriedly button them before zipping up. I adjust myself so that I'm as comfortable as I'm going to get, check to make sure my knife is still where it belongs, then start for the door.

I make it three steps before Savannah's voice calls after me.

"What happens now?"

I look over my shoulder at her. She's standing, arms crossed over her impressive chest, as she glares at me.

Damn it. I have to adjust myself again after the way that heated look goes straight to my cock.

Her attention dips, eyes drawn to the way I cup my groin. Since she's not looking at me, I don't bother concealing my smirk.

She can deny it all she wants, but at least she's drawn to me. I can work with that. There's a fine line between love and hate, and the fact that she already has some strong emotions regarding me will work in my favor.

I want this woman any way I can take her, and if I have to use every tricky, manipulative maneuver I can to get what I want... I *will*.

"I am going to check on my sister. You can get ready for bed."

Her eyes darken as she takes one noted step back.

"I already told you. You can't make me fuck you. If you do, that's rape—"

"I'm not going to rape you. When I fuck you... and, believe me, Savannah, I *will* fuck you... it'll be because you opened your legs for me the same way you just opened your mouth for my cock. If that's not tonight, fine. That's a disappointment, but I'm a big boy. I can wait—"

"You'll be waiting until your dick is shriveled up then."

"If you let me live that long. Hmm?"

She doesn't say anything to that. Certain that I made my point all the same, I start for the door again.

And, again, she stops me.

"That's really your sister? Not your girlfriend?"

Oh, Savannah. Did she really think I was that much of an asshole that I'd cheat on my romantic partner by forcing Savannah to marry me, then manipulating her into going down on me?

From the look on her face, the answer is yes—but that's not all I see.

I raise my eyebrows at her. "Jealous, wife?"

She scoffs. "What? No. I'm just trying to figure out how I'll ever face her again if she really is your sister. You might not give a fuck, but I don't perform sex acts in front of an audience. Her first impression of me is sucking her brother's dick. You don't see why that would make me feel like shit?"

Interesting that my murderous wife cares about

what Genevieve thinks about her... and that she honestly believes I'll let her get near my baby sister.

"Don't you worry about her. My sister is my business."

"And she's used to walking in on you getting your knob polished? Is that it?"

No. And that's precisely why I have to go check on her.

But first—

"Deny being jealous all you want, Savannah. I'll set your mind at ease regardless. Genevieve is my sister. Vincent is my cousin. You are my wife. I have no... mm... arrangements with any other women. Before tonight, I wasn't married. I don't have a girlfriend... and if I did? I'm fucking forty. It's a little ridiculous to refer to my partner as a 'girlfriend' if we're exclusive, don't you think? Anyway, I much prefer the title of 'wife'. And, in case you still think this is all a bad dream, I assure you that it isn't. You're my wife, and if you want a happy husband, you'll do what you're told and stay put."

She didn't say a word the entire time I spoke, but she swallows roughly when I finish.

And then—

"And if I don't?"

I reach over my torso and run my finger along the hilt of my stiletto, drawing her attention to it and trying like hell not to preen a little when she can't help but focus on the way the muscles in my chest flex as I do.

"Let's just say, you're not the only one who knows how to wield a knife, ragna mia."

I THOUGHT I WOULD HAVE TO HEAD UPSTAIRS TO FIND Genevieve. Hoping that I'd put enough fear into Savannah to keep her from trying to leave the manor, I was prepared to take the stairs as quickly as I could without aggravating my stitches—but that wasn't necessary.

Not when I find Gen in the hall, with her back to my door, forehead pressed to the wall opposite me.

When she was younger, my sister had a bad habit of putting her ear against my door, trying to listen to what I was doing. I know from experience that hormones are a bitch, and sex is a mystery when you're a teenager.

I was twenty-five when I took her in to live with me after our dad was killed. She was only ten then. I didn't think she had any idea what I was doing with the women I brought home, but once the thirteen-year-old smartass that she was asked me why she heard my date screaming my name the night before while we were eating breakfast, I found out I was wrong.

I also choked on my toast that day, but from that moment on, I refused to let any women come over when Gen was around. Eventually, it just became easier to have sex in a hotel, then head home when I was done. When I had a relationship, I would spend time at her place, but anyone who tried to get close to me had to deal with the fact that Genevieve will always be the most important woman in my life.

She's grown up knowing that her big brother will always be there to protect her. And because I've been careful to shield her from both syndicate life *and* my sex life, it probably never dawned on her to knock on my closed door before she let herself into my room.

That was my mistake. So distracted by my new wife, I forgot to lock the door. I only have one on the inside—which isn't helping me now that I have someone I'd like to see stay in there—but if I'd have turned the lock before I whipped out my cock, I wouldn't be talking to the back of Gen's blond head right now.

"Gen? Sorellina?" I ask, slipping into Italian. I don't often do it because I've always felt like it made me a walking stereotype, the Italian gangster, but sometimes —like when I slipped and referred to Savannah as 'my spider'—it just comes out. Like now, calling Genevieve my little sister. "What are you doing?"

"Oh, nothing. Just willing myself blind."

Willing myself blind... I sigh. "Really? Because you decided to walk into my bedroom without knocking, it's my fault that you—"

"Saw my brother getting his dick sucked by some stranger? Yup. That's your fault alright. What the fuck—"

"Language," I say mildly.

Without even turning around, my sweet sister flips me her middle finger.

"Genevieve..."

"What? In all the years I've been living under your roof, you never brought a woman back here. Not even when you were dating that golddigger, Damien. You spent the night at *her* house. How was I supposed to know you were busy?"

She's not wrong.

Well, not about that.

"Besides, she's not a stranger. She's my wife."

That gets her attention. Pushing away from the wall, she spins around, her eyes—light blue like mine—going fucking huge.

"Wife?" She folds in on herself, looking even smaller beneath the winter jacket she still has on. "What do you mean, *wife*? What... are you telling me that my brother... my *only* brother... had a serious relationship behind my back, then ran off and got married... and he *never* told me?"

"Genny—"

Suddenly, those baby blue eyes fill with tears. "I rarely get to leave the manor, and the one time I would've loved to... to see my big brother get *married*... and you kept that from me?"

If there's one thing I can say about my sister, it's that she got most of the emotions in the family. While I'm a stoic bastard most of the time when I'm not turning on the charm, she can switch her moods on a dime.

I'm not surprised she's hurt to think I hid something so significant from her. Mainly because she's so used to being iced out on the day-to-day Family business, she's at least sure I'll tell her about the things that truly matter.

Like, oh, being *engaged*.

"It's not what you think. I didn't know I was getting married until a few hours ago."

"How does that make sense?"

Admittedly, it doesn't. Not to anyone but me, that is.

I try to explain anyway. "You heard Vin and I talking about the woman who gave him a ride the other day?" When she doesn't deny it, I'm not surprised. I've learned that anything discussed in the manor is overheard by my sister, whether I want it to be or not. "That's her."

"Wait." She blinks, and the sadness turns to disbelief in a heartbeat. "*Her*? That's the woman who's been following you? Didn't you only just learn her name?"

"Yes."

"And now she's your wife? Without, like, dating her first?"

I nod. "That is accurate."

Genevieve bites down on her bottom lip, a slight furrow to her brow. She opens her mouth, probably to call me out on my bullshit, when she suddenly pauses for a moment. Lifting her hand, she points at my side.

"Damien. What's that?"

Fuck. I ran after Genevieve to make sure she was all right, but the only thing I stopped to do was pull up my pants. I'd left my bloody shirt and my suit jacket on one of my chairs. I didn't bother grabbing either, and I completely forgot about the bandage on my side.

"It's nothing," I begin, but when Gen reaches for the bandage, I step away before she can see the extent of the two-inch slice and all of my stitches. Instead, I try to soothe her curiosity by saying, "Just a little cut."

I don't mean to coddle her, and I know how much it pisses her off, but I like to protect my sister from the violence in the life—and that very rarely works because, like other Libellulas, she is very perceptive.

A glance at the gauze, a glance at the door, a glance at the stiletto in my holster that I would normally remove before I was being intimate with a date...

She's perceptive, and she's smart, and she guesses it in one.

"She *stabbed* you?" Genevieve squeals.

I don't even have a chance to come up with an alternate explanation for my knife wound before she's marching in front of me, hands perched on her hips.

"What did you do to her?"

Revenge List

TEN
FAMILY

DAMIEN

"**M**e?"

"Of course," Gen snaps. "Don't you play innocent with me, Damien. I know what kind of man you are, even if you'd rather pretend I didn't. If that woman stabbed you, I'm pretty sure you deserved it." She gasps, her fingers covering her mouth. "And then not only did you marry her, but you..." Dropping her hands again, they go right back to her hips as she glares up at me. "Do you want her to smother you in your sleep?"

Genevieve's thoughts always go a mile a minute. Normally, I find that charming. But, normally, she didn't burst in on me as my new wife was sucking my cock. I love my sister, but if I hadn't stuck around to finish in Savannah's mouth, I don't think I'd have the patience for this conversation.

"She won't—"

"You forced her to suck your dick!"

I did not. Not... necessarily. "I assure you, she went to her knees willingly."

"Oh?" Stepping away from me, holding out her arms as if she's pretending she's as muscular as I am instead of a dainty slip of a ballerina, she plants her feet on the hallway tile. Then she thrusts out her pelvis and, in a voice that's a mockery of mine, says, "I'm Damien Libellula. All-powerful head of the East End. You'll never suck a more magnificent dick than mine. You should be grateful for the privilege, woman."

I cast my eyes toward the ceiling. Instead of denying that her imitation might have... a little merit, I ask God, "Where is my sweet baby sister?"

Genevieve straightens up, moving closer so she can slap me in my bicep. "She's right here, wondering when my big brother became such a perv!"

"Excuse me?"

"What? Look, I didn't expect you to be a virgin at your big age. I know about your 'late nights'. Your dates. I want you to find someone to make you happy —but I'm not so sure *this* is the way to do it. You said she tried to kill you, right? How do you know she won't try again? Remember? Pillow-smothering? Even pervs don't deserve to be murdered in their sleep." Gen pauses, then taps her chin as if she's reconsidering her point. "Except pedos. Fuck them. They can die. But your wife... she's not a minor, is she?"

I pinch the bridge of my nose. I cannot believe I'm having this conversation with Genevieve right now, and I finally understand why Savannah might have been a little ashamed to be caught in such a compromising position when Gen goes on to add, "With her face full of dick, I couldn't get that great of a look at her."

Patience, Damien. Search for patience.

"She's twenty-nine. Thirty in June," I tell my sister after a moment.

At least, according to her fake identity, Savannah is. I'm leaning toward that being the case if only because, in my experience, a fake identity works best when there's some semblance of truth to it.

"That's a relief." Gen blows out a rush of air. "And you really did it, Dame? Got married and everything?"

"It was in front of a judge," I explain before she can grow upset that she missed the simple, expedient ceremony. "But, yes. I did."

And it doesn't matter that Savanna's fake name is the only one I had to put on the license. As soon as I get her to trust me enough to learn who she really is, I'll fix that up as soon as I can.

The way I see it, I already decided she was mine long before I enticed her to approach me tonight. And maybe I did because I was sick and tired of waiting for her to make her move, or that seeing how devoted

'Rolls' McIntyre was to the Williams girl made me rethink my relationships with women—and my lack thereof. Tonight, I went through getting stabbed, then stitched up to claim Savannah.

Fuck it, I'm *keeping* her.

But there aren't any more tears coming from Genevieve at the moment. Not ones of sadness, at any rate, since, out of nowhere, she bursts into roaring, wild laughter.

Oh?

"Something funny?"

"It just hit me. All these years of women trying to figure out a way to lock you down and become Mrs. Libellula, and the only one who manages to do it is the woman who caught your attention by *stabbing* you."

I sniff. "She was trying to kill me."

She dissolves into another peal of laughter. "That's what makes it so much funnier!"

Despite the pull on my stitches, I cross my arms over my chest as I look down my nose at Gen. "Aren't you supposed to be loyal to your family?"

"Yeah, well, you made her my sister-in-law, didn't you? She *is* family."

ONCE GENEVIEVE FINALLY STOPS LAUGHING BEFORE disappearing upstairs, I press the intercom button in the hall to page Vincent while keeping my eye on my closed bedroom door.

Our home has three floors plus a basement. I had it built with my immediate family in mind. Genevieve has the entire third floor to herself; she was seventeen when the building on the house was finished and threw a temper tantrum until I agreed she could have her room, a massive bathroom, and her dance studio installed on that level. The second floor is mine, from my bedroom to my private bath, my office, and my television room. Downstairs is where Vin sleeps. The first floor hosts the kitchen, the living room, three guest rooms plus his master, and a dining room we rarely use.

It's wired so that I can reach either of them with just a touch of a button in case I need them and I don't feel like relying on phones. While I always have mine on me—like how it's in the back pocket of my pants right now—and Gen is glued to hers, Vin's from my generation. We didn't grow up with them and, if business didn't call for it, I'd happily toss it to the side and forget about it for hours at a time.

Vin usually does. Unless he's on duty, waiting for me to call and give him a particular job, he sets his phone down once he's home. So I page him, and when he grumpily answers, I tell him to get his ass upstairs.

Considering the most he's done is strip off his jacket, I'm sure he'd been expecting this assignment— even if he's still going to give me shit about it.

We meet in the hallway before I jerk my thumb at my closed door. "I've gotta go out for a bit, Vin. I want you to watch her."

I don't have to tell him *who*. That she's in my bedroom tips him off, and he isn't happy to hear that I moved her into my bed instead of trapping my new wife inside one of the guest rooms until I have a better idea of what to do with her.

And since fucking her seems off the table for the moment—and Gen's scandalized 'perv' is still ringing in my ear—I might as well make some effort to prove to her that, so long as she respects me as her husband, she'll want for nothing as my wife.

Except, perhaps, her freedom...

Vin narrows his gaze on the door.

He scowls. "My job is to watch your back, boss. Not some murderous twat."

"That murderous twat is my wife, Vincent."

And I'm sure he's dying to get me to explain just what the hell I'm thinking.

He did while we were in the car. Even if I did feel inclined to explain myself, I wasn't going to do that with Savannah absorbing every single word we said. I have no illusion that, just because she chose the option I wanted her to, she's lost her desire to kill me.

She's not the first. I doubt she'll be the last. But, usually, when one of my enemies tries to take me out, I at least understand *why*. Either because they're a rival, they want to move in on my territory, or it's an attempt at revenge because of something the Dragonflies did.

What's Savannah's story? I saw the look in her pretty brown eyes before she stabbed me. They went from heavy-lidded and seductive to full of hate in a heartbeat. At that moment, she wanted me dead more than anything else in the world.

At first, I thought she might be a hired assassin. The mysterious man behind the snowflake might've put her up to it. I doubted it was Lincoln; that's not his style. But there are countless wannabes who think that, if I'm gone, they can step into my shoes. Putting a woman in front of me who's that stunning... I'm only human. I'm only a man. She's just my type, and when she went for blood, I was done for.

She's already occupied my thoughts these last few months just because she was watching me so closely. I hesitate to call it an obsession, but when I stroked my cock to thoughts of who she might be, why she was always there... I was already attracted to her.

Then she tried to kill me, and she handed me the perfect opportunity to finally make her mine.

I meant what I told her before, though. This battle between us, it's *between us*. If she targets Vincent of Genevieve? She's dead. If she tries to escape me and her punishment? She'll regret it.

But if I can wear this woman down, find out what it is that had her willing to throw her life away if only to take mine... that's exactly what I'm going to do, and that's no business but my wife and I.

My cousin doesn't get that yet.

"That's my point. This girl knifed you with your own fucking knife and you *marry* her? You know I've never once doubted you, but—"

My cousin doesn't get that yet—but he will.

I give Vin a small smile. "Then I'd suggest you don't start now. I'm still the head of this Family. I make the decisions. I give the orders. I expect you to do what you're told."

In the entire Family, there are two people who get a pass on talking back. Both have Libellula as a surname, but I mean it when I say that I'm in charge—and they know it.

Vin nods sheepishly. "Yeah. Sorry."

Better. "I have a couple of arrangements to take care of. Stay here. Make sure she doesn't leave this room. You can head to bed when I get back."

"You don't want me to help?"

Normally, I would. Vin is the one I rely on for everything—but, right now, the most important thing to me is for him to keep an eye on Savannah.

Genevieve is upstairs, annoyed with me and probably still thinking it's hysterical that I married Savannah after she proved to be one of the first people ever to stand up to me and get away with it. Inside my room, my wife is probably already plotting her escape. I need my cousin right where he is.

"Trust me, Vin. You already are."

Revenge List

ELEVEN
BED AND BREAKFAST

SAVANNAH

I never meant to fall asleep, and when the careful clearing of a throat somewhere above me has me jolting awake, I want to curse that I was caught so unaware.

Because there's Damien. His suit is fresh, no longer bloody. His black hair, with its striking silver streak, is damp yet perfectly combed. He smells of a musky cologne that goes right to my head, and he's crouched down so close to me, he could've slit my throat and I never would've seen it coming.

"Good morning, ragna mia."

Good morning, asshole.

I rub my eyes, hoping it'll make him look more like an ogre instead of a distinguished mobster. No dice. He looks too good, giving me one more reason to add to the ever-growing list of reasons I have to kill this smooth motherfucker.

The fact that he's smiling happily as I glare at him is another.

And it's all my fault.

Last night, I didn't know what to do. Escape seemed pretty fucking obvious, especially when he left to go after his sister. I mean, I can't stay here. There are a thousand reasons why, but having my new 'husband' fuck my mouth, then leave me behind to chase after another woman... I still wanted to kill him, but torn between feeling embarrassed and furious, every instinct inside of me was thrumming to get the hell out of here while I might be able to.

Assuming he's not full of shit when he calls her his sister, I figured that might be my chance. Then they actually had the world's most awkward conversation to overhear before she went to bed and my fucking wonderful 'husband' set a guard dog at my door.

If I tried to leave, Vin would stop me. No questions asked. He had his orders, and though I'm sure the big guy would rather snap my neck and end this bullshit, he made sure to knock on the door every half an hour as if to remind me he was there, and I was trapped.

The idea of giving in and sleeping in Damien's bed with or without him had me deciding I'd much rather stay up and hope Vin knocks out first. I didn't want to torture myself, though—especially since that seems to be my new 'husband's job—so when it became clear he's like the Energizer-fucking-Dragonfly, I took a pillow, stripping the comforter from the bed, and made myself a small nest on the floor between the bathroom door and the bed while I waited for him to return.

He never did. And after hours of being on alert, the events of the day finally caught up to me. Hoping like hell he wouldn't go back on his word and try to fuck me while I was sleeping, I eventually passed out.

Now I'm awake, I'm confused, and I'm more than a little pissed to be ripped from my dreams and thrust back into this nightmare by having to confront his face again so soon.

"What the hell are you doing?"

He raises his eyebrows. "What happened to my sweet Southern belle?"

Fuck. I completely forgot. A whole damn year of faking that drawl and all it took was the shock of waking up in Damien Libellula's bedroom before my harsh Springfield accent comes roaring right back. I never even realized I had one until I purposely adopted that fake one, but it's so different, even he noticed.

I can fix this. The last thing I need is for him to realize I'm not who he thinks I am. He might have his own twisted motives for forcing me to marry him after I stabbed him, but as far as I'm concerned, he's just giving me another opportunity to get my revenge.

"Don't know what you mean," I say, slipping right back into the drawl as I shove the blankets away from, struggling to climb out of the nest. "But my question stands, sir. Why were you watching me sleep?"

"Mm. The 'sir's a nice touch. I think I like it."

In that case, I'll never call him that again.

"And I wasn't watching you sleep, wife. I was waiting for you to wake up so I can let the movers in. But you looked so peaceful in my bedding just now, I didn't want to disturb you. Sleep well?"

"It's the floor," I say flatly. "What do you think?"

"I think you would've been far more comfortable in my bed."

I let out a short laugh without a single drop of humor in it. "Not if there was a chance you'd sneak into it while I couldn't protect myself."

"Ci sta, Savannah."

I have no idea what he means. I don't bother asking, either, since my foggy brain finally caught on to something else he said. "Wait. Movers?"

Instead of answering me, Damien rises up from his crouched position. Cupping his hand over his mouth, he calls out, "Come on in, boys."

The door to his bedroom is open. I almost expect Vin to come in first, but while the four men—because fuck 'boys', these are all men around my age or older—all wear a suit and gun combo similar to Damien's cousin, none of them are the scowling giant from last night.

Damien said they were movers, but they're obviously Dragonflies. However, that doesn't change the fact that they're all bringing something into the room.

The first two are carrying the ends of a floppy mattress. The next two are muscling a put-together metal frame in through the door with a little more trouble than the mattress duo did.

Each one is careful not to pay me attention. Oh, no. It's like I'm invisible, which makes me wonder what Damien told any of them before he propped them up out in the hall with their—

Hang on. Is that a bed?

Uh. Yeah. Damien points to the far side of his bed, wordlessly giving the order for his men to put the frame down first, then the mattress on top of it. There aren't any pillows, sheets, or blankets, it's undoubtedly a smaller version of his bed.

"Get me the table next, Gio."

"You got it, boss."

The one called Gio grabs one of the other indecipherable suits by the arm. Both men leave, returning a few minutes later. Gio is holding a folding table. The other guy has one narrow, metal chair—kind of like a stool—in each hand.

"Right there," Damien says, pointing at a space near me this time.

I dance out of the way before Gio unfolds the table, snapping the legs into place. It's about the size of a card table, perfect for the stools that the other suit sets out on opposite sides of the table.

"Frankie?" calls Damien.

As if on cue, an older man with a thick Springfield accent, a divot in his right cheek, and a suit that doesn't hide his gone-to-seed build comes in next, carrying a covered tray. Damien gestures at the folding table. The man lays the tray down carefully before lifting the lid.

I see two plates: each with a pile of fluffy scrambled eggs, thick bacon, and golden brown toast. Salt, pepper, and a ketchup bottle are one side of the tray, with forks, knifes, and two glasses of water closer to the middle.

"Thanks, Frankie. That'll be all. Let the cook know I said it looks amazing."

"Will do, boss."

The suits are gone. The butler dude follows after them, tugging the door closed behind him.

And then it's just Damien and me.

He takes one of the seats. Grabbing a rolled-up napkin I didn't notice on the tray before, he snaps his wrist, then drops the napkin onto his lap.

He waves at the food before pointing at my seat.

"Sit down, Savannah. Eat with me."

"I'm not hungry," I lie.

"Let me make myself clear," he says, his tone pleasant while his gaze shoots daggers at me. "If there's one thing I won't tolerate, it's you lying to me. If you can't be truthful, stay quiet."

I can't help myself.

"And if I tell you that I hate you?"

Damien doesn't even bat an eye at that. "Then I'll know you mean it."

I glare at him, doing my best to ignore the delicious smells of bacon and butter wafting up from the plates even as I plop into the metal chair across from him. "I still want you dead for what you did to me."

"You didn't have to marry me, wife."

Yes. Yes, I did. But that's not what I mean, and eventually we'll both know it. That's assuming he doesn't already. I tried to kill him before he forced me into this mockery of a marriage so there's no way that's what I'm referring to. I'm not going to tell him why I've spent the last year plotting his downfall, though. He backed me into agreeing not to turn on him when we're in our bedroom. That's all he's getting out of me.

He pushes one of the plates closer to me. "You went to bed without any dinner last night. You will eat breakfast, and you will eat it with me."

"You first." Damien gives me a look, and I shrug. "How do I know you didn't do something to it? Maybe you finally realized you could've died and this is your revenge. Watching me choke on poisoned toast."

His expression goes flat. Without a word, he takes a piece of toast from my plate, bites it, chews it, then places it back down with a large bite mark taken out of the bread as he swallows. He does the same for the scrambled eggs, then half a piece of bacon, plus finishes by popping an orange segment into his mouth.

Only when he's done sampling everything on my

plate does he grab his, scoot it closer to his side of the table, then start eating his own meal.

I know what he's doing. He proved his point that my plate wasn't messed with, and by eating his now, his is safe, too. I could probably demand either and he'd let me have it—so long as I eat.

And, honestly, I decide to eat the breakfast after all because the continuous glint in Damien's eyes tells me that, if I don't, he has no problem jerking open my mouth and shoving the food inside. Besides, I tried a hunger strike when I was in prison. Not only did I get threatened with more time for my insolence, but when I did get weak enough to eat, I got the scraps until the guards decided I'd been punished enough.

He finishes first, watching me as I choke down every bite.

Revenge List

TWELVE
LIFE

SAVANNAH

A satisfied smirk finds its way to his face. "We will share at least one meal together in here every day. Most likely, it will be dinner unless I have a meet I can't miss, but the two of us will eat and talk. Get to know each other."

"Isn't that something you do before you get married?" I mutter, placing down my fork.

"There you go. The first thing you can learn about me is that I never do what anyone expects."

I glance over at the cot he has set up on the other side of his bed. "You mean like bringing that in here?"

"You're getting it. You see, after I spoke to my sister last night, she made a very valid point."

"That you shouldn't expect the woman you threatened into marriage to want to fuck you right away?" I say sweetly.

Surprisingly, his eyes light up in amusement. "That I should expect you try to smother me with my pillow first chance you get if I push the issue."

Huh. Smart sister. She probably will never get over watching her older brother get head—because if *I* wasn't an only child, that's something that would scar me for life—but at least she has a lot more sense than Damien does. "Okay. And?"

"I gave you a choice last night. Marry me or go to prison. Obviously, you said 'I do'. This? This is another choice."

"Choice?" I echo, even more suspicious than before. No way he's saying that he gave me a bed of my own... right? "What do you mean, choice?"

"I'm not just going to make you sleep with me. And I don't mean sex, either. I mean giving you somewhere to sleep by yourself that isn't the floor. So I arranged for a separate bed for you."

I wrinkle my nose at it. I shouldn't when you take into consideration what the bed in my apartment is like, but he has this bougie king-sized bed and I get a *cot*? "A dinky twin on a metal frame?"

"Of course. I didn't say it was a *good* bed. I want you to join me in mine, Savannah, and why would you do that if I gave you one just as comfortable? It is better than the floor, I assure you."

I guess we'll see about that.

Once breakfast is done, he takes the tray out himself, leaving it in the hall by his door. After checking his phone for the time, he announces, "I have to go. But you? You will stay here."

I assume he means in this bedroom. Thankfully, with the en suite bathroom right there, and the television mounted to the wall over the dead fireplace across from his bed, I have a toilet and entertainment. No phone. No computer or internet access, but at least I'm not left alone with just my thoughts.

And now that I have my own bed to lay in, I'll be a little more comfortable than I was last night.

Still, I don't want him to think I'm *happy* about being made his prisoner. "For how long?"

"Hmm?"

I know he heard me. "I said, how long do you plan on keeping me here?"

The joke's played out. If he thinks he can keep me here against my will only because he blackmailed me into that fake wedding BS? That's fucking kidnapping. And, yeah, I doubt Mr. Dragonfly here gives a shit that he's breaking the law. But does he really want to be responsible for me?

He thinks I agreed to this meaningless truce between us while we're in this room. Hell, no. Once I accept that I have no choice of surviving being Damien Libellula's wife, what's to stop me from smothering him in his sleep? Using my goddamn panties to strangle him. Waiting for him to let down his guard enough that I can get close, get that knife, and finish what I started?

I might be a dead girl walking, but his days are numbered. He's nowhere near as smart as the Springfield rumor mill suggests if he doesn't realize that.

Then again, how much do you want to bet that Damien *does*? He does know. He just doesn't care. This man is so sure that I'll never be able to get a jump on him again, he's already plotting some kind of insane future where I *stay* his wife.

Because I see it in that same steely glint. He doesn't answer my question, but he doesn't need to.

How long will I stay here?

Forever… or until death does us part, which is the one I'm banking on.

"Instead of answering any more of your questions, wife, I think it's time you finally answer some of mine."

Um. No. I don't think I will.

"Where did you get the gun? The one with the snowflake on the bottom that Vin found in your purse."

I fucking knew it! "Dunno."

"Okay. Let's try this one on for size. Why have you been following me? I've noticed it for months now. You have to have a reason, especially since you tried to gut me during our first interaction. Care to explain yourself?"

Through tight teeth, I grit out, "Not. Really."

He's not done.

"How long have you been in Springfield? It seems like you just appeared... where were you? Alabama? The Carolinas? Georgia?"

It takes everything in me not to react. I don't answer, either.

Damien rises up from the metal chair. Bracing his hands against the small folding table, he gives me a searching look. "Very well. We'll try this again later. When you decide to answer me—"

I perk up. "You'll let me go?"

In my excitement, the accent slips again. For a moment, I think he's going to call me out on it, but he doesn't.

Instead, he shakes his head. "No. You belong to me now. That means I'll never let you go. But you'll like being my wife a lot better once I understand you." Letting go of the table, he gestures around the room; it's a lot more home-y since I arrived last night. "And you understand that this? This is your life now."

IT'S NOT. IT CAN'T BE.

Especially when I see just how insistent Damien is that I give in to this insanity.

After breakfast that morning, he left after giving me instructions on how to use both his television and his shower. He makes it a point to tell me that he isn't locking me in—mainly because the lock he has only works to keep someone out... and why the hell didn't he lock it before his sister came in—but that I shouldn't take that as an excuse to leave the room.

Does he have cameras? He refused to answer me. What about an alarm system? He just smiled. I even asked if Mount Vincent was going to be blocking the door again so I can't leave, and his answer to that was a sly twist to his grin.

I quickly wiped it off his too-handsome face when I pointed out that I was still in the same clothes that I'd been wearing since the morning before, and unless he wanted me to swim in one of his suits or put dirty panties back on, I didn't see the point in taking a shower.

His lips thinned at the 'dirty panties' comment, though I could see understanding dawning at the same time. He was finally getting it. I'm not just some stray he could pick up off the street, feed, and give a bed. I needed a little more than that.

He grabbed a pair of shorts from his drawer and t-shirt that still had the tags on it, offering them to me.

Hell, no. Those shorts looked like they could've been *his* underwear.

"I'd rather go naked," I sneered at him, giving him the perfect set-up.

He took it. Chuckling as he tossed the clothes on his bed, he told me, "I'd rather you go naked, too."

Of course he would. And if he was disappointed when he returned later that night and saw that I refused to change out of my old clothes, he didn't say anything.

He also didn't stick around after dinner.

I thought he was actually kind of being a nice guy. Like, he realized just what a dick move it is, forcing an unwilling woman to act the part of his wife, so he decided to hunker down in one of the many guest rooms that have got to be in this huge place. He did let the maid in to make my cot up with a sheet, a comforter, and a pillow before he left with the friendly older woman, and I thought he was giving me some space.

And then, after he insisted on sharing pastries for breakfast with me the next morning, I discovered exactly what he did while I lulled myself into a false sense of security that I could sleep on that cot without fear.

Nearly every bit of clothing I own was moved into his closet while I was knocked out. To do that, they must've been as quiet as the grave in order not to wake me up, but once again, I only came to with Damien at my side, clearing his throat before he risked his finger by stroking my cheek.

Up until I saw my clothes in there, I kept thinking this was all a joke. Especially since Damien's tone was almost teasing as he gestured at our outfits—mine a mish-mosh of whatever I could afford alongside his row of expensive business suits—hanging next to each other and said, "Does that please you, wife?"

Yeah. *No.*

I held it together until he made his excuses about needing to tend to the Family before he left. That's when I dashed to the bathroom, throwing up my entire breakfast in the toilet. After he split the donuts I picked out to prove they were safe the same way he shared my breakfast with me yesterday, it was clear my sudden nausea had nothing to do with the food. Nope. It was the realization that Damien Libellula—on his own, or one of his cronies—was in my apartment, going through my *stuff*.

It wouldn't take much for them to get access. I left my purse in my car, but if one of the Dragonflies went back to get it, they'd have access to my wallet. The name on my ID might be fake, but my address is real. My keys were in my purse, too.

Did they see Orion? I've spent the last day and a half worried about him, but sure he was all right for now. I left him a full bowl of food and water, and there's always a toilet if he got extra thirsty. Food was a bigger concern, but while he'd be hungry, he could survive a couple of days without me.

I honestly thought I'd be home by now. But seeing the lengths Damien went to to prove that I'm not allowed to leave... my new 'husband' was dead fucking serious. I'm stuck here forever.

And I can't do that.

Screw those wedding vows he made me say. Forget everything he tried to push me into agreeing to.

Savannah made all of those promises to him; at least, he probably thinks she did. But you know what? I don't *have* to be Savannah. I can shed that identity as easily as I got rid of Georgia if I have to.

He warned me not to leave. Not to run. But so long as he doesn't have anyone guarding that door—and, as far as I can tell, he hasn't since the first night—it would be worth it to at least *try*.

For Orion, I think I have to.

Let's just hope I can pull it off and get the hell out of here before my 'husband' finds out.

Revenge List

THIRTEEN
ATTEMPTED ESCAPE

DAMIEN

My new wife might have spent months stalking me, but if she thought I'd stand by and let her leave me after I promised her I'd never allow it... she doesn't know Damien Libellula at all.

I pride myself on my honesty. I never say anything I don't mean. I told her, if she tried to leave me, there would be consequences.

Savannah will not make me a liar.

That she made it further than she should've only infuriated me more. The security on my house is high-end for Genevieve's sake. It has alarms and sensors, but I realize my mistake the moment my cameras catch Savannah dashing out of the side door, sending me a notification right to my phone. The security is designed to keep threats out, not to trap them in my home.

That's because Vin and I need to be free to take care of business at a moment's notice. Gen knows better than to leave on her own without a chaperone to keep her safe. And Savannah... she should've known better by now than to test me.

I was doing this for her own safety. She tried to take me out, and not only did I make her untouchable by marrying her, but I let her into my *home*. So what if I did so because I maneuvered her into a position that she couldn't escape without my help. She didn't have to agree, but she did—and now she's going to pay for it.

I was in the middle of a meeting with our top accountant, Noel, when I got the notification. With the influx of bad Eclipse spreading through Springfield, our sales have taken a dip, and I needed to see the numbers on what the fucking snowflake crew is costing me. So already I was dealing with bad news. Is it a surprise that I didn't take Savannah's attempted escape as well as I might have.

Frankie might be my valet, making sure things run smoothly in my manor when I'm occupied with other elements of the Family's business, but he used to run with my dad going back thirty years ago now. Closing in on sixty, he did his time out on the streets. A working retirement, he's not exactly a lieutenant anymore, but he does run the staff.

And when I called the house and told him that my

wife made a break for it, Frankie locked down the gates before she could find a way out. The garage was closed off, too. From what he told me, he caught Savannah trying to climb before he convinced her it was useless.

The gun he keeps tucked beneath his valet jacket probably helped.

Either way, Savannah didn't look at Frankie and see an even older man she could attack. She hung her head, followed him back inside, and went to our room without any trouble.

By then, I'd gotten in touch with Vin. He was checking on the latest batch of bills coming out of the laundromat so, technically, he was closer to the manor than me. He hauled his ass home, parking his big body in front of my door while waiting for me to arrive.

I had every intention of doing so. I only had to make one pit stop first.

Last summer, before our truce, one of Lincoln's men decided to switch sides. Robert Cullens got his dragonfly, and to prove his newfound loyalty to my Family, he told Christopher everything about the Devil of Springfield and his new bride.

I knew immediately it was Ava Monroe. I also could guess just how he got the woman he'd been obsessed with since he was a young teen—and who he left fifteen years ago after his brutal run-in with Skittery the junkie—to finally forgive him *and* marry him.

Joey Maglione.

Maglione, like Cullens, was a recent recruit to the

Family. He was also, for a time, Ava Monroe's boyfriend. He vanished shortly before Lincoln married her, and rumors ran that it was because St. Ava pulled the trigger on Maglione one night after he attempted to sexually assault her.

And why did that fucking moron do that? Because once he realized his Ava was *Lincoln's* Ava, Maglione wanted to bring her to me to use against our rivals in the Sinners Syndicate. He thought he was showing initiative. Maybe if he didn't try to get his cock wet first, I'd see that, but no. I didn't blame Ava for killing one of my men when I probably would've done the same thing if she hadn't done it first.

Lincoln didn't know that at the time. He was protecting his wife from the police *and* from me. So he kept her hidden away, locked away in the penthouse of Paradise Suites, and it was only a stroke of luck that I was able to use Cullens to nab Ava and bring her to me.

I wanted this truce. I would've done anything for it. Making Lincoln's new wife leverage to control my former friend turned rival? I knew she was in no danger. *He* didn't. I could've gotten him to promise me the world with my gun to Ava's head, but the only thing I wanted was for our two syndicates to work together to block out any others from heading onto our turf.

In one decision, I got rid of the biggest threat to me while also using Lincoln's crew to shield my Family from any others. It's something I've been working toward for years, and I was so damn pleased when it finally came to fruition—no matter how low I had to go to get that.

He'll never forgive me, but he knows enough about the life that he's done his best to move on. He also—as he told me smugly during one of our early dinners—made sure that he'd never love tabs on his wife again, all thanks to a particular invention his tech guy came up with.

Lincoln definitely caught my interest with that statement. And though I know he charged me through the nose to get a couple of prototypes of my own, I happily paid it to him in good faith, hoping it would help him get over the whole 'me putting a gun to Ava's head' thing that he still had an issue with.

Since I didn't want Genevieve playing with them, I kept my case with the injectors at my main office in the Dragonfly building where we have the base of our dealing operation. When I'm not home, having meetings, or being seen around Springfield, making my presence known, most of my time is spent there. Luckily, Noel's office is only two floors down from mine so it was only a matter of minutes to grab my case and head for my car.

I try to calm down during the ride back to the house. I also thought I'd managed to as I nod at Vin, waiting for my cousin to step away from the door. He mutters something about Savannah being quiet in there, but I barely listen.

Sure, she's quiet. My devious wife is probably *plotting.*

She's certainly pacing at the foot of my bed when I push open the door, shoving it closed behind me. Her head shoots up, and if she'd looked remorseful at all, I might not have scowled so deeply at her.

But she doesn't and I did, and when she opens her mouth, I don't want to hear it.

"I warned you not to leave. You were told you have to stay in the manor until I gave you permission to go. I trusted you to behave. You disobeyed me, wife. And now you will learn I never give second chances."

She tilts her head back enough to show the slender, pale column of her throat. "You want to slit it. Go ahead. Because I'm not going to apologize."

I didn't think she would. "I have no patience for this martyr act. I told you not to leave. I trusted you to listen. Now you've proven you're not worthy of that trust." Popping the case, I remove one of the primed injectors. "You've left me no choice."

Savannah frowns when she notices the needle. "What the hell is that?" Her eyes narrow. "Are you going to tattoo me?"

Scoffing, I keep my thumb on the plunger as I tuck the case back into my suit jacket. "In my Family, you earn your Dragonfly." Stalking toward her, I make sure she knows: "You haven't."

"Then what— *ow*!"

If I wasn't so angry, I would've been more gentle. She doesn't deserve that, either. Gripping her by the arm, I held her in place so that I could jab the injector into the meat of her bicep before pushing down on the plunger.

I don't let go until the injector is completely empty.

The second I do, she clutches her arm, staring at the red hole left behind from the large needle. A dot of blood wells up. Licking her thumb, she rubs at s at it— then glares at me. "What did you just do to me?"

Now that it's done, I'm a lot calmer. A lot more relieved.

"This?" I hold up the empty injector. "It held a state-of-the-art subdermal tracker."

A tracker that is now inside of my wife.

I don't have to explain the obvious. A moment later, it clicks, and she screeches. "You chipped me?"

"Don't flatter yourself." I take the case back out, drop the empty inside of it, then put it away again. "You're not the only one who has one."

She's just the only one who didn't agree to let me inject it into the arm.

"Wow... You really are a control freak, aren't you?"

A small smile plays on my lips. Oh, yes. Now that I'll be able to follow her no matter where she goes... I've more than earned that grin. "You're surprised?"

I'm a man who forced her into marrying me all because she caught my attention by stalking me first, then boldly trying to kill me. I stole her freedom, keeping her locked in my home until she willingly accepts me as her husband?

"No," she says, and I know she's being honest like I demanded. "I'm not."

Well. Now that we have that settled. "If you hadn't tried to escape the manor, I wouldn't have had to do that."

"I had to!"

"Where were you going? What was so important, you thought it was a good idea to betray your husband?"

She flinches at the cold way I say 'betray'. "It wasn't like that."

"Fine. Then, tell me, what *was* it like?"

Savannah clenches her fists at her side. "You don't understand. It's been almost three days. I have to go back."

Not happening.

Then again, something... something's not right. She seems far more frustrated about being caught and brought back to the room than that I grabbed her arm and forced a tracking chip under her skin.

And that makes me think she wasn't running *from* me, but *to* someone else.

No.

"Not my problem, Savannah. If you had a lover, it's too late now. You're mine. You signed on the dotted line, my dear. Don't forget that."

"I know, but... look. It's not a guy, alright? Not like you think." She lets out a sound of frustration. "I have to go. Don't you get that?"

If it's not a guy—and I take that to mean any other lover, either—then what is it?

A pit in my stomach forms as the image of Ava Crewes pops into my head. "A child—"

Her head turns to the side.

Fuck.

I grab Savannah's arm, tugging her just hard enough that she's forced to look at me. "Is there a kid?"

"What? No!"

I don't want to look too closely at the relief that rushes through me when she says that.

I want her loyalty. I *crave* it. If there was a man, I wouldn't worry. But a child? I know Savannah is broken. Twisted almost beyond repair. I'm working on straightening her out, but I can't imagine the woman in front of me harming a child. If she's a mother, I will never be the one she is loyal to more than anyone, and I *need* that.

I warned her. If she betrayed me, the consequence was death. But as she looks up at me, tears making her eyes go glossy, that part of me that's always had a soft spot for the goody-goodies, the kind souls... it sees something that she's kept hidden from me all along.

Beneath her tough exterior and unpredictable—and, fine, *murderous*—nature is a sweetheart who doesn't want anyone to know it.

I saw it, though. I know it's there. And if I'm surprised by that, that's nothing compared to how my growing temper cools the moment she makes her confession.

"It's my cat," she admits.

Her cat. She risked everything for her *cat*.

What the hell am I supposed to do about that?

Revenge List

FOURTEEN
UNDER THE BED

DAMIEN

The answer to that question is very simple: since I refuse to let Savannah leave my home, that means someone has to go retrieve her cat. And since I obviously can't trust my men to do the job, it looks like that falls on me.

After all, if you want a job done right, do it yourself.

Honestly. How did none of my guys realize that she had a cat? Even if her pet was hiding when they went to the address on Savannah's license, there had to be some sign. Bowls. Cat food. Toys. I'm even more frustrated when I let myself into her place with the keys Chester retrieved for me when he went and moved her car from outside the laundromat to my garage because the first thing I come across is an empty water fountain on ground level, perfect for a pet.

The second thing I notice? Is just how sorry of a place my poor wife was living in before I brought her to live with me.

I knew she didn't have money. Between the decade-old car she was driving and the fact that she worked as a driver for a rideshare app, it seemed like she was just scraping together enough funds to survive.

This building is Dragonfly-owned. The rent could be lower, but I didn't get where I am today by being fair. As a businessman, legitimate or not, I need profits. Being a landlord added to what we brought in with our counterfeiting operation and our drug deals with the added bonus that it's, technically, above board.

Savannah is renting a single bedroom. I want to think that my boys cleaned it out the other night, but I know better. I sent a crew over to retrieve my new wife's wardrobe and anything that it seemed like she couldn't leave behind. At the time, I mentioned obvious prescriptions or mementos that might make her a little more comfortable in her new home.

And while I admit a cat should've been obvious even if I didn't point-blank tell them to keep an eye out for one, when all they brought over to the manor were the contents of her closet, I trusted my top guys to do what they were told.

They wouldn't steal. To steal from me is the same as betraying me, and every Dragonfly knows better than to do that. Our resident tattooer even has a spiel he gives before he inks my symbol on a new recruit.

Unless they're willing to pledge eternal loyalty to my Family, they should rethink getting the mark. Once a man has my dragonfly on him, I own him.

Just like how my men put a similar mark on their women when they want to claim them as property, they get the idea because the dragonflies inked on their inner arms? That's a sign that they're *my* property.

I might look the other way if someone without my mark offends me. And if I'm only saying that now to justify not only allowing Savannah to live, but *marrying* her, I could give a shit. The men that came here do have my tattoo. If they stole anything of hers, that's the same as stealing from me.

They wouldn't dare.

But since the alternative is accepting that, apart from a cheap couch in what could laughably be called a living room, a television about a quarter the size of mine, a flimsy faux wood table, and a wire bed frame hosting a box mattress in the bedroom, there isn't much else in here. She has no decorations on the walls, nothing that shows any personality... except for an overflowing shit box that has my nose wrinkling as I peek into her basic bathroom, an empty bowl in the kitchen, and two tiny toy mice that peek out from beneath her even emptier fridge.

I understand the cat bowl being empty. If she'd fed her pet before she left, odds are it would've run out of food sometime in the three nights and two days I've kept her to myself. Same thing with the water fountain, though her toilet lid's up so, hopefully, the cat has had some water.

That furry bastard better be alive, I think, as I continue to search the house for it.

All the while, I can't stop thinking about the contents of her refrigerator. Savannah had no idea what was going to happen that night since *I* had no idea what was going to happen. It's not like she came back and ate, but if she didn't... how was she going to survive on half of a bottle of ketchup, a jar of pickles, and two apples?

Because apart from an expired carton of orange juice she was still nursing, that was all I found in her refrigerator. A quick peek in her cabinets reveals they're just as empty.

No wonder she fought back against me when I wanted her to eat. It doesn't look like she does much of that. I don't think it's a dieting thing so much as she couldn't afford to keep her kitchen stocked. In fact, as I continue looking for her pet, I find more stored bags of cat kibble than I do human food.

One of the bags has been ripped open by tiny cat teeth. Hoping that's a sign the furry bastard hasn't starved to death in the last two days, I renew my search.

Eventually, I have to admit that I'm being ridiculous. Trained from the cradle not to show any weakness by her gangster father, I'd walked around her cramped apartment, looking around as if the cat would just be sitting on a nonexistent chair or her flimsy table, waiting for me to find it.

It's a *cat*. Considering my men didn't come across it, it must be hiding. Why the hell am I favoring my injured side so that no one can tell I'm still stitched-up beneath my dress shirt when no one else is around?

If the cat is hiding, odds are it's under the bed or behind the couch. Maybe in a cabinet. Either way, I need to get a little lower.

No dice on searching the living room. Same with the kitchen. However, when I head back into Savannah's room, dropping down so that my belly is on the old wood floor, I swear I see something flashing back at me from beneath her bed when I use the flashlight app on my phone.

And that's not all...

What's that poking out from beneath the cat?

Because, yup. That's definitely a cat all right. With vivid green eyes that seem almost mirror-like in the gloomy shadows gathering under her bed when my light lands on it, plus the fluffy orange-and-white fur Savannah described, I know I've found Orion.

Now I just have to figure out how to get him out.

Before I headed toward Savannah's address, I had Christopher bring me a cat carrier. See? This is why I'm the head of my Family. One of us needs to have a brain, and if I came all this way to retrieve the cat and lost him because I had nowhere to put him, I could kiss any chance of softening my new wife up goodbye.

I saw that look in her eye. I know how much she cares about this glorified, puffed-up rat. This Orion might be the key to figuring out the mysterious Savannah Montgomery.

And only for that reason do I click my tongue and rub my fingers, trying to lure the cat toward me.

It doesn't work. The furry bastard must know that I'm the reason his mistress has disappeared because he absolutely refused to come closer... until I say *fuck it*, toss a handful of treats I found in one of her cabinets —because of course Savannah stocks cat treats, but not a damn loaf of bread in her kitchen—under the bed, and snatch the cat by the scruff wants it gets the nerve to get close enough to scarf them down.

Ha. Gotcha!

Once I have her cat firmly inside of the carrier, my curiosity gets the better of me. I do end up tugging on my stitches, but it looks like a piece of mail has found its way under there. If my men completely blanked on seeing the cat, I can't expect those shit-for-brains to have found this.

And, suddenly, I really want to know what that is.

I expect it to be trash. Junk mail, maybe, or an old envelope she used to jot down a grocery list. Once I grab it, it's easy to see that it's an open envelope. Pulling it out, I confirm it's an *empty* envelope.

Still, I turned it over and read the front.

I except the letter to be addressed to Savannah Montgomery. After all, that's the name she's going under, even though we both know it's gotta be fake.

And when I see the name scrawled in old-fashioned script? I think I might finally have something to confirm my suspicions.

Georgia Gayle.

Who the fuck is Georgia Gayle?

Savannah, most likely, but as I ignore Orion's pissed-off yowls, I plop my ass on the rumpled bedsheet, trying not to imagine my wife sleeping here —or who she might have been sleeping here *with*— before I made her mine.

Who did I marry? Savannah—or this Georgia person?

I don't know, and after Google is no fucking help, I stare at the front of my phone for a moment before I make a call.

Lincoln answers on the third ring, his snarl telling me that I've probably interrupted something my counterpart considers important.

Oh, well. To me, this is even more important...

"If you're calling me to see if Tanner's got any info on the snowflake, I'm only gonna tell you one more time: get off my ass. You think I'm not pissed that this fucker is sneaking in under my nose? My guys found three more guns, and it's taking everything I can to not involve Royce while Nicolette's recovering."

I'm glad to hear that the Williams girl is doing all right. After seeing the mess Kieran made of her face for no other reason than that she chose a Sinner over returning and being his property again, I can't even fault 'Rolls' Royce McIntyre for shorting me one enforcer.

"So, yeah. I'll get that to you when I get it. But my wife's gonna pop in another month, my second is busy, and that's not even half of what the hell is going on around here. Unless you got something else—"

Clearing my throat, a signal for Devil to cut off his ridiculous tirade, I wait for him to shut up before I say, "There's something else. I need a favor."

When Lincoln doesn't answer right away, all I can think is: huh. I've done the impossible. I've stunned a ranting Lincoln Crewes speechless.

It doesn't last long. Within seconds, he's back on the line. "A favor? Damien fucking Libellula is asking *me* for a favor?"

"Actually. This one is more for Tanner."

Lincoln chuckles. "Yeah. That makes more sense. Alright. What do you need from my guy?"

I glance down at the ripped envelope. "Anything he can tell me about a woman named Georgia Gayle..."

Revenge List

FIFTEEN

ORION

SAVANNAH

When Damien walks into the bedroom—or, as I can't keep from thinking about it, my new, updated *prison cell*—about an hour and a half after he walked out of it, I want nothing more than to work up the energy to hate him more than I already have.

And then I see what he has curled up against his chest—

"Orion!"

It doesn't even occur to me to pretend like I couldn't care less that he's carrying the orange and white cat into the room. I probably should have. The other night, he asked me if there was anyone I cared about, and I told him no. I'd been talking about people at the time, since prison cost me any friends and family

I had before and plotting revenge took up too much time for me to make any now. But Orion... at a time in my life when I was ready to just give up and end it, he was the reason I didn't.

Seeing him again after I was sure that my impulsiveness and need for revenge would be the death of my baby... I rush toward him, tears burning my eyes as I hold out my arms.

I swear to God, if Damien jerked him out of my reach, I think I might've gone for his throat. Doubt I'm strong enough to overpower and strangle him, but for my cat, I'd *try*.

That's not what happens. Instead, hefting my confused cat up, not even scowling when his claws snag on his jacket, Damien passes Orion over to me.

My cat lets out an annoyed *mrow* as I squeeze him tight, but he lets me love on him, my tears spilling out, dampening his fur as I bury my face against his back.

While I'm whispering apologies to Orion, Damien disappears again, but this time he's only gone for a minute or two.

I catch sight of him walking back into the room, holding a laundry basket full of shit.

No.

Orion's shit.

Damien drops it by my feet. "I brought everything I could find. The water fountain with the plug. The glass bowls. These two ratty toys that I'm assuming are supposed to be mice... and the food. I brought it all back."

He also has an oversized brown bag hanging off his wrist. Reaching inside of it, he shows me a large, fuzzy cat bed before adding it to the top of Orion's supplies.

"He didn't have a bed that I could see so I stopped at the pet store and bought one. I didn't know what to get so the girl at the shop helped me. I hope it's right."

It looks right to me. And there's a pretty good reason why Damien didn't see a bed: because I couldn't afford to get him one when he could sleep with me. All of my extra money went to food, treats, and litter. It seemed kinda pointless to buy him a bed.

But Damien... the lead Dragonfly himself... *did*.

"That's because he slept in my bed."

"I hope he was the only male who did."

I ignore that as I rub my chin against the space between Orion's triangle-shaped ears. My cat purrs for the first time since I got him back. It sounds like music to me.

"Ah, well. It doesn't matter." Oh. It doesn't, Damien? I'm not so sure I believe that... "He'll sleep in the bed I provided. I won't let some animal sleep in mine."

Is that so? "Don't you listen to the scary man, Orion. If you don't want to sleep in that bed, you can curl up with me."

"Scary man?" Damien almost sounds offended.

"After I got on my hands and knees to persuade this creature to come out from under your bed?"

Wait—*what*?

"You did it? I... I guess I thought you got one of your cronies to do it."

He's offended that I called him scary. A man who rules half of Springfield with an iron fist and a sharp stiletto... he doesn't want to be scary. And yet, when I point out he has cronies, he doesn't react at all other than to say, "I told you. I rarely do what anyone expects of me."

I'm beginning to notice that.

He forced me into marriage. He insisted that I pleasure him one way or the other, accepting my offer of a blow job before making one of his men act like my jailer.

But then he brought me a bed of my own. I pointed out that I didn't have any clothes. He got me them. I admitted my cat was abandoned in my apartment...

And I have him purring in my arms, with everything he needs in that basket, including a pet bed he bought specifically for Orion.

I'd brush it off that he was just secretly a cat guy, but then he says, "Just remember that, when you're in my bed, wife, he can't come with you," and I have to admit it's not that.

He wasn't trying to save my cat. He was retrieving Orion for *me*.

Because he doesn't want me to have a reason to

leave. That's all it is. And with Orion here, I just gave him another way to control me...

...and, right now, I can't find it in me to give a fuck. I have Orion. That's all that matters.

And if Damien wants to make an effort so that we don't murder each other outright, I guess I can, too.

For now.

"You've never had a cat before, have you?" I tease. "They're not like dogs. You can't tell Orion to stay out of your bed and think he'll actually *listen*." Especially not this cat. "Besides, who says I'm sleeping in your bed?"

"I said you could have a choice, Savannah. My bed or yours. Don't you think I get to choose, too?"

He's kidding, right? I can't tell with this man, who can be hot or cold, teasing or stoic, sometimes all in the same conversation. But he wouldn't have gone to the trouble of bringing a twin-size cot up here for me if he planned on joining me on it. I don't even think we'll both fit!

Spoiler alert: we *do*.

And you know how I know that?

Because about an hour after Damien insists that we both turn in—and he does settle down into his bed for the first time since I've been here, while I curl up on the cot with Orion—I'm still awake, reliving those long, awful nights in prison when it's like fucking deja vu.

In prison, I rarely slept. When I did, it was only

after I checked to make sure Portia was out at least five times. I'd woken up to her deciding to return the favor, licking my pussy to orgasm while I was half asleep too many times to count. Then, when I got mad at her for it, she played the victim—and insisted I give her head while we were both conscious as soon as it was lights out.

It was her way of being a consummate sexual predator. She got off on assaulting me while I was sleeping, then enjoyed the control factor of using her connections against me so that I would drop to my knees for her whenever she snapped her damn fingers.

I became numb to it after a while. The actual *physical* act of oral sex, I mean.

Close your eyes. Lick. Get it over with...

It's why I didn't care when Damien did the same thing. Penetrative sex with a penis is a little different, and I haven't had any since before I went to prison, so I had to stop him before he tried to fuck me. But blowing him? That was nothing.

Oh, no. I'm so twisted up when it comes to that kind of sex, it doesn't bother me. But when someone tries to slip into my bed...

The only reason I was able to fall asleep the last two nights was because I did, knowing I was alone in Damien's room. Now that he's in here with me... I'm waiting until I hear the soft snuffles of his snores before I even think about shutting my eyes.

They never come. And, after an hour, the moment I was dreading happens.

The cot dips and groans as a second—well, *third*—body climbs on top of it.

I guess he wasn't kidding after all when he said he'd choose my bed and expect to be allowed into it if he wanted to.

"You're still awake."

Into the darkness, I whisper softly, "Yes."

"You must be tired. Close your eyes. Nothing will happen to you while I'm here."

It's that he *is* there that's the problem.

He's spooning me. That's all. One arm nestling on my hip as we both lay on our sides, he's squeezed onto the bed—but he's not doing anything else.

"How can I trust you?"

Damien is silent for a moment. All I can hear is the thudding of my heart and Orion's gentle purr as he sleeps near my belly.

"I swear on Genevieve's life that you have nothing to fear from me while we're in this room."

There's a weight to his words that makes me want to believe him. *Genevieve...* "That's your sister, right?"

"It is."

The same sister he was willing to slice my throat open for after I made a tiny reference to possibly making her a target.

And he's swearing on her life?

"I'm just going to lay here. To hold my wife close. To know that I own you. Capisce? But, in return, I will protect you. From the nightmares that keep you awake, and from whatever made you like this." He doesn't say it, but I know what he means: desperate enough to attempt to kill a man like him. "That's all I ask of you, Savannah... until you ask me for more."

The soft way he whispers those promises into my hair has my stomach twisting. Where is the monster I spent so long believing he was? *Ask* him... "You mean beg you, don't you?"

"No. When I see my wife on her knees again, it'll be because she chose to be, not because she thought it would be enough to keep the brute away from her."

I arch my back, bumping my ass into his erection. In the silent darkness, the sound of Damien sucking in a breath seems impossibly loud.

"It didn't work."

He sucked in that breath, now he shudders it out. His hand lands on my hip, burning a brand through my jeans. "No, ragna mia. It didn't."

Ragna mia.

My spider.

And, with Orion curled up in front of me because Damien brought him to me, I can't help but feel a little less murderous toward my 'husband'...

I SLEEP THROUGH THE ENTIRE NIGHT LIKE A BABY, AND when I wake up and feel a body behind me, for the first time in years, I don't feel my stomach sink.

Worse, my heart flutters—and what the fuck is *that* about?

The twin is not big enough for all three of us, just like I thought. Orion is gone, and I'm scooted all the way toward the edge. Damien is still right there, though, spooning me. One arm is thrown over my waist, the other tucked under my head.

Oh my God. I've been using Damien Libellula's arm for a pillow.

Slowly, I try to sneak out of his embrace. Maybe, if I'm lucky, I can get away before he wakes up…

"Your cat is sleeping on my bed."

My eyes close for a moment. Damn it. "Huh?"

"Your cat, wife. He's curled up on my bed."

Part of me wants to tell Damien 'I told you so'. The king-sized bed is massive. Orion's probably never seen anything like it, and once he got booted from the cot, he probably was like: *score.*

But then I remember how he made it a point to say that he'd never allow Orion up there.

Uh-oh. I pull myself into a sitting position, ready to scold Orion and shove his rump onto the floor if I can reach him. Only, before I can, Damien moves, too, and I barely notice until he's suddenly gripping my chin, turning my face so that he can kiss me—which is exactly what he does.

Things like *morning breath* and *I hate him* and *what does he think he's doing* all rush through my mind... but that doesn't stop me from kissing him back, does it?

I do break the kiss first, though. I have a little pride, I guess, though not much because all it takes is the tiniest of winks from Damien before I'm wondering if it would really be so bad to take advantage of this situation while I can.

A kiss can't hurt. I might even be able to make this work. If he wants to kiss me, sooner or later, he might forget what I'm capable of and...

And...

"What the hell was that?"

"Another expectation, my dear. My wife will kiss me when we wake up in the morning, and before we go to bed at night. It's the least you can do for me looking the other way as Orion sheds all over my Egyptian cotton sheets."

But *why*?

And I don't just mean the kiss, either.

Why—

"Why are you doing this?"

"Doing what?"

Being nice to me. To my cat. Treating me like I really am your wife... "You know."

"Maybe I do." He runs his finger along the edge of my jaw. "And maybe, when you answer my questions, I'll answer yours."

Before I can think of a way to respond to that,

Damien is out of my bed and halfway to his closet. Shifting my weight on the cot so that I don't disturb Orion, I watch as he steps inside of the walk-in, returning in a moment with another one of the suits he wears daily on a hanger including the dress shirt, with a fresh pile of his underclothes—tank, underwear, dress socks—tucked under his arm.

Something must be wrong with me because I don't notice that he stripped down to his boxer briefs until I watch his sculpted back and his tight ass pass in front of me before he heads into the bathroom.

I blink. Did he... did he sleep behind me in his underwear and I had no idea? I guess that makes sense. When I think of Damien Libellula, I think of the styled hair, the charming smile, the tanned skin, and the suit. He's still human, though. Despite his immaculate appearance when he's out and about, why the hell would he sleep in a suit?

More importantly, how the hell did I not notice he was nearly naked behind me? Especially since he was certainly hard before I finally fell asleep—and, fuck, I can't believe I felt comfortable enough in a bed with the head Dragonfly to actually nod off.

By the time he finishes his shower and comes out in a cloud of tempting perfume, looking like he stepped off the pages of GQ, I've schooled my features into a look that says I wasn't affected at all by his half-naked walk to the bathroom.

"Leaving so soon?"

"Why? Are you going to miss me?"

I huff. "You wish."

His answer is a tiny half-smile. "I'm sorry, but I won't be able to join you for breakfast this morning. I'm needed at the office."

The office. He knows damn well that *I* know what kind of business he's in, and yet, he insists on acting like he has a legitimate job that he goes off to every day. Honestly? I think he's trying to get me so pissed that I finally blurt out that I wanted to kill him because he runs a mafia—but I'm not about to give him the satisfaction.

"That's alright. I'll share with Orion."

He didn't want my cat in his bed. He'll probably *hate* the idea of an animal eating off of his plate.

Come on, Damien. Say something bad about my cat. Remind me why I'm supposed to hate you so fucking much...

He doesn't.

Damn it.

"I'll be home by dinner, and that will be for just you and me. Until then, if you want to leave the room, I think it's only fair that you should be able to."

Really? "Why?"

He doesn't answer me. Going on as if I hadn't asked anything at all, he says, "The third floor is off-limits. You can go to the first floor if you'd like, but that's

186

usually where Vin is when he's home. Our cook, too, our maid, and Frankie, my valet, who's in charge of the staff."

Ah. The grey-haired man who brings me each of the three meals Damien insists I'm served, whether he's there to eat with me or not. I knew he was Frankie, but at least now I know what his job title is.

"As for the second floor where we are," Damien continues, straightening his blood-red tie. "Feel free to explore it. The television out there is much bigger, and I have a couch that, once you sink into it, you'll never want to leave."

Since he still is insisting I can't, maybe that's a good thing.

But why now? I've only been here four days. He trusts me enough to leave my gilded cell?

The tracker, I remember. Even if I try to leave, I can't without him coming after me. I can't even try to remove it, either. For one thing, no one in this manor will let me have a knife; trying to cut my steak during dinner with a spoon is proof of that. For another, the subdermal tracker is so fucking tiny, I could hack off half my bicep and still never find it.

"Aren't you afraid I might mess with some of your stuff?"

"Why would I be? This is your home now, Savannah. The second floor is ours. It belongs to us. Enjoy it."

I just... I don't get it. I don't understand him. I made it clear I hate him, even if I refuse to explain myself. So, no. There is no 'us'. There is no 'our'. There's only Damien versus me.

Isn't there?

Revenge List

SIXTEEN
GENEVIEVE

SAVANNAH

Call me paranoid and suspicious if you want, but Damien's offer to explore the second floor... it feels like a trap.

I don't know what he's getting out of it. Like, if I slip out of the bedroom and nose around, will he use that against me? Or will he see me giving in as a victory in this war between us?

Or is this war as one-sided as it seems?

Let's put it out there. We're almost at the week mark since my life got flipped upside-down. And apart from the flash of temper he showed after my escape attempt, he's been nothing but cordial. He's been kind.

And, damn it, he's been *seductive*.

Is this Damien's way of getting back at me for how I made it seem like I was into him so I could steal his knife? For a split second there, even I'd admit there was a spark... some chemistry even... before my revenge list popped into my brain and I remembered in the next instant who I am—*now*—and why I was as close to him as I got.

I've run that altercation in the alley over and over again. Hundreds of times since I've been basically trapped in Damien's manor. I don't doubt that he was attracted to the vibes I was giving off. But after I stabbed him?

The crazy bastard seemed even *more* attracted...

How else can I explain the way he's treated me since. With fresh stitches in his side, he would've fucked me that same night if I didn't refuse. The fact that I did and he didn't push it? That sex wouldn't have been a punishment, not like the way I thought of him fucking my mouth. It would've been because getting stabbed was like foreplay for him, and since I was the one wielding the knife, Damien Libellula locked on me.

But it's only been a week. To my shock, he's done everything he could to make me feel comfortable here. Mainly because the mafia leader one hundred percent means it when he says that he won't allow me to leave him. If I'm his prisoner, at least I'm a well-treated one.

Consider I tried to assassinate him? I should be lucky he hasn't just gotten sick of me, summoned Vin, and left him to it.

I haven't seen the big guy since that first night. I

don't think that's a coincidence, either. Now that I have a *tracker* in my arm, it's not like I need to be guarded, right? And if he's still pissy over Damien's stab wound, oh well. Damien doesn't seem to care.

Oh, no. Because my 'husband' has finally caught on to the fact that I'm amazed by the body he hides beneath his suits, he spends more time parading around our room both before and after his share than is good for my mental health. He preens like a fucking peacock—and it works. I can't deny I find him good-looking, and when he checks his stitches and changes his bandages, looking at the slowly healing wound with something that might shockingly be pride, I don't know *how* I feel.

So I do what I did when shit got rough in prison. I shut down, keep my mouth shut, and just try to survive.

Having Orion near helps. Being able to finally shower, brush my teeth, and change into fresh clothes helps even more. I know this can't last. One way or another, something has to give. I can't spend the rest of my life in Damien Libellula's bedroom, even if he sees that as a just punishment for my attempted murder of him.

In the end, it's because of Orion that I finally get the nerve to leave the room. After two days of him exploring every corner of the bedroom, my curious cat finally figures out that the door to the bedroom is different from the one in my apartment. At the apartment, he knew better than to leave so he rarely scratched at that door.

Here? Because of Damien's comings and goings, plus his staff coming in to bring food or make his bed or put the grown man's laundry away, the single brain cell in my orange and white cat's head flares as he discovers that there's more to this place than this one room.

And once he does, he wants to explore out there.

Since I'd rather not see Orion scratch the shit out of Damien's fancy wood door—or have my 'husband' tell me how I can make it up to him since I sure as hell can't pay for any damage—I open the door. He bolts, I chase, and the rest is history.

It didn't take me long before I saw my mistake. Damien warned me away from the first floor by mentioning that Vin resides down there, but he was very clear: the third floor is off-limits. And where does Orion go as soon as my fluffy idiot has free rein of the house?

Right up the stairs to the third floor.

I can't let him. Music is filtering down from upstairs, and during one of the dinners Damien insisted we share, he let slip that his sister is a professional dancer. Her studio is kept on the third floor, and when I hear music, it means she's rehearsing.

Here's hoping that she can't hear me running up the stairs, hissing my cat's name over the sound of—

Shit.

The music turns off the exact moment that Orion reaches the landing.

"Orion! Get over here."

He looks behind him at me, sees I'm chasing, and decides it's a game. I swear, he has a grin on his face, whiskers twitching, before he starts to run down the hall.

Orion, you *asshole*.

On the plus side, he doesn't get that far—but that's the downside. Because, just as he's about to dash past an open doorway, someone comes walking out of it.

It's a stranger. Orion's gotten used to Damien being in our space—because, to my cat, that room is *our* space—but he wasn't expecting someone else to move in front of him.

Especially not someone who looks down, squeals, and immediately drops to pet him.

Orion hisses, batting at the air because he's not a bad boy who'll actually scratch a human.

The girl laughs. "Nice to meet you, too."

And then, turning her head, she smiles at me. "And you."

Fuck. We're caught.

Even if I hadn't already seen her face countless times while she was out with Damien, or had the image of the blonde hair and horrified expression after she burst into his bedroom that first night seared into my brain, her outfit would've given her away. She has on a pale pink leotard complete with a gauzy skirt, cropped tights that show off a pair of gnarly dancers' toes that are painted black, and a white towel draped around her sweaty neck.

Genevieve Libellula.

"Um. Hi."

"I know, I know. It's so awkward that we've been living in the same house and this is the first time we're really being introduced. That's because my brother told me not to bother you until I was sure you wouldn't be embarrassed about..." She makes a crude gesture, shaking one hand by her mouth, using her tongue to make her cheek bulge at the same time. "You know."

Oh my God. "Yeah. I know."

"Thought you would. And since *I'm* never forgetting that, I thought maybe we could finally meet on your, like, fiftieth wedding anniversary? I might be senile by then and it wouldn't matter. But I guess your cat— this is your cat, right? And you're Savannah?"

I nod.

"I'm Genevieve. Most people call me Gen. Vin calls me Genny." She pauses for a moment. "Don't call me Genny."

Okay, then. I gesture at the cat. "This is Orion."

At the sound of his name, his tail goes right up in the air, and he eases his way toward me as if realizing that he's a) in big, big trouble right now, and b) running in his condition was probably a bad idea, and now that he's stopped, he's feeling it.

Genevieve frowns. "What's wrong with your cat? Is she supposed to walk like she's bow-legged?"

"Orion is a he."

"Sorry. I didn't see any balls so I thought she was a girl." Lowering her voice, almost as an aside, she adds, "Don't tell Dame I know what balls look like. He might have a shit fit."

I swallow my laugh. I'm sorry, but how in any world is this girl *Damien's* sister? I'm not even talking about her being blonde while he has super dark hair. Their tanned skin is the same, so are their eyes and a few facial features, but their personalities?

Worlds fucking apart.

I like her. Maybe I shouldn't. Maybe I need to just pick Orion up and carry him back downstairs.

Or maybe...

"Maybe I should take him to the vet." I bend low, stroking his head. "You're right. I noticed he's been walking a little weird since your brother went to my apartment and got him for me." Peeking up at Genevieve, I check her reaction. Huh. She doesn't seem surprised that Damien would do that. Because she already knew? Or because that's just what kind of a man he is? I shake my head. "Now that I'm thinking about it, his litter box hasn't really been full. I thought it was the stress of a new place, but maybe he's constipated. A vet visit's probably in order."

All of that is true. I wasn't worried because this isn't that unusual for Orion. When I got him as a kitten, he ended up so full of shit, I had to scrape my pennies together to take him to the vet for an enema. Talk about a three-hundred-dollar dump by the time he was done.

But if I could convince Damien's sister that it might be essential to take him now? I'll keep her secrets, she can keep mine, and instead of taking Orion to the vet, I can get a headstart out of Springfield.

He doesn't give a shit about me. Not really. If I leave his turf, tracker or no tracker, he wouldn't chase after me. I'd only be a loose end if I stayed in the city, but even if I have to give up on my revenge, I'd do it if only to get away from Damien while I still can.

Lifting her towel, she dabs the underside of her jaw. "Know what? That's a good idea. We've got, like, six cars in the garage. I know where Damien keeps the keys, too, if you want to take him. I'd hate to see the kitty in pain."

"Really?"

"No."

It's the flat tone of voice that has me doing a double-take, especially since Genevieve hasn't lost her friendly smile.

"Um. Sorry. What?"

She reaches out, patting my arm.

"I'm not sure if Damien told you about me, but if we're going to get along, I should make something perfectly clear. My big brother still looks at me and sees a four-year-old in a tutu. He thinks I have no idea what's going on half the time, and I'm happy to let him. Yeah? Yeah. But you're not my big brother. Honestly, I'm not really sure who you are except for the woman who stabbed Dame."

Oh, shit. And to think I couldn't understand how these two were related. Right now, I see her brother in the way she's looking at me. Overprotective. Ruthless. Merciless.

"I—"

"Hey. Don't worry about it. That's between the two of you. If he gets off with a little pain, I'd rather not know. Okay? You do you. But, please. Don't think because I let him treat me like a kid, that you can, too. For some reason, Damien wants to keep you around. I'd like to have some more estrogen in the manor for a change. So don't fuck it up, kay? And trying to use me to leave my brother? Not gonna happen, babe."

Know what? She was honest with me. I might as well return the favor.

I own it. "Hey. It was worth a shot."

"I know. And I respect that. And I really am worried about your cat."

She points. Orion is sucky as backup. While Genevieve was threatening me, he decided to plop down, kick up a leg, and lick his asshole. And while I know he's doing that because there's a good chance he really is constipated, the optics are super annoying.

"I wasn't kidding when I said he's constipated."

"Is there anything we can do about it?" Before I can answer her, her eyes light up. "I know! Stay right here."

Okay. I guess.

Genevieve runs gracefully back into the room that she had just left. I don't know what she's doing in there —or how it'll help Orion—but she has her phone out, on speakerphone, and she's already talking by the time she returns to the hall.

"Hey, Dr. Liz. It's me. Genevieve."

Dr. Liz? From the clinic?

"Gen! How are you doing, sweetie? How's your ankle? Giving you trouble?"

"I'm okay." As if to prove it, she goes on point on one foot, flexing the other, testing her ankle. "Yup. All good. But, listen. I'm here with Damien's wife—"

"Wife? I didn't know he was married."

"Oh, yeah. It's new, but it's been a little hush-hush. You know what I mean."

I wish I did. I wish I had any idea what the fuck was going on right now.

"Genevieve—"

"Shh." She waves her hands at me to hush since Dr. Liz is still talking.

"—did bring this quiet brunette with him to the clinic a few days ago. But *wife*—"

"Yup," Damien's sister cuts in. "That's Savannah. Hey. She's right here." Genevieve nudges my shoulder. "Say 'hi'."

I cannot believe this is happening. Leaning forward, speaking into her phone, I mutter, "Hello."

"Hello, Savannah," Dr. Liz says warmly. "Sorry that we met under such stressful circumstances, but I'm glad to see that your date must've ended well. Congratulations on the nuptials!"

Someone kill me. Kill me now. "Thanks. Um. Genevieve said you might be able to help me."

Right? I mean, she seemed like she had a brilliant idea to help Orion's clogged-up pooper, and she came back with Liz on the phone, so maybe she has some vet experience or something.

"Of course. What do you need?"

"It's not me," I begin before Genevieve angles the phone toward her mouth.

"It's a cat," she announces. "The cutest, fluffiest orange and white cat. And I'm pretty sure he's all stopped up, Dr. Liz. Now, I know you're not a vet or anything, but do you have any idea what we can do about a cat that won't shit?"

For Orion, I tell myself. I'm going through this right now for my baby.

It's worth a shot. I know what my vet says to do, and I'd hoped that plenty of fresh water, a little less stress, and some time might fix him, but if she has an idea... why not?

Surprisingly, she does. And after Dr. Liz rattles off all the home remedies we can give Orion to help him out, I'm so thankful and amazed by her expertise, she laughs and admits that she grew up in a home that always had two or three cats. She's firmly a people doctor, like I thought, but she has the necessary experience anyway.

That done, Genevieve begins to finish the phone call when, suddenly, Dr. Liz says, "Will I see you guys at Damien's dinner next week?"

Huh?

"Of course," his sister says quickly. "Because it's being hosted in the private room at La Vita Vino, I get to go. You'll be there, right?"

"I already have my dress picked out, and a note printed to put on the clinic door that we're closed for the evening."

"Awesome. See you then!"

"You, too, Genevieve. Oh, and Savannah? If you need any more help, please feel free to give me a call."

Yeah. Maybe if I had any idea what happened to my phone, I might. "Sure."

I think Genevieve realizes that, too. After she hangs up, she's careful to tighten her grip on her phone as if I'm going to snatch it from her.

Not right now. I'm a little bit distracted by what the doctor and the dancer were talking about.

"So, uh... what dinner were you guys talking about?" I ask her.

"Damien's fortieth birthday dinner. His birthday was last month, but we didn't have enough time to make the arrangements. Though that's a crock of shit if you ask me. I think he just didn't want to admit he was the big four-oh. But he agreed to a dinner instead of a party, and we're having it next Saturday."

"Really?"

"Yup. But don't worry about it. We've got plenty of time 'til then." Swooping down, picking the now-dozing Orion up before he can realize it's Genevieve and not me, she starts to flounce toward the stairs. "Now, come on! Let's see if the cook has any pumpkin."

And because Damien's younger sister runs off with my cat, I have no choice but to follow her.

For Orion, I remind myself. For *Orion*.

Revenge List

SEVENTEEN
SELFISH

DAMIEN

Another night at Il Sogno. Another steak dinner while ignoring Lincoln's piss-poor mood. Only this time? He's not the only one eager to get home to his wife.

I can tell almost immediately that he has news for me. Which makes sense. Our next meet wasn't supposed to be until two weeks from now, and it's Devil's turn to host. So when he called me this morning and asked if I could get a reservation at Il Sogno because 'they made a good steak', I knew there was more to it than just meeting the terms of our truce.

Doesn't mean he's happy to be here. Just means that, if he did what I thought he did, I owe him a debt. I'm sure he *will* be happy to call that in one day.

The moment the waiter takes away our plates, and

we both wave him off for dessert, Lincoln grabs something he kept tucked under his seat.

Watching me closely, he slides two folders onto the table.

One says *Georgia Gayle.* The other? *Jimmy Winter.*

"Which one do you want to look at first?"

Jimmy Winter. As a sign of good faith, when Lincoln arranged this meet, he let me know that Tanner finally came through. After weeks of research, he learned exactly who's running the crew that uses a snowfall as a symbol.

As the head of a Family, I should want to know about the man behind the mysterious snowflake. But, fuck it. I've devoted fifteen years to building my mafia. I've poured blood—mine and others—sweat and tears into this life, and I've put the Dragonflies first time and time and time again. If not the Dragonflies, then the Libellulas.

Just once, why can't I be completely selfish? Do something for *me*?

I tap Georgia's. "This one."

Lincoln makes a soft noise.

"What?"

"Nothing."

It's not nothing, and we both know it. "Spit it out. I'm sure you have something you want to say."

He shrugs, sliding Winter's back toward him. "Not really. I guess I just figured you'd want to know about the man behind the snowflake more."

Really? Since he has Georgia's folder, I'm willing to bet he's figured out why I asked him to have Tanner look her up. He'd be an awful boss if he didn't read through the folder before he set it down in front of me, and since Tanner is a pro at what he does, there's no doubt in my mind that he hasn't linked Georgia to Savannah if they are—as I suspect—one and the same.

Add that to the sly congratulation Lincoln slipped into the conversation earlier, the Devil of Springfield knows that I, too, am married.

How? Because Judge Callihan decided to take a trip down to the Playground and run his mouth.

I don't care. Let the city know that one of its most eligible bachelors has finally settled down. I'd be proud to show off my murderous wife if I didn't accept that, by doing so, I was putting her in danger.

She's already hiding so much from me. Without knowing what it is, how could I risk someone going after her the way she went after me?

That, at least, won't be in this folder. But what is?

Before I reach for Georgia's folder, I ask Lincoln, "If Ava was hiding things for you, wouldn't you choose her?"

"First of all, even when I was serving my penance, Ava didn't hide shit from me. She might not have no idea I was out there watching, but the only time I got caught off-guard was when she blew Maglione away and I saw his dragonfly."

He waits to see if I'm going to comment on that.

When I don't, he continues. "Second? Fuck, yeah, I'd choose Ava. But I fucking love that woman so she'll always be my first choice in everything. What's your excuse?"

Apart from being irrationally obsessed with a woman who makes no qualms about how much she loathes me? I don't have one.

But once I open the folder...

One glimpse. One glimpse at the photo that's placed on top of the half-inch thick pile of paper inside of the folder. A print-out of a driver's license, it lists the woman pictured as Georgia Gayle, with a Springfield address.

It's Savannah, thought. Her hair is a lovely shade of brown with golden streaks, her smile is a lot more innocent, and her features are softer, more rounded... but that's her. That's my wife.

Just like I expected.

I slam the the folder shut.

Lincoln cocks his head at me. "All that work and you just needed a picture? That it, Damien?"

No, but I find that I don't want to explain myself to my old friend right now. "Let's just say I saw what I needed to. I'll go through the rest later." When I'm alone. When I can read it carefully, processing what it says. Sliding the folder away, I look at Lincoln. "Okay. I'm ready. Tell me all about Jimmy Winter..."

Revenge List

EIGHTEEN
FORTIETH

SAVANNAH

When Damien never mentioned this birthday dinner of his, I tried not to be offended.

Why should I be? I'm not really his wife. I'm basically his glorified prisoner. This is a celebration of forty years of his life while I've only been in it for, what, a little more than two weeks?

Of course, if you ask him, he's decided that we've known each other for months. He counts it from the first moment he spied me watching him, even when he didn't know my name, only that I was stalking him. Why? No idea, except that annoys me, and he seems to find that funny.

Dick.

What makes it sting a little more is how it's not like

he didn't have time to tell me that his entire Family—plus those affiliated with the Dragonflies, like Dr. Liz—was throwing him this elaborate dinner. Because of his insistence that we share at least one meal a day before I inevitably end up sleeping beside him in either his bed or my cot, he could've mentioned it at any point.

He didn't—and that's why I'm so confused when Damien arrives home on the afternoon of the party, frowning when he finds me watching the next episode of a series I've been binging on his big television.

In his arms, he's holding a dry-cleaning bag that's probably his outfit for tonight. Because, knowing my new husband, he probably had to get *another* black suit for the occasion.

"Savannah? Why haven't you gotten ready yet?"

I'm wearing a sweater and jeans, my hair pulled back in a ponytail because I'll be damned if I try to get myself all dolled up. I'm already having a hard time not falling for his charm—which, I'm sure, is part of his plan... to make me not only give up my plan of revenge, but to actually start liking him a little before he decides his fun is over and he finishes me off. To give him a reason to start his seductive, sexual onslaught?

No, thanks.

But he seems so surprised that I'm vegging out, I almost feel bad for him. "Why would I be getting ready?"

It's not like *I'm* invited to this dinner—

"Because we have to leave in two hours to be on time. Here. I stopped in early to make sure you have this."

Ignoring how he seems to think I'm going anywhere with him, I'm curious enough to take the dry-cleaning bag from him. I honestly thought it was a suit, especially when I could see the black material through the plastic, but once I unzip it, it's obvious it's *not* a suit.

It's a strapless black cocktail dress—and it's just my size.

I glance up at him. "What's this for?"

"Dinner. Since this is the first time you'll be meeting some of the other members of my Family, I thought it called for something special."

His matter-of-fact answer has me confused now.

"Wait? Why? You think I'm going to it?"

Damien's lips thin. "You're my wife. Where else would you be?"

"I dunno." Where else would I be? With the tracker in my arm and eyes watching my every fucking move.... "Here. With Orion."

For some reason, that answer only seems to piss him off more.

"Our cook has the afternoon and evening off. So does Frankie and Annette. Vin will be at the dinner. Genevieve, too. Is this your way of trying to leave me? Stay behind and escape? Because I should remind you, my dear... I can always find you."

Trust me. I don't need the reminder.

"Hey. Don't be an ass. I didn't think you wanted me there." Just in case it isn't clear... "You never told me about it."

"Why would I? My sister told me that she did."

No. Genevieve mentioned it, then we got distracted trying to find a can of pumpkin puree to help Orion poop. That ended with Damien's cook calling someone up to make a trip to the store, bringing us a can so that Genevieve could feed spoonfuls of the dark orange mush to Orion by hand.

He had a monster shit that night, and a tentative friendship between Genevieve and I was formed.

So long as I understand she'll use her powerful ballerina legs to kick the shit out of me if I ever try to hurt her big brother again, and she gets that I'll let her play with Orion, but she better never hurt *him*, we're good.

Plus, she's the one who turned me onto this new show. When she's taking breaks from rehearsing upstairs —or when her ankle injury flares up—she usually comes down to the second floor, plops onto the couch with me and Orion in Damien's big television room, and asks perkily, "So, what are we watching today?"

The dinner? Hasn't come up, and I was struggling with *why* I was feeling so rejected for not getting an invite, I didn't have time to mention it to Gen.

I don't want to explain all of that to Damien.

Honestly, I don't owe him an explanation, either. Just because he thought Gen brought it up to me, doesn't excuse him from doing the same.

I think he comes to that same conclusion at the same time. He sighs. "A miscommunication on my part, then. But that doesn't change things. I want you at the dinner. You will join me." He gestures at the dress in my lap. "And you will wear that."

You know what? I will. For two reasons, too. One: I haven't been out of the house since Frankie caught me trying to hop the gate; even then, that doesn't really count because I never even got off the property. I'm not planning to run or anything—especially since I'm sure Damien will have at least a few someones watching me —but if the opportunity provides itself, you never know. And two: I still haven't put on all of my weight back, but I still think I can rock this dress.

Maybe show Damien what he's never gonna have.

Clutching the dress to my chest, I'm careful to avoid brushing it along the top of Orion's furry butt so that I don't get more cat fur on it than I already have. I get to my feet, meeting the dare written in every line of his face.

"Two hours?" I think of what's in the bathroom. He has a blow dryer and, not surprisingly, my meager make-up bag also made it to Damien's house after the Dragonflies visited my apartment. It's not much, but it'll do. "I'll be ready in an hour and a half."

I JUST MAKE MY SELF-IMPOSED DEADLINE. AFTER shimmying the dress on, I blew out my hair, forming tousled waves using my brush and my fingers. A little mascara, eyeliner, some blush, and my favorite lip finish the job, and I'm looking the best I have in a long, long time as I leave the bathroom.

Damien's sitting on the bed, looking at his phone when the door opens. His head snaps up, and I have to swallow my grin when he sucks in a breath.

"*Savannah...*"

I run my hands down the sides of my hips, smoothing the dress. "You like?"

"Very much." He tosses his phone to the bed, then gets to his feet. "Let me look at you."

I turn so he can get the full effect, but that's not what he means. Taking me by the hand, I stumble in my bare feet until he has me right in front of the floor-length mirror in his room.

"Bellissima, ragna mia. My black widow, you are *beautiful*."

Damien moves so that he's behind me, gazing at my reflection in the mirror with me. Swooping up my loose hair, he sets it over my shoulder before bending down to press a kiss to the bare back of the other one.

I can't stop myself from reacting. Closing my eyes so that I don't have to see the lust in them reflecting back at me, I angle my head so that I'm giving him better access to my throat.

Damien's hot mouth as he suckles my skin burns me up from the inside out. I keen a little, and he chuckles against my neck.

Then, as suddenly as the moment began, it's over. He's lifting his head up, though with my eyes still closed, I only can tell because I suddenly sense movement as he reaches around me.

My heart stutters in my chest. Is this it? Did he finally decide he was tired of me and was getting into position to... what? Stab me? Choke me? *Strangle* me?

Something settles on my chest. My eyes spring open in time to see that he's looped a silver chain around my throat. In my panic, I think *garotte*, but it isn't. It's a gleaming silver chain with a pair of charms hanging off the center.

Wearing a pleased smirk, Damien fastens it, then runs his thumb along the top of my shoulder.

I'm still staring at the necklace he just put on me.

"What's this?"

"I had it personally made for you, wife. A dress like this calls for accessories, don't you agree?"

And because he *did* have it made for me, the pair of charms are quite fitting.

The larger one is a silver dragonfly. And the other? Is a *knife*.

My breath catches in my throat. In his way,

Damien's marked me as his just as much as the scar on his side from his knife is proof that he decided to make me mine.

"Well?" he murmurs, nuzzling my temple as I do absolutely shit-all to stop him. "What do you think?"

I think that, if I honestly believed that I might win this war against Damien Libellula, I was fucking fooling myself.

It's not a tattoo that marks me as his property like every other woman who gets suckered into joining his Family. Oh, no. I haven't *earned* that yet... but he's marked me all the same, and any hope that I might be able to annul this fake marriage and start my life over with Orion flittered away the moment the silver dragonfly touched my chest.

And the worst part is, I'm not so sure how I feel about that at all...

———

THE HIGH FROM DAMIEN'S REACTION TO MY appearance lasts through the second course of dinner.

I'm surprised it lasted as long as it did. From the moment I follow at Damien's heels, walking into the elaborate private room at La Vita Vino, I already know I'm way out of my element. The dress, shoes he also bought for me, and the necklace help so that I fit in; most women in this room are wearing a variation of my evening wear, except for maybe Genevieve, who's gorgeous in a flowing, pale pink dress that looks striking with her blonde updo.

It's Damien's party, but she's the belle of the ball. Her outspoken, vivacious personality has her talking to everyone, and if I was anything like that, she'd be dragging me by the hand, showing me off to all of the guests.

I've never been like that. Even before my stint inside, I've always been more of an introvert. A loner. That's why I ran my store by myself, too. I don't really like people.

But that doesn't mean I'm not just a little bothered that, as soon as we arrive, my 'husband' ditches me almost immediately.

He has a place at the head of the main table. Two suits are sitting next to him, and the only thing stopping me from being irrationally jealous that I'm tucked all the way at a small circle table across the room is the fact that everyone at that main table is a guy. Not even Genevieve is sitting with Damien, though that might be because she's flitting all around the place, joining whichever table has an empty seat.

Just because Gen is occupied and, between courses, Damien is obviously still avoiding me, that doesn't mean I'm sitting by myself.

Oh, no. I have a babysitter.

I should've expected as much. When Vin plopped down in the seat next to me for the hors d'oeuvres course, one look at his scowl and I know that Damien put him up to it.

I'm not fooled by the scowl. He might hate me because he was the one who was seconds late to stop me from turning Damien's knife on him, but he's nowhere near as scary as he wants me to think he is. I've seen him with Genevieve, and even if I could brush that off as him taking care of his baby cousin, I caught him tossing one of Orion's catnip mice for him.

After the appetizers, but before the salad, Gen decides that I need to be a part of the socialization.

I get introduced to Christopher, Genevieve's friend whom I've actually already heard a bunch about, plus his boyfriend, Paul. Gio stops over to ask how I'm liking the bed he and his boys put together, and I find out that one of the other dark-haired suits who was there that day is an enforcer named Oliver who congratulates me when he notices my necklace.

Apart from that, no one makes any reference to the fact that I'm Damien's wife at all.

That's not a surprise, either. I get the vibe that, for weeks now, I've been his dirty little secret. Just because he insisted I come with him to this party, that didn't mean it was going to change.

So it sucks, but I force myself to eat my salad, refuse any offers of alcohol, and try my fucking best not to look around the room in search of dinner.

Even Dr. Liz stops by my table to say 'hello', a flute of champagne in her hand. She's wearing a cream-colored dress that shows off a surprisingly flattering shape. I guess, since I only saw her while she was wearing scrubs and a white coat, I shouldn't have assumed, but she looks really good—something that Vin obviously notices.

Her friendly smile is a welcome when mostly everyone else in the room is either watching me curiously or, following Damien's lead, pretending I'm not even here.

Once she drifts away, heading off to talk to someone else, Vin grunts out bluntly, "Gotta take a shit. I'll be right back. Don't go anywhere."

I don't say anything. I'd suspect he's really trailing behind Dr. Liz, trying to get her alone for a moment, but even if he *does* have to poop? I didn't need to know that, and I really don't care.

Vin takes my silence as an agreement that I'm going to sit tight like a good little girl, then pushes himself out of the seat.

We're between courses again. At the rate this is going, dinner is going to take five hours by the time it's done since there's a good twenty minutes between meals where everyone gathered can chat. I resign myself to sitting alone, waiting to see if the main course gets served first or Vin comes back to babysit me.

Two minutes after he got up—and not enough time for him to go the bathroom—someone takes Vin's seat.

"I've been waiting all night for a chance to talk to you."

Oh? Shifting in my seat, I look at my new companion.

He's about my age, maybe a year or two younger. He has dark blond hair in a money cut, deep brown eyes, and a winning smile that might've worked on Georgia as he slings his arm onto the back of my seat, trying to pull me into it.

It might've worked on Georgia.

Savannah doesn't have time for his shit. "That's nice. But I'm here with someone, so..."

"I know. I saw you with Vinnie. No knock on him, but I think I might be a better catch. Besides," he adds, using his other hand to trail down my nearest *empty* forearm, "if he liked you so much, you'd be marked as his property before he brought you around the rest of the Family. Since he didn't, you're fair game."

I *am*?

I don't bother correcting him that I'm here with Damien, not Vin. It's none of his business, and regardless of how these Dragonflies treat their women, I'm not about to let him treat me like he can own me.

"Thanks, but no thanks."

His hand is still close enough to my arm that, when I go to get up, he tightens his fingers around my wrist. "I don't think you understand. I didn't come here with a date. They didn't give me a plus one. I'm getting laid tonight, and I picked you. So instead of trying to play hard to get, just be grateful that I'm paying you any attention."

Idiot. Doesn't he realize that attention is the last thing I want, especially from some creep?

I break free of him, taking a few steps away from the table. There's an exit not too far on this side of the private room. It leads to a hall where the bathrooms are, plus an employee's only door at the end of it. If I have to hide out in the ladies' room to get away from this prick, I will.

He doesn't like this idea.

His hand is like a vice on my arm as he latches onto me again. "I *said*—"

I don't give a fuck *what* he said.

Jerking my elbow out of his hold, I whirl on him. I knee him in the dick, hoping that the pain will be enough to get this asshole to let me get away from him. I'm not even thinking about the fact that the room is full and I'm probably making a scene. I just want to e*scape*.

On the plus side, it is. Grunting out a, 'you fucking bitch', under his breath, he immediately releases me. Unfortunately, that leaves his hands free—and almost as if it's an unconscious reaction on his part, he fucking backhands me.

It doesn't feel the greatest. The slap of his hand against my cheek is almost deafening, and I gasp more because the force of his hit has me falling to my knee than because it's that painful.

I catch myself before I overbalance and land flat on my face.

And that's when I see a familiar pair of dress shoes in my line a vision a split second before someone grips my arm possessively, helping me back to my heels.

But it's not that creep.

It's *Damien*.

Revenge List

NINETEEN
MY WIFE

DAMIEN

I t took everything I have to stay on the opposite side of the room from Savannah the entire night long.

The reason was simple. If I didn't? I was going to find an excuse to whisk her away and fuck her in that little black dress she has on.

So desperate for her, I scared myself with how badly I needed to bend her over the nearest surface and take her. The make-up only made it worse. Talk about a temptress. I was already under her spell. Now? I never want it to break.

But what kind of guest of honor would I be if I dipped out of the party to bang my bride? Especially since Savannah has made no sign that she'd welcome me—and after going through that folder, I'm beginning to realize she never will.

So I distracted myself with business. Everyone here is either a Dragonfly or an associate of ours. If I can't have Savannah, the least I could do was find out more about Jimmy Winter and the threat he poses to my Family.

Lincoln's not here. My former rival actually laughed when I tendered him and Ava an invitation. Not only because his wife never wants to be in my company again, but she's so close to her due date, he hates the idea of her leaving Paradise Suites—which means he's not going anywhere, either.

That man would lock her up in a tower like Rapunzel if he could. And, honestly, now that I have Savannah, I'm beginning to see the merits of a plan like that...

I didn't think she would mind that I was staying away. I didn't think she'd even notice. And if it's a huge boost to my ego that, whenever I'd dare a glance toward the table where I had Genevieve put her, she was watching me closely... well, I was just hoping that she wasn't planning on taking one of the dinner knives and going after me with it.

I had Vin watching her anyway. Since I couldn't trust myself near Savannah, I had my most trusted enforcer on the job. He knew that there was only one excuse he could use to leave her: going to the bathroom. Other than that, he needed to be on her like flies on shit.

That must be what happened. I'd notice some of the newer recruits swarming around Savannah, but seeing Vin so close scared the soldiers off. One of them, though, waited until Vin slipped away for just a second to act.

That's all it took. Next thing I knew, I saw Savannah getting up from her seat out of the corner of my eye. She said something to the younger Dragonfly—Ricky, his name is *Ricky*—and whatever it was, he didn't like it.

And then he did something he never should've done.

He grabbed my wife.

Fuck staying away. I was already on the move before she *did* something that had him twisting away in pain mingled with fury, and just as I was closing the gap between me and Savannah, Ricky whirled around and *back-handed* her.

I caught her. It was pure luck that I did, and the thing that sealed his fate at the moment more than anything else was the flash of relief I saw on her face as she realized it was me.

That's how much trouble she thought she was in. She's actually glad to see *me*.

Setting her on her feet, I turn all of my attention to the boy.

"You hit my wife?"

Ricky's cupping himself, but over the noise, those two words make it through. "Your... your *wife*?"

"Listen to me, son. You didn't answer me. I'll ask you again. Did you have your hands on my wife?"

"Boss, I—"

My voice could drip icicles, it's that fucking cold. "Answer the question. Did you touch my wife?"

He can't deny it. I wasn't fast enough to stop the hit, though the evidence of it was clear. I had to lunge to grab Savannah before she landed on the floor. Even now her cheek bears the mark of his hand.

He can't deny it, so he tries to place the blame on her. "She tried to knee me in the cock—"

Dumb fuck.

"That's only because I have her knife," I tell Ricky, cutting off his excuses with my casual words. Dipping my hand under my jacket, I pull the stiletto out of its holster.

Twisting my wrist, showing him the knife, I give him a hard smile—and then my hand moves.

There's no resistance. The sharp blade cuts right through his throat so efficiently that Ricky doesn't even know he's dead right away.

When it catches up to him, though, he clutches his throat. Blood dribbles down his pale skin, covering his fingers, bubbling up in the massive gap that's stretching ear to ear.

He gasps. His knees fold.

I check the sheen of the blood on the knife as Ricky

falls forward, landing on his belly, inches away from Savannah's shoes.

I turn to my wife. "See that? That's how you kill someone with this stiletto, my dear."

The entire room goes silent. It probably was before, but after a moment, someone claps—probably my sister—and the chatter starts up again.

We're Dragonflies. We expect murder and mayhem at our gatherings. It's one of the reasons we always host them at a property we either own or have a stake in. Because, despite my need to appear debonair and classy, we're a bunch of violent criminals at our core.

And now my wife knows that.

Her lips are parted, mouth hanging open. Her gaze darts to the corpse clutching his throat on the floor. Ricky is dead, and since her stab wound didn't end me, I'm beginning to think this might be the first time she's ever been so close to one.

This might be the first time she's ever seen anyone die.

I feel this sudden urge to protect her from the reality of my Family. That's what I've been doing for weeks now, keeping her locked up in my home, but she's here now. She's a part of it. But maybe it's too much. Maybe she needs a moment to process it all.

With the knife still in my hand, I grab Savannah by the wrist. Knowing there isn't a single soul in this room that will stop me, I tug on her hand. I almost expect her to dig in her heels so that I can't. She doesn't. As though she's a zombie behind me, she just stares ahead as I navigate our way through the crowd.

She was halfway to the hall when Ricky grabbed her. I continue that way. Once we leave the private room behind us, I see the men's room, the ladies, and the employee's only door.

I own this place. I'm the highest fucking level of employee, and if the manager needs her office? Well, she can wait.

Savannah purses her lips when she sees where I've brought her, though she doesn't say anything as I open the door and shuffle her into the office.

Only when I've slammed shut the door behind her, locking it for good measure in case it all becomes too much and she decides to bolt, does she speak up.

"You killed that guy."

"He hurt you," I answer simply. Calmly.

I wait for her to get hysterical. That's what women do, right? So unused to the brutality of the life, now that she's got over being numb, she'll start crying—

She slaps me in the arm.

"So did you, Damien! And what happened? I tried to kill you... I tried to give you the same justice you just dealt out for me... and you didn't fucking die. And now I'm here, that asshole tried to *claim* me, and you're trying to act like my hero? No. *No.* If you think someone should die because they hurt me, you should be first in line."

Is that how she feels? I'm so glad that, for once, my wife is being honest with me.

"Fair enough." I hand her the hilt of the stiletto. "Go right ahead."

Savannah takes it with trembling fingers; not because she's upset, though, but because she's *furious*. She's steady enough as she closes them around the top of the knife, eyes locked on the splash of shiny red blood that coats the blade.

For a moment, I don't know what to expect. I'm ready to dodge if she does strike, but there's a better chance that she's bluffing—

Without telegraphing her move, she slashes at me. It's wide, though, not even close to my skin, even if the murderous look on her face makes it clear that it was a good attempt.

To be honest, I would've been disappointed in her if she didn't at least *try*.

I lash my fingers around her wrist, jerking it down so that she can't try to stab at me again.

And it hits me a second later.

She could've killed me. I handed her the weapon and, if she really wanted to, I highly doubt I could've dodged it so completely that there wasn't even a scratch left on my skin.

Savannah could've killed me—and she didn't.

And everything that happens next is because she had the chance *and she didn't take it*.

I twist my hand roughly, forcing her to drop the

stiletto to the floor. The *clang* echoes around me as I throw her arm up, pinning her against the door at her back. My other hand goes to her throat.

"What's that, *husband*?" she bites out, and I can't tell if she's frightened—or excited. "You're gonna choke me now?"

If I did, it would only be because it heightened her arousal to cut off some of her air.

"And let you out of this life when you promised it to me?" I coo. "No fucking way."

Her eyes flash angrily. "Then what do you think you're doing?"

"*This.*"

I kiss her. With my hand a necklace for her pretty, pretty throat, I squeeze just enough to make her gasp in a breath. Once her mouth is open, I dive in, taking advantage of it.

I kiss her, plundering her mouth with my tongue. Our teeth clash, this intimacy another battle, but the way I swallow her breaths, tasting her tongue, sucking her lips until I'm sure they'll be swollen... I kiss her and, in this position, there isn't anything she can do except take it.

And then she proves me wrong. Because Savannah doesn't just take it.

She kisses me back.

I have one arm thrown up over her head. Her other hand goes right to my side. For a second, I think she's squeezing me there because she's trying to find my healing scar, see if I'm still in pain from her stab.

I'm wrong. The deeper the kiss gets, the more she touches me. Her hand on my side. Her heel rubbing up and down the length of my calf. Her head angled as far back as she could move it so that our chests can connect at the same time as she wordlessly begs me to kiss her.

I don't know if this is another trap. If she's trying to lull me into a false sense of security. Only knowing the stiletto is on the floor and there's no way she can reach it is the reason why I finally let go of her hand.

I needed one of my own. If she's touching me, I'm going to take advantage and touch her. Squeezing her tit through her dress, I break the kiss just enough to press my wet mouth against her cheek.

"Tell me to stop, wife. If you don't want this... I won't stop on my own. You have to tell me to stop."

She doesn't say anything. She doesn't say 'yes'. She doesn't say 'no'.

She doesn't say 'stop'...

Letting go of her tit, I grab the hem of her strapless dress. One shove. One shove and there must be a God because Savannah went without a bra. The material goes down, her breast comes out, and like a starving man who'd long been denied a feast, I drop my head and suck her entire nipple into my mouth.

And even then she doesn't stop me.

Instead, she does the opposite. Panting softly, just about trying to climb me with her legs, Savannah starts to yank on my dress shirt. Now that she has both hands, she finds it easy to do. My dress shirt is out and, next thing I know, she's fumbling with my button.

My button, then my zipper.

My erection springs free as if searching for her hand like it's a goddamn magnet. She shifts her hand, rubbing her thumb around the crown, gathering up the precome I'm not too ashamed to admit is already there.

Fuck. If she keeps playing with me, I might just blow my load before I find out what it's like to be inside of this woman.

No. I can't let that happen. She might complain later that it all happened too fast, that she didn't want it, that she regrets being with me... but that's later. At this very moment, I have her tit in my mouth, her hands on my cock, and my bloodlust from a few minutes ago turned to straight-up lust now.

I let go of her throat. Both of my hands drop to her waist. I'm still sucking on her tit, swirling my tongue around the nipple, kneading the mound of flesh with my nose. It doesn't take me long to notice that his strokes—as jerky and frantic as they are—go in time to the amount of suction I use on her breast. So, of course, I use that to my advantage, keeping her distracted as I hoist her up.

Her back is still to the door. I use my body to keep her in place. She groans into my neck, obviously annoyed that she can't keep tugging on my cock when that and her hand is trapped between our lower bellies.

I let her tit slip out of my mouth with a soft *pop*ping sound.

"Don't be impatient, wife," I tease, using my free hands to take hold of the bottom of her dress.

"Shut up, Damien," she hisses into my ear. "Shut up and fuck me."

Anything for you, ragna mia.

I yank the skirt of her dress up so that it doesn't hinder the movement of her legs. Once she realizes she can move them wider, she instinctively wraps them around my waist.

Savannah might have gone without a bra, but she has a pair of silky black panties on. They're fucking *soaked*. I can see the moisture along the edge of them and smile into her hair. Even if I doubted that she wanted this now, there's proof that she's as turned on as I am.

If I had my stiletto, I'd slice off the panties to save time. I don't, and I'd rather not draw Savannah's attention back to the weapon, either. So, instead, I hook my finger under the wet material, shoving it to the side so that I can access her pussy.

I don't want to give Savannah the chance to change her mind. Not when I'm so close. Besides. I'm ready to explode, she's basically creaming herself, and it doesn't take much for me to push most of my cock inside of her in one thrust.

There's a small amount of resistance. Not enough to make me worry that my wife is a virgin whose first time is in the manager's office of one of my restaurants, but I'm sure it's been a long, long time since she's had sex.

Probably even longer since she's been thoroughly fucked by a man.

And she wants it. No matter how she reacts later, the moan she lets out as I shove myself the rest of the way in, fully seated inside of her as she wraps her arms around my neck, tugging me up to kiss her again, she *wants* it.

It takes a few messy seconds where I try to get the right rhythm going while also kissing her. I might've bit her one. She hisses out a breath, but if it hurts, she doesn't complain. Oh, no. She actually squeezes my cock as I thrust up into her.

As much as I wish it was otherwise, once I knew that this would be our first time together, it was always destined to be a quickie. I'm still so worked up over Ricky's disrespect, plus the mark he left on Savannah's beautiful face. I've spent months dreaming of fucking this woman, too, and I'm racing my certainty that she'll realize she lost her mind and invited the man she hates most in the world into her body.

Most importantly? I wouldn't blame her one bit. I read the files. I pored over her folder. I know the truth.

I know why she tried to kill me, and if I was Savannah? No amount of blustering and bluffing from the man who became my captor would stop me from reaching for the pillow after all.

Not when I learned what I took from her, and how I had no idea until Tanner ran that name for me.

So for as long as I can have her? For as long as I can delude myself that this magnificent creature truly is my wife? I'm going to take it, knowing that it won't last.

And, damn it, it *doesn't*.

Once I sense that I'm close, I make sure to slip a hand between our bodies. At first, I flick Savannah's clit. When she jolts, then tightens her hold on me, I can tell she's close, too. I start to rub roughly, stimulating her, ripping an orgasm out of her before I nut.

Once she starts gasping into my mouth, her keening whine fucking music to my ears, I know she's coming around my cock. The sensation of her inner walls fluttering around me is too much—as is her desperate need to kiss me again while she climaxes—and I follow right behind her, filling her up with everything I have.

Only then, when I jerk my hips one last time, sure that I've emptied myself does she react like a switch has been flipped.

No more hug. No more kisses. She reaches between

us, tucking her breast back into her dress before patting me on the chest.

Understanding the signal even if I don't like it, I pull out of her.

Savannah slides down my body, pushing against the wall to move me away from her.

I instantly miss the warmth of her in my arms.

I'm panting. Coming down from my climax... I'm shuddering, too. I haven't come so hard in longer than I want to admit, but she pushes off my chest and gives me her back, all while I have the silent promises to give her the world tucked in the corner of my mouth.

Once there's some space between us, Savannah pats her dress into place. Then, without a word to me, she starts to totter across the room. One heel came partly off her foot while I was pinning her into place against the door, fucking her like mad, and she pauses just long enough to adjust her shoe before she straightens her back, gripping the doorknob.

She's going to leave me. She's going to walk out of the manager's office like that didn't just happen.

Like I didn't finally *fuck* her.

Not in this lifetime, wife.

There's only one way I can think to stop her. If I demand her to return to me, she'll keep going just out of spite. But if I do *this*... it might mean I'll have to show my cards sooner than I wanted to, but it's a sure-fire way to get her attention.

Stopping only to fix my pants so that I don't have to confront her with my spent cocking hanging out, I take two steps and call out the one word guaranteed to stop her in her tracks before she can get far enough away from me:

"Georgia."

Revenge List

TWENTY
GEORGIA GAYLE

SAVANNAH

Georgia.

I haven't heard that name in almost a year, but my *husband* just used it.

Husband. Right. For weeks now, I've been telling myself that our marriage is a sham. A fucking joke.

Whatever it is, there's no denying that we just consummated it.

That's a nice way of saying that Damien Libellula just fucked my brains out—and I wanted him to. I was into it all the way, and even now that I'm walking away on wobbly legs, I can't deny that.

He killed a man for touching me. Didn't even hesitate. Swiped his stiletto across Ricky's throat, blood dribbling down his throat, and instead of being the cold Damien I've gotten used to, I got to see the fiery side of him before he lost the last of his control.

But that Damien is back now, and I can hear it in the way he says my old name.

"Georgia—"

"Savannah," I say firmly, turning to face him. "Please. Georgia is dead."

"Because I killed her. And that's why you're so determined to kill me." He crouches low, grabbing the stiletto from the tile. "But you couldn't. Could you?"

I hold out my palm. "So I missed," I say, bluffing like hell. "They say third time's the charm. Pass it over, Damien. Let's see if I miss again."

Damn it. With a daring look on his gorgeous face, he calls my bluff. Placing the hilt against my palm again, he backs up, spreading his arms wide. "Do it."

"No." I drop the stiletto back to the floor.

"Because Georgia Gayle isn't a murderer, is she?"

My empty hands flex, and I almost regret dropping that knife after all. With fire in my eyes, I glare at him. "You don't know anything about her."

About *me*.

"Is that so? Okay. I didn't expect to have this conversation right after I finally got the chance to fuck my beautiful wife, but if you want to do this now? I can't think of a better time."

I can. *Never.* "Stop this."

"You started this, my dear. Remember that. Your name is Georgia Ann Gayle. Adorable, by the way, and

I finally understand the inspiration behind Savannah. I'll call you Savannah if that's what you want, but if you decide to go back to Georgia—"

I'm already shaking my head.

"Very well. You're twenty-nine. Your birthday is next month, and if you want to forgo a dinner like this because... well... obviously... I understand. It can just be you and me—"

Is he fucking serious? "Damien."

He continues as if I hadn't said his name. "You were born in Springfield, just like I expected. Your accent was cute, Savannah, but it slipped far too frequently."

I open my mouth.

"You were in prison," he says next, and my teeth click shut. "A four-year stint at Madison, and suddenly your comment about someone slipping into your bed at night is crystal clear. It wasn't an ex-boyfriend you were talking about, was it?"

Somehow Damien has all the fucking receipts about my life, spouting them off as if there's a book on Georgia Gayle and he read it cover to cover. He's looking at me like he expects me to provide him some footnotes, but he might regret that one.

I shrug. "I had a store once. Healthy Habits by Georgia. Your gang got me mixed up with their counterfeiting, and I got hit with a four-year sentence. My first cellie wasn't bad, but then they stuck me with Portia. She's kinda like you, Damien. She was in prison for white collar crime... embezzlement which was so fucking funny because she had all the money in the world before she fleeced her employer... and she thought her name and her money and her *power* meant she could rule the prison."

And she did, too, which makes it so much worse.

He swallows a little, losing some of his cockiness. "And she was the one who..."

From the man who had me sucking his cock the same night we officially met, it's almost funny that he can't say the words. "Put it this way, if you don't like pussy when you go in, you learn to deal. You learn to look out for yourself."

Damien kicks aside the stiletto, moving toward me before I can even think to get out of his path. His hands land on my upper arms, tugging me toward him. "That's my job now. You hear me, Savannah? Lo faccio. I do that now."

His fingers dig into my skin. Not because he wants to hurt me, but because he doesn't want me to push back, to fight against him, to *escape*.

But I don't. I can't.

I collapse into him, letting him hold my weight at this moment as easily as he did when he had me hoisted and pinned against the wall.

His hands move, cradling my elbows. "Savannah? Are you alright?"

No.

Burying my face into his shoulder, unable to look at him as I make my confession, I murmur, "Fuck it.

Alright? You know the truth now. You know *everything.* You win."

Holding tightly to my elbows, he moves back, forcing me to look up at him. "What are you saying?"

"You're right. Okay? I couldn't... I couldn't kill you. When you were just the head of the Libellula Family, it was all I wanted. I plotted, right? I planned. The whole time I was in prison, I wanted you dead. I got out? I followed you. I *stalked* you. I visualized what it would be like to take you out and know that the rest of your gang would be finished. You stole four years from me. I would steal you from them. But then—

"Then I made you my wife," he says.

Right. "And you weren't just the head of the Libellula Family anymore. You're Damien. You're Gen's older brother. You're Vin's big cousin. You let Orion shed on your expensive pants. You pay so Liz can run her free clinic."

Damien scoffs. "You're making me sound like a good guy."

I snort. "Oh, no. You're definitely a bad guy. I mean, you just killed a guy for grabbing me."

His expression goes dark. "I killed him because you're mine. And he scared you, my wife. I couldn't let him do that."

Because he still is the head of the Family, and betrayal means death. It doesn't matter that only a few people in that room knew I was Damien's wife. Technically, he wasn't doing anything that countless other

Dragonflies haven't done. I was a woman at a mafia function without the mark that said I belonged to one of them. Fair game, right?

Not to Damien.

And since I'm dark and twisted enough now to see the romance in such brutal possessiveness, I'm still incredibly turned on that he killed Ricky for the crime of touching me.

"See? You're a bad guy, but that doesn't make you a villain. Not to me."

Releasing my left arm, he uses his free hand to tip my chin back. "I'm glad to hear that. Seeing as how I am also your husband."

"No," I say softly. "You're Savannah's husband. And now you know... Savannah doesn't exist. Not really."

The night I married Damien, I considered that my ace in the hole. No matter what, our marriage couldn't be legal because the woman he married just didn't exist. But now... I can't deny the twinge of disappointment that our marriage really is fake. Somehow, I've grown to like being his wife, but now that I know he knows the truth, how can I be?

Simple.

His other hand moves. Suddenly, he's gripping me by the jaw, angling my face up so that he can kiss me deeply.

When he breaks for a breath, he presses his forehead to mine. "You are Savannah. And that means you're *mine*."

"But why," I whisper back. "Why the hell did you marry me?"

"Because I wanted a wife, but out of all the women I've ever known, I've never felt the desire to tie myself to one until you." He caresses the edge of my jaw with his thumb. "You were beautiful. *Feisty*. I caught you spying on me almost immediately, but I'm sure there were times I didn't. Do you know how rare that is? Even for someone to try? And then you stabbed me... even with my knife in my side, I was already imagining you as my wife. So that's what I did."

And all that's well and good, but you know what I didn't hear him say? That he *loves* me.

That's just further proof that I really have lost my fucking mind. Because why would I care if he loves me or not?

I won't kill him. That's as much as I can offer him. I won't cheat on him, either. I'll be the loyal wife he wants... but that's all.

I need to change the subject. I need something else to focus on that's not how he's touching me as if I'm precious, as if I mean something to him. Considering how thoroughly he just fucked me, it's like he's trying to give me some aftercare.

And that makes me realize something I hadn't noticed before.

"Shit."

"Hmm?"

Planting my hands against his chest, I give him a

small shove. I don't put enough oomph in it to really move him on my own. Luckily, he takes pity on me and lets me go.

Right away, I reach under my skirt, dipping my pointer finger inside of my tender pussy. It's way wetter than it should be, and I glare over at Damien.

"You nutted in me," I accuse.

"Yes. What? Did you think I would pull out? You let me give you my cock, cara mia. There was only one place I was going to finish and that's inside of you."

I should've expected that. After all, he enjoyed himself finishing in my mouth during that fateful BJ. Why wouldn't he give me a creampie?

Oh, that's right. Because this marriage is already so dysfunctional, why shouldn't we throw a fucking kid into it?

"Are you serious? You weren't wearing a condom!"

Duh. With how fast everything was happening, protection was the last thing on my mind, too, but now that I'm coming down from the high of banging my gorgeous husband... "Shit. I need Plan B."

"Don't be ridiculous."

Me? "Okay. Next time wear a goddamn condom."

His upper lip curls. At first, I think it's because I basically just reassured him that that wasn't a one-time thing, but it's more than that, and I find out when he tells me bluntly, "No. If there's one thing I'll insist on, it's that nothing will ever come between us."

Damien is a smart man. Why doesn't he understand why I'm suddenly freaking out?

"Yes, but I'm not on any birth control!"

He has to know that. I mean, he already proved that—somehow—he knows *everything* about me. Add that to how he had his men bring over my clothes, then he went to get Orion himself... oh, yeah. He knows I'm not on birth control.

And when he flippantly waves his hand, telling me, "It's fine, I had a vasectomy," I know why that tiny little tidbit doesn't bother him.

But the bomb *Damien* just dropped?

"What? You... you did? When?"

"Five years ago? Maybe six. I can't recall."

Okay. I feel a teeny bit better that it wasn't since he married me, but... "Why?"

"It was a precaution after the first woman tried to claim her child was mine. I was careful. She wasn't my wife, and I insisted on two forms of birth control at all times: condoms for me, and pills for her. I wasn't surprised when the paternity test said her child wasn't mine, but I learned my lesson. I got snipped so no one else could try to take advantage of me or my Family."

"Yeah. Sure. That makes sense."

Right?

Damien tilts his head as his gaze runs over me. A small smile tugs on his lips. "Disappointed?"

Am I?

"What? No. I was... I was just worried about STIs from all your previous partners," I lie.

He knows it, too. "There aren't as many as you think. As for diseases, I'm all clear. Though, if you ask me, I think it might just be the 'previous partners' part that's really got you pouting all of a sudden. What's that matter, Savannah? Jealous?"

I sniff, patting my dress again. "I'm not even going to dignify that with a response."

"Be careful, ragna mia," he says teasingly. "You're acting like you believe you *are* my wife."

I'm not. It's worse than that.

I'm *panicking*.

Okay. I fucked him. I kissed him. I admitted that I'll never be able to kill him... but the way my heart sank when I thought about Damien never having children with me?

I'm not jealous of his previous lovers. Sure, I was curious when I thought Genevieve might have been one, but anyone else? That's not my business. So long as my *husband* doesn't fuck around on me while he believes we're married, I'm not jealous.

But the vasectomy? The pregnancy scare? The fact that, despite being a man who lives and dies by his last name, he had surgery so that he wouldn't have kids?

In a million years, I never thought that would bother me—but it does, and before I could examine that too closely, I blurt out, "Are you ever going to tell me what that means? Not 'spider', 'cause you already did. But of all the things you could call me, why that?"

"You haven't figured it out yet?"

If I had, I wouldn't have asked. "No."

His icy blue eyes warm over. "Because the dragonfly has very few predators. But its biggest threat? Is a spider."

Oh.

I can't think of anything to say to that, and while I stand there, quiet, Damien takes my hand, placing it in the crook of his folded arm. "Let's go back to the party."

What? My hair's a mess, my dress is crumpled, and I bet every single person in that room knows exactly what happened after Damien marched me out of it.

"I don't know—"

"If you're worried that you'll have to face Ricky's body, don't be. I'm sure Vin would've taken care of that while we were... mm... distracted."

Is it bad that the dead Dragonfly didn't even cross my mind? "That's not it," I begin.

"Well, I'm sure it's not you being embarrassed about your husband's attraction to you. Because you shouldn't be. No matter what this... unconventional relationship of ours looks like, never doubt that there isn't anything I won't do... any man I won't slaughter... just to have you smile at me. To know that pussy belongs to me and only me? I'd risk my life and more, and now my entire Family knows it."

Damien pats my hand, smirking slightly at my continuously stunned reaction. "Your secrets are mine as much as your body is. If I can't have your heart, I'll at least earn your loyalty. And that starts tonight by showing you that you, Savannah Libellula, mean as much to me as Genevieve and Vincent do. And it's about time I make that clear."

I swallow roughly. *Savannah Libellula*... it's got a nice ring to it. "To the rest of your gang?"

His smirk widens. "To you, wife. *My* wife."

Oh.

Revenge List

TWENTY-ONE
REPRODUCTION

DAMIEN

I made a personal wager with myself about how long it would take for Vin to bring up the events of my birthday dinner. Knowing him, he's been wrestling with loyalty to me, to the Family because we lost one, and guilt since none of that would've happened if he hadn't left Savannah at the table by herself because he had to take a shit.

I don't blame him. Looking back on it, I think I would've rather had a public display so that all of the Dragonflies know that Savannah is off-limits—especially since it ended with the two of us finally consummating our marriage.

Still, I know Vin, so I gave him upwards of a week.

By day five, he walks into my office in the Dragonfly building, closes the door, and gives me a look that says it's time.

He couldn't have picked a worse moment to go through this, but because it is Vin, I don't snap at him to get out.

Instead, I cut him off at the pass.

"Ricky Ferris was an average soldier with a reputation for taking things from women that they didn't want to give him. I looked the other way because he made sure to offer them protection and make them his property first. He didn't do that with my wife. He tried to take what he wanted from her, and back-slapped her when she tried to protect herself. Then he had the nerve to deny it as if I hadn't seen it all happen."

Seen it happen, and been too late to prevent it...

And there's the truth. Ricky Ferris was dead for all of those reasons, but he was assassinated in front of the Family because I lost my cool and became judge, jury, and executioner the second I heard the slap, my wife fell, and I saw the red mark standing out against her cheek.

Vin can't deny I had the right to do it. She's my *wife* —but he's also not wrong when he points out that, apart from a handful of Dragonflies (and anyone that big mouth Callihan told), no one else is aware of that.

"You can't blame Ricky for not knowing she was your property."

But that's the thing. Savannah isn't my property.

Not the way that Vin means... and that's all my fucking fault.

I let that happen.

See, I always wanted the Dragonflies to be a family. Despite being a full-blooded Italian American, when I created my syndicate, I had no ties to the actual mob. It became a crime Family—an organized crew of criminals, but with a level of dedication and loyalty that I insisted on—and, though it wasn't my *intent* for it to be so misogynistic, it happened.

I wanted to protect my sister. In a way, I thought the other men would do the same for the women in their lives. It's an old-fashioned mindset, but one I grew up with after seeing the way my dad tortured himself after losing my mom.

I wouldn't let anything happen to Genevieve, and if I had to call her my property to get my rivals to understand that I'd go scorched fucking earth if anyone targeted her, that's what I did. She was too young to understand, anyway, and it worked.

It also birthed a culture where my men just had to mark the women they wanted to claim to give them protection... unless you were a bad seed like Kieran Alfieri.

Women in our Family have to *consent* to being property. They have to choose. That's why what Ricky did was so messed-up.

And that's also why Savannah *isn't* my property...

"She's my wife," is all I say after a moment's pause.

"And even if she doesn't have my mark, the necklace should've been enough of a warning."

"So you gave her a dragonfly necklace. You get her a ring yet?" Vin jerks his chin at me. "Where's yours?"

Okay. Ci sta. Fair point. "Women are protected in our Family. It shouldn't take a ring for my men to know to keep their hands to themselves."

"Right, boss. The ones who wear the dragonfly are protected."

And Savannah doesn't have it yet.

"I know. Luckily, she doesn't need my mark on her to be safe. You know why?"

The way Vin rubs the top of his buzz cut tells me that he has a pretty good idea. "Don't tell me you want me back on guard duty. I... I mean, I can't be the only one who hasn't forgot she tried to *kill* you."

He's not. But considering he's spent nearly his whole life in crime, I'm surprised it still bothers him. I mean, if *I* got over it... "She stopped," I say helpfully.

Vin snorts.

I smile. "Doesn't matter anyway since you're right. You're my most trusted enforcer, Vincent. My family. I want you watching her when I can't."

All I keep thinking about is how easy it was to get to Ava Crewes. I don't think Lincoln would pay me back by going for Savannah; if I did, I never would've handed him her birth name to check out. But we still have Jimmy Winter trying to muscle his way onto our turf, and though that nobody is the hardest push we've had to deal with in a while, he's not the only upstart who thinks he can take a slice of the Springfield pie.

"The Family knows she's mine now. How much longer before my other enemies do?"

Vin sighs. "Yeah. Of course. You know I'll do anything for you, boss."

I knew he'd say that.

"Good." Rising up from my desk, I grab my suit jacket from the back of my chair. Even if I'm going to get my dick worked on, I'm going in style. "Because I'm going to be out of commission for most of today."

He takes a few steps back, obviously stunned. "What? A day off and you're not spending it with her? What's going on? Where are you going?"

"I actually have a doctor's appointment."

"Going to visit Dr. Lizzie? You sure I can't come? I can come. One of the other guys can watch your wife."

Poor guy. Can he make it any more obvious?

It's a shame, too. Elizabeth Harper is married to her job. After escaping her junkie ex, she basically swore off cock to the disappointment of more than one of my guys. Half of the Dragonflies who stop in at the clinic could be patched up with a little iodine and a gauze pad, but they go to Liz because they're sure, this time, she might bandage them up, then go home with them.

It hasn't happened in the seven years I've known the woman. I've even had to step in a time or two when one of the soldiers got a little handsy with our doc.

She's happy to do her job and go home to an empty bed, just like I was before I had Savannah in it.

Vin, on the other hand, would be more than happy to fill Elizabeth's.

My cousin's last fling ended around Halloween. I didn't think he even had Liz on his radar, but since the fateful night Vin, Savannah, and I went to the clinic together, he's been circling around the doc.

With that puppy-dog eager expression suddenly on his face, you'd be hard-pressed to recognize him as a thirty-eight-year-old bruiser with eleven leaves on the back of his bicep. He's got a crush, and I only hope it doesn't end up crushing him.

"Sorry, Vin. I'm not going to see Elizabeth. But you know what?" Savannah is safe for now. It might only illustrate how obsessed I am with my wife, but I check her location constantly. Same with my cousin. Gen, on the other hand... my sister warned me that, if I ever put a tracker in her, she'd jump in front of a train—and my highly emotional sister doesn't bluff. She'd do it, too, so that's the one element of protection I never insisted on... yet.

Like she constantly throws in my face, Genevieve rarely leaves the house. She's home; most likely rehearsing for her next performance. Savannah's dot puts her firmly at the manor.

And since she doesn't need someone watching her back right now, maybe I should take Vin with me to watch mine.

I nod at him. "My pre-surgery check-in is in about half an hour. You want to come with?"

"Of course, Dame. Yeah." Suddenly, he stops, then blinks. "Wait. Your *what*?"

WHO WOULD HAVE THOUGHT THAT, BETWEEN A vasectomy, the reversal, or being stabbed with my own knife, the reversal would be the one that hurt the fucking most.

What goes on with my cock is my business. I made sure Christopher knew that I was unreachable for the day, that if it's an emergency, he could either handle it on his own or rely on some of my most loyal lieutenants, like Bruiser, Sly, or Cameron; more brains than the muscle my enforcers are, they have proven themselves over the last decade to act in the best interests of the Family.

Vin was with me.

I was having surgery on my genitals. I chose local anesthesia because no way in hell was I letting a doc that didn't work for me put me completely under, but I find that if those not in the life don't find my lean form intimidating, they pay attention when Vin is standing at my back.

Just in case they decided to pull a Savannah and try to take advantage of me in a rare vulnerable state, my cousin won't let them. I doubted that would be the case

—and I vetted this outpatient surgery center outside of Springfield years ago when I decided to go with the vasectomy in the first place—but I didn't get to where I am by not being a suspicious bastard.

They gave me all the run-down. How I should expect to be sore and swollen and achy for a few days after the hours-long outpatient procedure, that I needed to ice my junk and off for the next forty-eight hours, and how I can't do anything strenuous for the next two weeks.

The idea that I can't fuck Savannah again for that long after I finally did for the first time hurts me almost as much as my achy scrotum.

But I did this for her. As a gesture to show my wife that I consider this marriage both binding and lasting, I got the vasovasostomy. That way, if it's kids she needs to stick around, I'll breed her as soon as my pipes are in working order again.

I'll do *anything* to make it so that woman can never, ever leave me.

The doc made it clear that I shouldn't expect miracles. I'm older, it's been years since I first got the snip, and odds of my reversal not quite taking is in the twenty percent range, give or take. But it's better than zero—and until I can recover enough to get tested and see how the procedure fared, I decide not to say anything to Savannah.

I don't want to get her hopes up. I also don't want to push her away with how serious I am about her. Up until the dinner, I thought I'd been doing a good job—and then I showed her just how ruthless you need to be to lead a syndicate.

Ricky touched what was mine. He *hurt* her. Savannah tried to fight back, and maybe if I hadn't confiscated her weapons, she might not have needed me to step in... but I did.

I promised her. When I first climbed into her bed after I noticed she refused to fall asleep first while I was in the room with her, I promised that—as her husband—I would protect her. Lord knows I had no idea what I was protecting her *from* then. How I inadvertently triggered the trauma she experienced from her time in prison, and how I didn't know that my Family and I were the cause behind all of it.

And then I tore through the folder of gathered intel Lincoln got for me, and I fucking *knew*.

Portia Daniels. Forty-eight. Worth two million dollars before she went into Club Fed; somehow worth *three* million after nine years in. Doing twelve to fifteen for an embezzlement charge, she was scheduled for a parole hearing in October.

Was.

I'll own my part in breaking Georgia and turning her into Savannah. If my guys hadn't poured too many fake hundreds into her small store, if my hold on the SPFD wasn't as iron-tight back then... if the bank hadn't pretended not to notice all the bad bills like they do now... she never would've been an innocent woman caught in the crosshairs on my business.

But this bitch? She's the reason my wife flinches when I stroke her neck from behind in the dark. She's the reason Savannah took *weeks* before she allowed herself to fall asleep before I did. She's the reason an innocent twenty-five-year-old woman—the same age as Gen is now—went into a minimum security prison only to come out, feeling like murdering a mafia leader more than a decade her senior seemed like the only way to quiet the noise inside her head.

Savannah was and is murderous. And maybe I'm just as broken as she is, but I *like* that about her. So long as she's not spilling Dragonfly blood—unless they've done enough to earn death—I can give her the outlet for this dark side of her.

Even better, I can *teach* her how to do it. To protect herself when I can't, and to make sure that no one will ever, ever hurt her again.

And though I'm sure she'd have rather make Portia Daniels a victim of her own, she's my wife—and I wanted that kill.

So I sent Oliver to Madison with enough money to buy a crooked correctional officer, plus a syringe full of so much dirty Eclipse, Daniels would die of an OD in minutes. My newest enforcer—Kieran's replacement— was eager to earn his first leaf, and since I've always been the type to delegate, I let him do this for me while

I had a very firm alibi of having my vas deferens put back together.

Once the surgery was done and I got the okay to be released, I grit my fucking teeth and walk out of the surgery center as if my sac wasn't screaming. The local anesthesia had worn off enough for it to be noticeable, and the instruction told me if it got too bad to take an ibuprofen.

Fuck that. I'll be fine.

To prove it, I not only drove myself home, but I also dropped Vin back off at the manor before I headed to the office. Oliver had express instructions to return there after he finished up in Madison, and I wanted to talk to my enforcer in person to hear how the job went.

It went. It was actually pretty impressive. He'd made contact with a few 'maybe' guards last week, testing out who'd be interested in doing a favor for a hefty sum of cash. Madison is near enough to Springfield that our distribution operation already had a foot in the door there. Even in a min sec prison like Madison, drugs are rampant, and the Dragonflies supply.

Portia Daniels's nasty death would be unexpected, but not impossible, and when I meet with Oliver in my office, he shows me the pictures the guard sent him after the deed was done.

As I smile in satisfaction at a job well done, I think about how Savannah will react to hearing I had her biggest nightmare murdered. Not that I'm going to tell her. Not yet, at least.

Not until I'm sure she can handle it.

It's one thing for her to see Ricky get killed in the heat of the moment. She understood that. But for the death to be so cold-blooded, so meticulously planned... I see the darkness inside of my beautiful, deadly spider, but is she as dark as I am?

I'm used to being in charge. In *control*. It's part of the reason I never really sought a partner other than for an occasional release. I didn't arrange for Daniels's death as a way to manipulate Savannah any further.

I did it because, after how that woman treated my wife, she didn't deserve to live—and I'll kill anyone who thinks they can do the same until I've taught Savannah how to protect herself.

Even then, *I* will do it.

I am her husband. It's my job.

And I'll do it happily.

At that point, the ache in my cock was becoming more annoying than anything, so I pat Oliver on the shoulder, gave him the okay to head down to the Coyote Den to get his first leaf on my order, and went the hell home.

I can't fuck Savannah. Not yet. But that doesn't mean I can't share a meal with my wife, proud that she trusts me enough that she'll finally eat off her plate before seeing me do the same—or taste-testing her food—and, if I'm lucky, hold her close while I sleep.

But then, when I ease my way up the spiral stairs to the second floor, inwardly cursing myself for not thinking to put in an elevator during construction all those years ago, I hear laughter coming from the television room and head in that direction.

I move carefully but purposefully so that, except for Vin, no one in this room would have any idea I've just gone through surgery.

Because Vin *is* in here. His big body thrown in one chair, his face twisted in an 'oh shit' expression as I eyeball him as he sings along to 'Grease Lightning' from the old 70s movie, *Grease*.

He finishes the line, cutting himself off before he can say 'pussy wagon', before sinking back in his seat. "What can I say? They suckered me in, boss."

He's not the only one watching the musical on my big screen television. On the large couch, Savannah is curled up on one side, a bowl of popcorn in her lap. And if I wonder why it's the popcorn she's holding and not her cat, that's because Genevieve is sitting cross-legged on the next cushion, snuggling with Orion.

My sister snorts. "Boss, schmoss, Vinnie. In this house, Damien's my brother, your cousin, Savannah's husband, and Orion's bitch." She leans over, running her fingers through the cat's scruff. "Isn't that right, Orion? And don't knock musicals, Damien."

Clearing my throat, I say, "I didn't know Vin could sing that well. That's all."

The heights of Vin's cheeks burn red. "Ah, jeez, Dame. Really?"

"Really."

Genevieve gestures at a young John Travolta as he bounces around the car on the screen. "Come on. You didn't miss much."

Savannah tosses a handful of popcorn into the air, catching maybe... one kernel?

It's fucking adorable.

"Gen said we can watch 'Grease 2' when we're done," my wife tells me. "I've never heard of it, but supposedly it's about bowling, and there's a song called—"

Genevieve looks dead at me, a smug expression on her face. "'Reproduction'. It's *hysterical*."

My head shoots toward Vin. His shoulders go tight, but he gives a tiny shake of his head.

So he didn't tell my sister about my surgery. But does she know? Or is this somehow one hell of a coincidence?

It doesn't matter. Because you know what else? My sister's right. And I don't just mean how, as soon as I find room on the couch to sit down right next to Savannah, Orion leaves Gen's lap to bump against my thigh as though he can sense my nuts can't handle his weight right now... Genevieve was right about *all* of that.

I'm here with my sister. My cousin. My wife. My adopted cat. And, if everything works out the way it's supposed to, one day I might have a kid of my own to watch a movie with...

I've spent so many years building my Family.

But this?

This is my *family*—and I will do anything... *kill* anyone... to keep it.

Revenge List

TWENTY-TWO
SILENZIO

SAVANNAH

I look around the basement.

"Okay," I say out loud after a moment. "If I knew about this, I wouldn't have been surprised by how jacked you were under your suit."

"Just because I'm forty now, doesn't mean I can't take care of myself," he says smugly.

Yeah. And with a set-up like this, I understand *how*.

If I hadn't just followed Damien down the stairs of his house myself, I'd have thought he'd somehow teleported me to the local gym. That's what he has down here. A full-on commercial gym, with mirrors, equipment, and mats padding one side of the large space.

"How often do you come down here?"

"Before I was told to rest per doctor's orders? Five days a week. Religiously. I've seen too many in the life get used to the cushy parts that come along with it. The good meals. The civilians who do anything to make your personal life easier so that you scratch their backs in return. They get lazy."

"Hire staff?" I tease.

He shoots me a look out of the corner of one of his icy blue eyes. "Frankie needed a job. Annette's his wife, and he looks after her. I look after them. Mary's boy Jack was a good friend of mine who got blown away when we were twenty-three. I remember eating dinners at her house. Now she feeds my family since she doesn't have one of her own."

Oh. "Damien, I didn't mean—"

"No. Don't apologize. I know what you meant. And you're right. They make my life easier because I can afford to have them do so. But they only get to work for me because I trust them. Because I trust them, I can use the time I'm not busy with the Family working on myself."

He's certainly done a good job of it.

His face shows his age. There's experience in the depths of his eyes, plus fine lines bracketed them. That silver streak in his hair that beckons me to touch him... he's obviously not as young as I am. But that sculpted body? He looks good for forty. Really good.

Damien had his stitches removed two weeks ago, give or take. He had a doctor's appointment, and when he came home, he no longer had the black thread curving through the puckered scar standing out against his tanned skin.

I knew something was up when he told me to put on workout clothes earlier this morning. I didn't have much, just an old sports bra and a pair of too-big sleep shorts, but since he put on a muscle tank and baseball shorts of his own, I figured that would do.

And, okay. Maybe I ogled him in his exercise clothes more than I should've. Can you help me? Except for being naked or just wearing his boxer briefs, I've only ever seen him in a suit. Damien walking around with the jacket off was as casual as he's been, even at home.

Until now.

As if I'm finding it harder and harder to keep myself from jumping him, now he wants to show off his toned arms and muscular legs?

Down, girl. With the exception of the night of his birthday dinner—when, once again, Damien got turned on when someone got knifed—he hasn't made any move to be intimate with me again. Sure, we're still sleeping in the same bed. And, yeah, somehow the cot became designated as Orion's while Damien and I started to lie together in the big bed. But sex?

There hasn't been any since then.

Fucking hell. Is he a tease? Because, right now, I think my husband just might be.

Either that, or he's found a new way to punish me...

"Okay. You got me down here. You want to tell me why?"

"Of course. I thought it was time to start your self-defense lessons."

I'm sorry... what? "What do you mean?" I look around, expecting him to have a personal trainer or something pop out, just another Springfield resident on the Dragonfly payroll. "Lessons? With who?"

"With me." He gestures at himself, holding his figures over his palm. "Come on, Savannah. Let's see what you've got."

Is he kidding?

One look at him and... no. Damien's not kidding at all. He's really inviting me to attack him.

Not with any weapons, obviously. But he's lowered himself in a fighting stance, telling me to try to knock him down.

Holy shit. I might never get this chance again.

Trying to tap into the dwindling feelings of rage that kept me going for so long, I throw myself at him shoulder first.

Woosh. Suddenly, I'm flipping through the air before landing on my back on the mat with a slapping sound and a jolt that knocks most of my bones around.

What the fuck—

Damien's face appears over mine. "Is that all?" he smirks.

Oh. It's *on*.

Five times. Five times I get up, and five times he

knocks me back down again. It becomes clear that he's not trying to hurt me. The opposite. After each confrontation between us, he makes it clear how he's able to control it to the point that, before I know it, he has me down.

He's teaching me. And maybe it's being knocked down that many times, but I'm not really understanding what this is coming from all of a sudden.

The fifth time, I end up flat on my belly.

He nudges me in my ass with his toe. "Come, come, Savannah. How did you think you'd kill me up close if I can knock you on that pretty ass so easily?"

Gritting my teeth, frustrated as all hell at how easily he's throwing me around like a goddamn rag doll, I have to remind him as I climb back to my feet, "I almost pulled it off."

"You distracted me with your cleavage that night. I've had my mouth on those tits since then. It'll take more than that for you to seduce me for my weapon."

I look him up and down. Between the muscle tank and the basketball shorts, it's pretty obvious the only weapon he's carrying is the one that's notably bulging against the slick material.

He gives me that crooked half-smile when my gaze lingers on his dick a second too long. "I'm all yours, ragna mia. When you're ready to try again, go ahead."

"You want me to try and kill you?"

Right after I decided that I couldn't even if I had the chance, he's *daring* me to do it?

Damien shakes his head. "Not at all. But I'm more than willing to be seduced."

Oh.

A shiver courses down my spine at the way he lowered his voice on that last word. If I didn't know better, I'd think that all of this 'training' is really foreplay. But how can it be? Since the party at the restaurant, he hasn't made a single move toward me except for his solemn insistence that his wife sleep with him in his bed.

That's all we do, though. He spoons me, wrapping me up in his embrace, all while careful to keep his lower half as far away from me as possible. I tremble every time he lays soft kisses along the back of my throat, viscerally aware that he's not putting his mouth anywhere else.

I thought... I thought it was a fluke. That I got the totally wrong idea when he killed Ricky. He wasn't possessive over *me* because he cared, but because he considered me his property. That he fucked me so thoroughly to show the Dragonflies that he owned me instead of any other more sentimental reason.

That, once he nutted and nonchalantly mentioned his vasectomy, he regretted being intimate with me at all.

Why else had he kept his distance since then? Even if it was hate sex, it was *good* sex. I wouldn't have stopped him—but he never even *tried*.

So seduce him now... why bother? Unless this is

just another way for the Dragonfly to manipulate me to get what he wants: his would-be murderer under his complete control.

I shake my head. "Let me try again. I think I almost got you down that last time."

Light on his feet, ready for me to come at him again, Damien smiles. "No, you didn't."

I ignore him.

The sixth time? Not only does he use my arm to flip me and my momentum to have me on my back, but my wonderful husband shifts his heel before pinning me with his body.

I groan. Out of pain or because his weight pressed against me is delicious, I can't tell. But it's a groan all the same.

He climbs off of me, and I groan again. This time, though, I know it's because his weight is gone.

Sitting up, I glare at him. "Are you trying to kill me? Be honest. This is revenge for me stabbing you."

"Not at all. This is teaching you how to protect yourself. You'll thank me later."

I doubt it.

"You know, if I still had my gun, I wouldn't need this," I point out.

"Don't worry, wife. That's next."

I do a double-take as I stand again. "What? You're going to give it back?"

"Eventually. Once I'm sure you know how to use it.

We have a shooting range for new soldiers. I want to set you up with Bianca."

My stomach twists. "Bianca? Who's Bianca?"

Damien never mentions other women. The only exceptions are Genevieve and Dr. Liz, but almost as if we've come to a silent agreement never to mention previous lovers, he makes it a point not to.

Am I jealous? Fuck. I don't know... I think I might be.

And he *knows* it.

"Bianca is a talented marksman at the range. One of the best. But *the* best is a handsome young man named Chad. I refuse to introduce you to Chad, cara mia. My dear. My Savannah. So you will work with Bianca to teach you to shoot. I will teach you how to go hand-to-hand with anyone who might try to harm you. And, one day, when I'm sure you won't use it against me, I'll teach you to wield my knife."

He's serious, too. Like, really serious.

And I thought he must've lost his mind *before*.

"You really *are* trying to teach me to hurt you."

"Not just me, Savannah. *Anyone*."

"I don't understand—"

He places his finger beneath my chin, tilting my head back so that I'm forced to see the emotion lurking in the depths of his icy blue eyes. "Ricky could've really hurt you. Vin could've hurt you. Fuck, but *I* can hurt you. I won't allow it, ragna mia. You're mine, and I *will* keep you. That means you must know how to protect yourself if I can't. So I will teach you how to really kill, and so long as it keeps you alive, I don't give a shit who you turn on."

I swallow roughly. "Even you, Damien?"

His gaze drops to my lips. "You're my wife, Savannah. 'Til death do we part.'"

I've lost my mind. I left it behind at Madison Correctional Facility five years ago, but when I have Damien Libellula inches away from me, his breath whispering over my face as his lethal yet beautiful body is *right fucking there*, hurting him is the last thing on my mind.

Oh, no. Instead, grasping his muscle tank, closing the gap between us only because he allows it, I go up on my tip-toes and press my mouth to his.

For the first time since I've known him, *I* kiss *him.*

Damien is the first to pull back, moving so quickly that he rips the fabric of his tank out of my grasp. His eyes flash beneath the fluorescents that light the gym as he backs out of my reach next.

And then, with a taunting expression twisting his gorgeous face, he beckons me again. "Again, Savannah."

Fine.

I don't know if he let me overpower him or if Damien decided he wanted to spar a little before he knocked me down for the *seventh* time. Something changed after I initiated that kiss, though, and after we wrestle for a few frantic moments, it ends with Damien on his back for once.

At least, I thought that was the end. But my husband? He has an entirely different idea.

Pressing his hand to the small of my back, he keeps our groins connected. Through our shorts, his cock is a length of steel pushing against my pussy. In this position, it wouldn't take much effort at all for me to start riding him if we were naked—

—and I'm pretty sure Damien is thinking along the same lines as me.

His stiletto appears in his hand as if by magic. How? I have no idea. He's definitely not wearing his holster, but I recognize the knife.

I gasp, the sound turning into a throaty moan as he drops the blade alongside my thigh before slipping it beneath my shorts. One hand gripping the material, the other working the knife, and it doesn't take more than a few forceful jerks on one side, then the next before he's *cut my shorts off*. Pulling them out from under my ass, he flings them to the side.

"Damien—"

"Silenzio," he whispers huskily. He does it again, and there go my panties. I'm completely naked from the waist down now. "Ah. Much better."

Revenge List

TWENTY-THREE
TOO MUCH

SAVANNAH

That's what he thinks. Me? I might not have my hands on that knife, and he vanishes it as quickly as he used it to get rid of my clothes, but I don't need to destroy his basketball shorts to move my weight so that I can dip my hand past the waistband and release his cock.

The last time we fucked, Damien was in complete control. I was with him all the way, but there's no denying that I just went along for the ride. Right now? My chest is heaving, my pussy is soaked, his dick is in my hand, and there's a dare mingled with anticipation written all over his face.

He wants me to take the lead. One of the most powerful men in all of Springfield, and I have him at my mercy. He's dying for me to fuck him, but he's leaving this one up to me.

As if I can resist.

I'm so wet, it takes a little concentration to line his cock up with the entrance to my pussy. He slid the first time, bumping into the top of my mound, hitting my clit. Probably because he's not even trying to help me, either.

It's as though he's decided that, if I want to fuck him, this time he's going to make *me* do the fucking.

No doubt I'll regret this later. But in the moment, I finally lodge the head of his cock inside of me. Rising up on my knees, I adjust my angle, then sink down until I've taken all of him inside next.

I had no choice. Gravity helped me out on that one, but the fact that I'm so damn hot for this man... with the amount of juices I created in preparation for fucking this man, there's no resistance once I have him right where I want him. I sink down, my groin touching his now with nothing between us, and I dig my fingers into the material of his tank as I hold myself in place on top of him.

"Dio mio," breathes out Damien as I squeeze him. "I didn't think anything could be as good as it was when I took you at the dinner, but I was wrong."

I stick the tip of my tongue out between my teeth. "I gotta make note of the date. Damien Libellula admitting he was wrong... that must be a first."

"No," he says, jerking his hips so that he can thrust

a little. "I know when I'm wrong. An honest man will admit his faults. But if you want to see a first... it's a desperate man begging his wife to *move*."

"You want me to climb off of you? I mean, if that's what you want..."

His hands have been on my waist, holding me in position while I worked on getting his cock inside my pussy. He kept them there after I swallowed him whole, but while the left one stays in place, the right one moves.

Thwack.

I jump, and the result is that I squeeze his dick again, leaving him to moan under his breath.

That's not all. He slapped my ass, I did move, and because I moved forward, that plus the pressure of his cock pushing against my inner walls sends a massive jolt of pleasure toward my clit.

Holy fucking shit, that's *amazing*. So amazing that, chasing the high of that sensation, I start to ride Damien's cock.

"Look at you. I wanted you to move, ragna mia, and you thought you were being smart. But a nice spank was enough to make you do just what your husband wanted you to. Such a good girl. You deserve another one. Yes?"

I swallow roughly. "*Yes.*"

Thwack.

"Damien—"

"Husband. Savannah, I am your *husband*. When I'm inside you, call me that or else—"

I raise my eyebrows as I lean forward, changing the angle of his penetration as I continue to fuck him. "What, *Damien*? You'll spank me again?"

Lifting up, meeting my thrusts so that it's more like I'm bouncing on top of him than moving at a slow, leisurely pace, he slides his hand down the curve of my stinging ass. "No. If you don't call me your husband, I won't spank you at all."

That's fucking low. Now that I know how amazing that feels?

"Fine. *Husband*."

Thwack.

"Fuck. Fuck, fuck, fuck. Why does that feel so fucking good?"

Damien laughs as he reaches between us, using his magic hand to rub my clit now. He must be able to tell that I'm already chasing my orgasm, courtesy of his slaps, and the way he controls my body so easily in other ways has me clenching down on him as I explode around his cock.

"Because you're fucking your husband, wife," he says as I keen out a whine, too distracted by the sensations rushing through me to really pay attention to what he's saying—until he takes advantage of my lapse to flip me onto my back as easily as he did before.

"And now it's time for your husband to fuck *you*, Savannah."

My legs are already feeling weak from my climax. That doesn't stop Damien from lifting up one of them, hooking it over his shoulder so that he can fuck me even deeper.

And even though I can't bring myself to believe that this man will ever truly be my husband, I let him.

Because, at this moment, I can pretend...

I LAY ON THE MAT, TOO BONELESS TO ROLL OVER AND find my shorts. Then I remember that Damien used his stiletto to slice through the fabric of both those and my panties so that he could get to my pussy easier. They're basically useless now.

Oh, well.

Damien is perched on his side, propped up on his elbow so that he could look down at me with that daring half-smile of his. Apart from the sweat slicking his hairline, and the way his tank is molded to his chest, he looks as perfect as he did when we started. This man has a whole decade on me, but I'm the one who's panting heavily as I come down from my orgasm.

Smirking now, he moves his free hand so that he's playing with the curls covering my pussy. At least, that's what I *thought* he was doing until he dips his pointer inside of me.

"There."

"What are you doing?"

"Making sure that stays inside of you where it belongs."

His come? Why would he do that?

Propping up on my elbows now, I say, "It doesn't matter. Your swimmers are cut off. You're shooting blanks."

"I was. My surgeon told me that it could take anywhere between a month and a year before sperm returns to the semen. I have an analysis scheduled at the two-month mark, but I just got the all-clear to return to strenuous activities." He runs his hand over my thigh, squeezing the inner side of it. "And I think we can both agree that was pretty strenuous."

I'm confused. Did he just fuck the sense out of me? He might've, because I don't know what he's talking about.

"Huh? What?"

"My vasectomy reversal."

"You got it reversed? When?"

"Two weeks ago. Didn't you notice how careful I have to be with my cock? I promise you, those two weeks were hell, knowing that I wanted nothing more than fuck my wife, but I couldn't until the swelling went down. But for you, I did it."

I'm sitting up straight now. "You did? Why?"

"Because I saw the look on your face when you'd learned I'd had one done. I only have it done because, if I did have children, they would be with my wedded wife and no one else. Like it or not, you *are* my wife. So

I had the reversal procedure done. It's not a foolproof guarantee that we will have children one day, but in case you want to try... I'd give them to you if that's what you want. I'd give you anything."

Anything, it seems, but my freedom.

The reality of that is like a bell clanging deep inside of my mind. It echoes, making me want to cover my ears. But since Damien would probably take that the totally wrong way, I just use my hands to start climbing back up again.

"Savannah?"

"I'm okay." No, I'm not. "I just... that was a lot. The training, I mean. I think I'd like to go upstairs, shower, change, and maybe take a nap."

Or, you know, try to make some sort of sense of what Damien just told me.

"Of course." Quicker than me, he gets to his feet. "Here. Let me help you up."

"No. I got it."

Damien makes a noise in the back of his throat. "Please, amore. Let me help you."

Amore... I don't need to know any Italian to take a stab at what *that* means.

I hold out my hand. Without a word, he lifts me easily so that I'm now standing.

And that's when I realize that I don't have anything to cover me from the waist down.

It's fine. The only people allowed in this house are members of Damien's immediate family. Genevieve will turn her back and cover her eyes at any reminder that her forty-year-old brother fucks, and if Vin happens to catch a glimpse of my bare ass, I don't think Damien will care—

He holds up a finger. "One moment, cara mia." He pulls off his baseball shorts, then his boxer briefs. Handing me his underwear before stabbing his legs back into the shorts, he commands, "Put these on."

Damien's used underwear?

I just had his bare cock inside of me. He came, too, and used his finger to make sure his creampie didn't immediately drip down my thighs. It is now—and I'm so sticky, I can't wait to shower—but I draw the line at pulling on his boxer briefs.

"I'm good, thanks."

A muscle ticks in his jaw. He gestures at my lower half. "Fine, but if I find out you paraded around like that in front of my cousin, I will slap that ass red—but not before I pluck out his eyeballs for seeing something that's meant only for your husband."

Oh. Um. Maybe I was wrong.

Maybe he *will* care if Vin sees.

"Are you serious? He's your *blood*."

"He was born into being a Libellula. You were *chosen*. Never forget that for a moment."

Chosen? "What are you on about, Damien? You didn't marry me because you wanted to or some shit like that. You were punishing me for trying to kill you. That's all."

And I've never forgotten *that* for a moment.

I have to go. I also don't want to be the reason Damien turns on his cousin so, as gross as it is, I shrug on his warm boxer briefs so that I can get out of here without him trying to stop me again—

"Is that what you think?"

Shuddering out a breath, my back to Damien, I admit to myself that's what I *know*.

Next thing I know, he's there. His hands are on my shoulders, easing me around so that I'm facing him, and *he's there*.

"You're wrong. I didn't marry you to punish you. If anything, I was punishing myself."

"I don't... I don't understand."

Damien lowers his hands so that they're on my back again. Pushing me toward him, tucking me under his chin, he suddenly has me in an embrace so comforting, he could whisper in my ear that he's lying, that it's his turn to stab me in the back... and I'd let him.

But he doesn't. Instead, he says, "What is love if not obsession? From the moment I first saw your face, there was something in it I saw that I wanted. That I *recognized*. I've spent so many years looking for the perfect partner... for Gen's sake, for the Family... and I'd just about given up. Sex was about release, not affection. But then you... I looked forward to seeing you watch me. Of course, I didn't know then why you hated me. Why you had a perfectly good reason to blame me for your stay in prison—"

My stomach lurches. "Damien, I—"

"Shh. Let me finish, amore. I didn't know any of that then. To be honest, I don't think I would've cared. I've ruined many lives to get where I am."

"You've helped some, too," I have to admit. "Liz. Frankie and Annette. Your cook—"

"Again, making me the good guy. But since I met you, Savannah... I want to *be* that guy. But how could I when you only married me because I gave you no choice? It wasn't a punishment. It was an *opportunity*. You stabbed me, and in that moment of clarity that followed the excruciating pain, I saw my chance to make you mine. So long as you didn't kill me, I could have the one woman who's caught and kept my attention over the years."

I gulp, threading my fingers behind Damien's back. Because, somehow, I'm clinging to him as tightly now. "Me?"

"You," he agrees, dropping a kiss to the top of my hair.

Pulling away just enough so that our eyes meet, Damien tells me, "I thought I'd get over it. That I would wake up and realize that I willingly tied myself to a woman who could never love me because of how much she hated me... but that never happened.

"And now," he murmurs, his forehead pressed to mine, our sweat-slicked bodies almost as entangled now as they were when we were fucking, "I don't ever want it to."

I almost tell him that he has nothing to worry about. That Savannah agreed to a sham marriage, already looking for a way out, but even if I had the chance to escape again? I wouldn't take it.

But I can't find the words.

That's okay.

Damien does.

"Understand this. My life belongs to you, ragna mia. Do with that what you will. Love me. Kill me. Just never, ever regret me. That's all I ask of you."

That's all?

But it might just be too much.

Revenge List

TWENTY-FOUR
PART ONE

DAMIEN

I tell myself that I couldn't care less that Savannah doesn't love me the way I love her.

Look at that. I guess that woman made a liar of me after all because if that isn't a crock of shit, I don't know what is.

I want to say everything changed at my fortieth birthday dinner. That would be another lie. From the moment I had her standing in front of Judge Callihan, I was already prepared to do whatever I had to to keep her. Obsession was enough; I didn't expect to fall in love. But I did, and now a part of me won't stop until he loves me, too.

It's hard. To convince her to trust me, to fall for me, to *love* me... that's a full-time job. Throw in the self-defense lessons that I insist on, plus those cozy moments when I can forget the weight of the world on my shoulders and just watch a silly musical with Vin, Gen, Savannah, and Orion... that's time I never would've spared before.

Not when my entire life was devoted to turning the Libellula Family into what it is now.

I'm still a workaholic. Nothing passes through the East End of Springfield without my stamp on it, and with Jimmy Winter still finding a way to push his shitty product through *my* city, I'm busier than ever.

Two nights ago, a pair of my soldiers got invited to a dice game downtown. It was run by Winter and his guys, and it was obvious he was looking for new recruits. He saw the dragonflies on their skin and didn't care, either. That means he's looking to poach, and that bothers me more than hearing he's expanding his operations, bringing the hard drugs like coke and H into Springfield instead of sticking to party drugs like Breeze and Eclipse.

Fuck, no. The real shit is a Dragonfly special. Lincoln's already desperate to shut him down because of the cut in profits he's seen since Winter started gun-running on his turf, but for this upstart nobody to come for me?

He's dead. The second I can get my hands on him, I'll make an example of him for any other shit-for-brains who think they can take me on.

Only one problem. Winter snuck out of the dice game before my guy could tip off the rest of our Family.

By the time I got there with Vin, Oliver, and Tony, Winter was gone, and the one sacrificial lamb he left behind refused to give up his boss.

Even when I used my stiletto to cut out his tongue, choking on his blood as Vin tipped his head back to allow it to pour, that dumb fuck never said a word beyond an agonized, then garbled yell.

That pissed me off. I wanted to shut him down, knowing that once the snowflake threat was over with, I'd have more time to dedicate to Savannah. As it was, despite the fact that now we're actually sleeping together instead of just sleeping side-by-side, I can't help but feel like she's drawing away from me again.

Gen, too. She's as bubbly as ever when she's not in 'dance' mode, obsessively performing a routine until her toes are bloody and she's a sweaty mess, but lately... she seems to be hiding something from me.

I don't like it. I also don't like how Savannah will fuck me, but anytime I try to treat her like my wife, she pulls away.

And then I remember what Vin said to me before I had my snip reversed, and I had a brilliant idea to show Savannah just how dedicated I am to making this marriage work. It's a two-parter of a plan—and if I guess wrong and she's been fucking playing me all along, I might be dead at the end of it—but, to me, it was worth the risk.

It took another week and a half before I could get everything set in motion, plus find the time to actually do it. But I finally did, and though she seems a little hesitant when I tell her we're leaving the manor after dark, I see the tiniest hint of trust in her soft brown eyes as she says, "Okay."

Fifteen minutes later, my wife looks up at the neon sign hung over the door of the shop. She takes it in—**Coyote Den Ink**—and then shakes her head when she sees the cut-out piece of vinyl shaped like a dragonfly that's tucked away in the nearest window.

"One of your businesses?" she asks.

"Something like that. It's more like we give Roger most of his business, and because of that, it's a welcome place for my men in case they need one."

I would've thought that she figured out what we were doing here once she saw it was a tattoo parlor, and maybe she did, but that doesn't stop Savannah from asking me, "And why have you brought me here?"

With one hand on the lower back of her jacket, I use my other to open the door. Normally, Roger closes up his shop at six. It's after eight, but the door's unlocked because I asked him to give me an eight o'clock appointment as a favor to me.

"I told you once that you have to earn your dragonfly," I murmur, guiding her into the clean shop. The scent of disinfectant slaps you in the face as you enter, as does the bright light Roger uses so he can see what he's doing, but those are all marks of a shop where I trust the ink. "It's time."

Savannah bites down on her bottom lip. For a moment, I wonder if my murderess will fight me on this. To wear the Dragonfly... she spent years plotting how to take us down. With my mark on her skin, it'll be a reminder that she didn't. That she actually *became* one.

I won't force her. When it comes to this... this has to be her decision.

I wait on bated breath, only to feel my chest puff up in pride when my wife simply says, "Can I pick the colors?"

Brushing my lips over the shell of her ear, hiding my smile of relief, I tell her, "Naturalmente."

I'VE HAD THE PLEASURE OF SEEING SAVANNAH IN THE nude. Before now, she didn't have a single tattoo, a fact that did not pass me by as she agrees to mar that beautiful skin with *my* symbol. She goes through it all like a champ, not even wincing when Roger starts the outline on her inner arm.

She ends up picking colors similarly enough to mine. There's purple and green in her dragonfly, with a hint of yellow and orange, too. Half the size and almost *dainty*, it's perfect by the time Roger is done.

Like he does for every Dragonfly, he made sure she understood just what she's signing up for when she gets her tattoo. For a moment, I think she might back out, but all she did was thrust out her wrist and say, "Ready."

Now she's been given instructions on how to care for it, her new tattoo covered up with second skin, and she seems ready to go—but I'm not.

Roger swaps out his gloves. "One moment, Mr. Libellula, then we can get started on you."

Savannah's head snaps my way. There's a question on her lips she doesn't quite ask, though that's all right. I'll answer her anyway.

"You didn't think you would be the only one marked tonight, did you? Ragna mia... if you are my property, I am yours. And I will wear your mark proudly on my skin."

I jerk my chin at Roger. "You prepared the stencil I approved?"

"Got it right here, sir."

"Then, please, show my wife."

It's a spider. Nothing too graphic, or detailed—not like my large dragonfly tattoo—but its undeniably an illustration of a black widow spider.

"Where are you planning to put that?"

I smile at Savannah. I'd already removed my jacket in preparation for my appointment, and my fingers fly down my shirt, unbuttoning it so I could take that off next.

One I have, I trace my finger over the scar on my side.

She swallows notably. "You're covering it up?"

"No. I would never cover up my wife's handiwork. But I will put the spider right next to it as a reminder not to piss my personal black widow off again."

I thought she'd laugh or roll her eyes. Only... unless I'm mistaking it or it's the fault of the bright lights, it seems to me as if those pretty brown eyes are shiny with unshed tears instead. And then she blinks a few times, and I know I'm right.

Even better, part one of my plan is a clear success.

And once the tattoos have healed enough, it'll be time for part two.

Revenge List

TWENTY-FIVE
PART TWO

DAMIEN

Long before I knew anything about my wife except for her false identity, I knew that she was the perfect woman for me.

In so many ways, she's like most I've known. She loves chocolate, and is sweet on Mary's infamous death-by-chocolate cake. She'll sit on my couch with a box of tissues and purposely watch a sad movie. Her cat is her best friend, and isn't even bothered when I tease her that he is.

But in other ways, she's unique. Savannah doesn't want flowers and candy from her husband, though. She wants to spar with him, to practice her punches while he wears the padded gloves, and spend time lunging with a blade in her hand so that, if she should ever choose to take a life with a blade, she knows precisely how to.

So long as it's not my throat she's aiming for, that is.

We tried lessons down at the shooting range. Bianca was a saint, despite Savannah's obvious and instant dislike of her, but it became obvious early on that the gun wasn't her weapon. She yipped whenever it went off, could hardly hit the target, and said the weapons Bianca selected for her were too bulky in her hand.

So I brought her Glock, and she hated shooting with that so much, she handed it back to me when the lesson was done.

No trying to convince me to give it back to her for good. No making a sly comment about how she could blow me away with the weapon. Just a wrinkled nose and a sigh as she shook her head and said, "Well, that was a waste of two hundred bucks."

And that was about when I first had the spark of an idea to win her over...

Like preparing the tattoos, it took some time. Then I didn't want to start up our self-defense lessons until they were healed, not because I cared about the pain, but because I didn't want to cause Savannah any.

They are now. And, this morning, I picked up my latest gift for my wife. I keep it in the pocket of my exercise shorts during our warm up, but before we start our lesson, I pull the leather case out and dangle it in front of Savannah.

With a curious tilt to her head, her ponytail settling over her shoulder, she snatches it from my grip. "What's this?"

"It's a holster."

She rolls her eyes at me. "I know that, babe."

Babe? "Did you just call me 'babe'?"

"Sure did."

"I've got ten years on you, wife."

"So? Does that mean you can't be my 'babe'?"

I lift her free hand, pressing a kiss to the top of it. "So long as I am yours, you may call me anything you want, ragna mia."

She sticks her tongue out at me.

I laugh. "Unless you're willing to use it, keep that pretty tongue in your mouth where it belongs."

"Why?" she says, daring me. "You gonna spank me again?"

My cock twitches. No matter how often we find the time to train in my gym, between the scent of her sweat and her musk in the air, plus the sports bra that molds to her tits so perfectly, I'm constantly aroused down here. It's fair to say that I'm constantly aroused whenever I'm near my wife, but something about her trusting me to take full control over her body, knowing I could never bring myself to hurt her... there's a reason why she teases me that I think of our sparring sessions as foreplay.

It's because it *is*.

But spanking? I've never had a partner that I wanted to take over my knee and spank before—until the first time she rode me after a training session. Since then, I haven't had the reason to bring my hand down on her ass again... but, oh, do I want to now.

Later, I tell myself. When I see how she reacts to my gift...

Without realizing how suddenly desperate I am for her, Savannah runs her thumb over the initials embossed on the leather. "S.L.?"

"Savannah Libellula," I tell her. "It's yours. So is what's inside of the holster."

Her cheeks flush. As though she doesn't know what to say, she busies herself with unsnapping the full holster so that she can see the hilt poking out from the top. Grabbing it, she checks to see if the blade's attached—as if it wouldn't be—then looks up at me again.

"You got me my own knife?"

"No. I'm giving you *my* knife."

Savannah sucks in a breath. Her hand twitches, and I press the bottom half of the holster against her palm so she doesn't drop it.

"Damien—"

"Don't try to tell me you don't want it. I won't hear it. You need protection. If the incident with Ricky proved anything, it's that not even having me near... or my bodyguard watching you... is enough to keep you safe. You don't want your gun back. But you seem very comfortable with a blade."

She gulps. "And you're not afraid that I'm going to stab you again?"

I fold her fingers over the holster. "No. I'm not."

Savannah stares down at the knife in her hand. She's quiet for so long that I wonder if I fucked up—but then her head snaps back to mine, her hand tossing the half-open holster to the floor. The stiletto falls out of the sheath a little more.

We both pretend not to notice.

Savannah starts to jog in place. "So... are we going to spar now?"

This isn't the reaction I was hoping for. Savannah taking my giving her my knife as some grand gesture of my affection for her and being so overwhelmed with gratitude that she strips and fucks me with the mirrors surrounding us... I'd been leaning toward that one.

But this is Savannah. Ragna mia.

And she's perfect.

I roll my neck on its stump. "I'm ready when you are, my dear."

"Okay. But first... let's make a bet."

Oh? "A wager? Gambling is usually the Sinners' domain, but all right. I'm game. What are your terms?"

"We wrestle. If you pin me first, I'll let you spank me. But I pin you—"

My upper lip starts to curl on its own accord. "I'm listening."

Her eyes seem to sparkle mischievously. "You'll have to let me win to find out."

"You know better. I can't just *let* you win."

"Oh. I know. But, believe me, you might want to."

Savannah is probably right, but since I'm suddenly very interested in baring her ass to me and watching her squirm as I bring my hand down on it again whether I'm inside of her or not... I can't see how I lose either way.

She's gotten so much better since we started. It's not as easy for me to overpower her, and she's taken my tips to use her speed and slighter weight against her opponent. There's also no denying that her time in the gym has made her stronger, too.

And, for some reason, she seems to really want to win this match.

Then again, so do I....

Just when I'm about to pin Savannah, the devious minx takes hold of my cock. Already so hard I felt a mixture of pleasure and pain as we tussled, when she grabs me and *tugs*, it's all I can do not to cream my pants like a goddamn teenage boy.

I don't know how she does it. One second, I'm on top of her, grinding my hips as if I can fuck her fist. The next, she yanks, I moan, and now I'm on my back. I miss her touch as she releases my cock. Before I can lunge for her, though, she's on top of me. Straddling me with a leg on each side, she presses her pussy against my lower belly, allowing my cock to nestle against her ass.

Her workout shorts are so tiny and so thin, it's almost like she's not wearing anything at all. Only she is, and so am I; otherwise one well-timed thrust might have my cock finding a hole of hers to lodge in.

Pussy. Ass. Right now, I'm so desperate to be inside this woman, to *claim* her again, that I'd take whatever she offered me... and, almost out of my head with lust, I start rocking my hips so that she knows it.

One hand plants on my chest. The other grabs for something. I can't even tell what it is. My sole focus is grabbing at Savannah's shorts, trying to shove them aside before I grab my own to free my cock—and that's when I see a flash of fluorescent light against metal, see her hand move, and curse when my left ear suddenly feels like it's on fucking fire.

It takes me a second to understand what happened. Well, that and seeing Savannah lift my stiletto to her lips, tongue darting out to play carefully with the tip.

Did she... was that *blood*?

"Wife?" It comes out shaky because, holy shit, I'm about to combust. "Did you just cut me?"

"Yup."

"On purpose?"

She snorts. "Please. I know you barely felt that. You took a blade to the gut and acted like we were discussing the fucking weather."

She's not wrong, but that's only because I was stubborn enough to hide my pain. What she just did now, though... it didn't hurt. Not really. Not after I got over the initial fiery feeling as she nicked my ear. But for her to use my knife to play with me, to lap at my blood the same way Orion laps at his water bowl?

"Tell me, my dear. Did I make a mistake in trusting you with that knife?"

Her weight shifts a little as Savannah lifts up, then scoots back, rubbing her pussy along my erection. "I wasn't trying to hurt you, babe. I just wanted your attention."

"You certainly have it now."

"Good. Because I just want to point out something."

"Go right ahead."

"The first time you had me on my knees, it's because I was trying to get out of fucking you. You know that. *I* know that. But I'd be lying if I said I hadn't thought about your taste a million times since then."

I find it hard to swallow right now. No. Fuck swallowing. I can't *breathe.* "Is that so?"

"Mm-hmm. And, well, since I have you pinned... I get to do what *I* want."

And what Savannah wants to do is dip her hand beneath the waistband of my pants, pulling out my cock before she shimmies down my body, finding a spot for her in the cradle of my legs.

I don't get up. Instead, folding my hand behind my head, not even caring that my ear stings from where she cut it, I let my beautiful bride worship me with her mouth.

Her face is buried in my crotch. As if she's trying every trick she has to make me explode in her mouth, she devotes the next few moments to laving my cock with her tongue, playing with my balls, humming against my length as she sucks.

I want to hold out. To continue this unexpected moment as long as I can, but there's a marked difference between the first blow job she gave me and this one. Instead of going through the motions, acting like a fucking fleshlight, Savannah is as into giving this oral as I am being on the receiving end. So I want to hold out, but before I know it, I'm running my fingers through the top of her hair, letting her know that I'm about to release.

She mumbles something around the head of my cock, and the vibration has me spurting right into her mouth.

Only after she swallows every drop of come I have to give her does she meet my gaze.

She looks so proud of herself, I have to assume she just told me to go ahead and give her my jizz. But there's more to it than that, and I have to know.

"Why?" Usually it's Savannah with the questions. But I just don't understand why she would do that without me finding a way to get her to. She said she wanted it, but... "*Why*, ragna mia?"

Savannah squeezes my hip before laying her hand over my spider tattoo—and my scar.

"Why?" she echoes bluntly, and I adore her notable Springfield accent far more than the fake Southern drawl she's thankfully dropped. "Because I guess I don't hate you after all."

It's not the same as her telling me she loves me, but it's a start.

Revenge List

SAVANNAH

It's closing in on the end of May, spring getting ready to trade places with summer, and all I keep hearing about is *Winter*.

I didn't realize how big of a problem this guy is. Most of that has to do with Damien trying to treat me like Genevieve, pretending as if he doesn't deal in drugs, blood, and bullets. He wants us both to have this idealized version of him, not understanding that I learned more than my fair share about what he does during prison, then after I got out and made him my target.

That means my husband keeps trying to keep his 'business' life separate from his 'personal' life, and because it's easier for me to accept this *new* life I found myself living when he does that, I usually let him.

But it's harder for him to do that these days. And I guess one part of being a mafia leader's wife is being there for him when he doesn't have the bandwidth to continue to hide the realities of who Damien Libellula really is from me.

And that means I keep hearing about Jimmy Winter.

Jimmy Winter is a wannabe gangster who seemed to come out of nowhere. Damien is sure this guy is being bankrolled by someone even bigger for him to be able to infiltrate as much as Springfield as he has, and it bothers my husband that he can't squash this threat to his empire like a cockroach. Even when he does get his hands on a member of Winter's crew, another takes his place, and he's no closer to extinguishing the head of the gang than he was before.

I try not to smirk and point out that I know exactly what he means, though I don't often manage it. On the plus side, he doesn't mind my sass—and I'm becoming a fan of letting him spank me to get out some of his frustration.

Like earlier tonight.

He got a phone call while we were getting ready for bed. Because the Dragonflies usually speak in a code when they don't want anyone to understand what they're discussing, he doesn't leave the room if he has to answer and we're together.

Lately, he hasn't been using the code as much as he has been. That makes sense to me for a few reasons.

One: because most of his discussions had been about him planning our tattoos and having my personalized holster made and, now that he's done all that, he doesn't have to keep it a secret any longer. And, most importantly, two: because now that I have no desire to kill *him*, he trusts me enough to speak more openly about Dragonfly biz.

Of course, his innate overprotective nature means that he wants to keep me as coddled as Gen. Instead of confining me to the house so that he can keep his eye on me—or Vin's—he doesn't want me to leave because I might be in danger.

And we have Jimmy fucking Winter to blame.

I never understood why Damien seemed so obsessed with the snowflake that was marked on the bottom of the gun I bought from the pawn shop. I finally admitted where I got it from after another disastrous morning at the gun range, and while I accepted I'll never be a marksman and my former fantasy of putting a bullet through Damien's skull was just that, he was more interested in the weapon itself.

I have no use for it. Since Damien gave me his stiletto, I've worn the holster he gave me on my hip whenever I'm dressed.

I'm naked now, curled up on his chest. He seems a lot more relaxed now, though I've learned that my older husband has quite the stamina. He'll be ready to fuck me again before we turn in for the night, but for the moment, he's content to stroke my hair as he confesses to me what the earlier call was about.

Turns out, two soldiers caught a pair of Winter's men sneaking around Il Sogno. They tried to act like they were down for some Italian, but they were caught with a kilo of cocaine on them. Damien didn't hesitate while he was on the phone. He gave the order to send an enforcer.

In his Family, enforcers are the sly assassins who kill on Damien's orders. He doesn't have that many, and he prizes the ones he has. The night I met him, he'd lost one to his rivals on the West Side of Springfield. Of course, then I realized the man was killed because he'd beaten that poor blonde girl half-to-death and I understood why Damien didn't retaliate.

He did, however, enlist Oliver to be his next enforcer. But Oliver, it seems, disappeared after he was dispatched.

Whether he was killed, poached, or just decided not to be a syndicate murderer anymore, Damien doesn't know—but it bothers him that one of his men went missing and he can't track him.

I lay my head on his chest, listening to his heart beat. "I don't know why you can't," I muse. "Don't you have all of your guys chipped like me? You said I wasn't the only one."

"You're not, but the technology was too expensive to insist on it being a requirement to join the Family. Only a few of my most trusted men have it."

Really? Sitting up so that I'm next to Damien, I gaze down at his face. "Like who?"

"Vin, for one. Christopher. As part of the truce, I have Lincoln Crewes's code. Tony accepted. So did Gio. A couple of my lieutenants said they were willing to test out the tech, too. But that's all." He pauses for a moment. "I have one, too, but the only one who has the code is Devil."

"Because of the truce."

"Mm-hmm."

"Not Gen, though?" I ask. Then, thinking better about what I asked, I answer my own question. "No. She'd never let you do that. And she'd probably kick you right in the balls if you ever did that without her permission. You know that, too, so you wouldn't. You wouldn't do anything to push your sister away."

Damien chuckles. "Very perceptive."

I shrug. "I guess."

I don't mean to sound so forlorn all of a sudden. Now that I don't pretend to use the Southern drawl anymore around Damien, I rarely police my tone, but that came out on its own.

Worse, he noticed.

"Savannah? Amore... what's wrong?"

I shake my head. "Nothing."

"Cara mia..."

I've learned that the more Damien slips into Italian, the harder I find it to resist him.

"*Fine.* It's just... you just told me Oliver went missing. If the only one who can track you is your rival—"

"We have a truce," he reminds me.

And it could easily be broken one day. "What if something happens to you? What if he won't give up your location? What if I can't find you and you're gone like Oliver?"

Damien grips the side of my face lightly, stroking my upper cheek. "You would care? If one of my enemies came after me... and in the unlikely circumstance they managed to overpower me... you would care?"

I could lie. I could pretend that I didn't give a shit about him... but why? Ever since he told me that I could expect him to be honest no matter what, he has, for the good and the bad. I've tried to do the same. If I couldn't tell the truth, I kept my mouth shut.

I could do that now. I could say nothing, allowing Damien to come to his own conclusions. I could—

"I would."

Another brush of his thumb on my skin before Damien grips the comforter, tossing it away from us. He slides across the sheet, the motion seeming to echo in the dark bedroom, before his bare feet land on the floor.

I watch his sculpted back and gorgeous ass move across the room to reach the pants he shucked off earlier. Digging around inside of it, he pulls out two phones. He glances at them both, then tucks one back into his pocket.

The other stays in his grip as he joins me back in bed.

Once I'm snuggled up against him again, he shows it to me.

"I always keep an extra burner around in case I need it. I got the idea from Lincoln Crewes years ago when I saw he always had two phones on him. If I needed to lose one, I wasn't without another. Here. Take it. You can have it."

"Aren't you afraid I could call someone? Tell them I need help?"

"You could. That's a risk I'll have to take. But you've been no contact with your parents for years, you have no siblings, and I'm sure you wouldn't want to drag any friends you might have into this life, hmm?"

I'd have to have friends first... "What about 911?"

In the shadows of our bedroom, he gives me that crooked half-smile I can't help but adore. "Tell Deb I said 'hi'. Or Shannon. It's usually one of those two who field calls on the East End as the dispatcher."

Why am I not surprised that he has 911 in his pocket, too?

Whatever. It isn't worth bluffing anyway when we both know that I won't do that. Not now. Not anymore.

"Why are you giving me this phone?"

"Two reasons. One: my number is programmed into this. I should've thought about this before, but if you need me and don't want to ask Gen or Vin or Frankie to get in touch with me, you won't have to. You can call me yourself."

That's a good thing to be able to do if I want to start accepting that I'm his wife and not his prisoner. "Okay. And the second reason?"

"There's an app on here. Look. This blue one. If you click it, then click on my name, you can track me down wherever I go."

Wow.

I... I'm touched. I'm fucking *touched*.

The head Dragonfly himself, who guards his location so fiercely that only one other soul has it, just offered it to me because I accidentally made it obvious that I'd feel much better if I knew where he was—and not because it would be easier to ambush him and kill him?

Oh, how the tables have turned. All those weeks ago, I never would've expected it, and a part of me is still struggling to accept how much our relationship has changed.

"What if I decide to do, like, social media? Go online with my old accounts. Call some old friends who might want to hear from me?"

"Please, Savannah. This phone is completely clean. I had yours erased and tossed right after our wedding. In order to do that, you'll need to know your user-names, passwords, and contacts." He gooses my side. "Do you?"

Asshole, I think, and there's actually a hint of affection to it. "What about you? You're ten years older than me. Your memory's gotta be going, babe. You're telling me you remember *yours*?"

"Most of them."

"Bullshit."

"Not at all, wife. As you so kindly mentioned, I am older than you. That means I remember a time before cell phones. When, if I wanted to call someone, I had to memorize the number and hope they answered." Damien drops a kiss to my lips, tasting my smile. "I didn't even get my first phone until I was twenty and I stole it. I remember it, too. A blue Nokia brick, and I bashed in a guy's head with it without even denting the thing."

I giggle. "That image shouldn't be as sexy as it is."

"That's only because, deep down, you're as violent as I am. But that's okay, ragna mia. I like that about you." Then, before I can make a comment on his fairly apt assessment of 'Savannah', he asks, "What about you? How old were you when you got your first phone?"

Oof. Most of the time, I don't notice the age gap between us. But when he asks something like that...

"Nine," I admit.

"Nine! With a phone?"

"I had soccer practice, okay?"

Damien sucks in a breath. "Soccer? Oh, amore..." His shoulder moves, arm sliding until he has his hand on my thigh. Tugging me closer with his other hand, he uses the first one to caress as much of my leg as he can reach. "Is that where you got these gorgeous legs? Mm... so strong. So powerful. So delicious, especially when they're wrapped around your husband."

His fingers guide upward, finding their way to my pussy. Like Damien, I'm still naked from earlier. Naked and, when he dips his finger inside of me, testing to see how wet I am, fucking *soaked*.

"Ah..." His breath is warm on my skin as he exhales. "I have an idea. Let's see if this old man can show his young wife how my generation entertained ourselves before smartphones took over. What do you think?"

I let the phone Damien gave me slip out of my hand, falling to the other side of me as he eases me to my back.

"I think that sounds like a great idea..."

Revenge List

TWENTY-SEVEN

WHERE IS HE

SAVANNAH

Last night was great. Damien more than made up for his boasting, and after I was panting beneath him, I finally muttered something about how I'm glad I met him when he was forty. I think a later-twenties, early-thirties Damien would've been the death of me.

But that was last night.

Today? I'm freaking out.

I can't find Orion.

At first, I figured he was still exploring the house. It didn't take my cat long to learn that off-limits didn't apply to him; honestly, it doesn't apply to me, either, anymore. More often than not, he's upstairs, keeping Genevieve company while she's stretching, practicing, or working on her choreography. If not there, he's following Mary around the kitchen, hoping the kindly cook would drop some scraps for him.

I've double-checked the first floor three times already. Vin's door is closed, whether he's home or not, but when I knock on the door and realize he's sleeping off an all-night search for Oliver, I slink away after he confirms Orion didn't slip in when he got home this morning.

Frankie promises he'll let me know if he finds my cat, though I shouldn't worry since Orion usually finds some out of the way corner to nap in, especially when he's having another flare-up. But he's been good lately which is why I'm so concerned when it seems as if he's up and disappeared.

I want to ask Genevieve if she's seen him, but I figure I'll have to wait until the music stops before I head upstairs.

I've learned that, when the music is playing and the door is closed, it's better to leave Genevieve be. She can go from bubbly to demanded in a heartbeat, then blame it on the stress of being interrupted. I don't blame her, either, and it's better for me to find something to do on my own while I'm waiting for Damien to return home.

Once Vin came home and gave him an update on the search—which yielded no sign of Oliver so far—the two men traded places. My husband kissed me goodbye while Vin went to bed.

It's late afternoon now. I tried to distract myself

with television in between getting up to look around for Orion. It made it harder to focus because, usually when one of us is in here, so is he.

Finally, right when it's about six o'clock, the music finally dies. I don't hesitate. Launching myself from the couch, I head right upstairs, going so quick that I nearly slam right into Gen coming out of her studio.

She looks fairly fresh for having danced all day, but I barely clock that. Not when I'm way too worried about Orion.

When I don't see him trotting at her feet, my worry only worsens. Even if he was sleeping, if Gen left the studio and he was in it, he'd be right behind her, thinking it was time for food.

"Where's Orion?" I ask. "I've been looking for him all day, and I haven't been able to find any sign of him that he's around."

Did he get out? With all the cameras Damien has surrounding this place, Frankie would've caught sight of my orange and white cat sneaking out. But he hadn't, and he wants me to believe that Orion is just hiding in the house somewhere.

But where?

Genevieve doesn't seem too concerned. "I don't know, but did you check the shit box?"

"Yeah. I did. There was nothing in it."

"Hm. That's weird. I would've thought he'd have filled it by now. I mean, I gave him his medicine this morning."

Record scratch—

"Medicine? What medicine?"

"You know. The poop medicine."

"Orion doesn't have poop medicine. Gen, what are you talking about?"

She tucks a lock of blonde hair that had escaped her bun behind her ear. "Remember? When he was constipated?"

"That was weeks ago. He's been okay since then. And when he gets a little stopped-up, Mary lets me have some canned pumpkin for him." Damien's cook is a sweetheart, and she's been stocking it up for me ever since Genevieve burst into the kitchen, shouting we had a pumpkin emergency.

Gen frowns. "Then what was in that shot?"

Panic makes my voice rise. "What shot? What are you talking about?"

"Okay. Let me explain. Last night, I tweaked my ankle again. Okay? So, this morning, Christopher came over and went with me to see Dr. Liz at the clinic. She told me to take a couple Aleves, then stay off of it if it was still bothering me. Before I left, she told me that she'd been talking to this vet tech she knows about Orion. The vet tech got some medicine from the vet she works for, then gave it to Doc Liz as a favor for us. She said... she said I should go home, scruff him, and give him the injection right away. It would help him stay regular for the next month in case he has problems again. That..." Her brow furrows. "That was the right thing to do... wasn't it? She told me to give him the medicine."

I can't imagine why. We only called her about the cat once; since then, I only saw Dr. Liz one more time, at Damien's birthday dinner. Neither of us brought up Orion.

If there was such a thing as a shot that did everything Genevieve just said it did, why hadn't any of the vets I brought Orion to as a kitten mentioned that?

Something... something's not right.

"I'm sure it'll be fine," I lie, trying to keep Damien's sister calm. "Where did you give him the medicine?"

"Well, my room. He likes to hang out on my bed sometimes, but I'm sure he would've left by now. I left the door open while I went to my studio—"

I'm already rushing for the open door. I've never been in Genevieve's room before since I've never had a reason to, and I wasn't going to just walk in there to search for Orion earlier. I'm kicking myself now because there he is—

—*and he's not moving.*

My beautiful boy is sprawled out on his side, legs kicking out in front of him. His eyes are half open, and unless I'm panicking too much to notice, his body is completely still.

No!

I run over to him, Gen right on my heels.

"Oh my God. Oh my *God*. Did I kill your cat? Savannah, did I fucking kill your cat?"

I... I don't know. I lift him up, a small burst of relief rushing through me when he's not stiff. Rigor mortis hasn't set in, and he's still warm. Putting his face up to mine, I can tell that he's breathing, but barely.

I whirl on Genevieve, trying not to freak her out any more than she is—and that I am. "He's alive, but I'm not sure if he will be for much longer. What was in that medicine?"

Her eyes are wide as she takes a step away from me. A moment later, she seems to collect herself. "I don't know. But I know who can find out."

Before she says another word, she dashes out the door. I poke Orion, trying to wake him up. He's not responding at all. It's almost like he's been sedated or something, knocked out so entirely, he didn't even close his eyes.

"Come on, Orion. Wake up, baby. I know you're okay. Please. Please, please, please..."

He doesn't answer, and I'm seconds away from throwing up all over Genevieve's floor.

This time, when she's on the phone, she doesn't even bother with the speakerphone. Slightly panicked by more than a little firm, she's already speaking to someone on the other end as she rushes back in, patting Orion's head with her trembling fingers.

"Dr. Liz? It's Genevieve. Yeah. Hi. No, it's not my ankle again. It's actually about that shot you gave me this morning. The one you said was for the... Right. The cat." I whimper as she pauses. "Uh-huh. What was in it? You... you don't know. Well, something's wrong with Orion. He's... he's, like, passed out or something. Who was the vet... what do you mean, they're on vacation? Doc, we need *help*."

Gen is quiet for a few seconds before she starts to nod. "Okay. I guess that's better than nothing. We'll be right there."

She hangs up the phone, and I cling to my cat. "What did she say?"

"To bring him to the clinic. She might not be a vet, but she swears she can help. The vet who prescribed the medicine left for a cruise this morning. Dr. Liz has the bag it came in, though, and medical knowledge."

Liz was the one who helped us when Orion got constipated...

"What are we waiting for? Let's go!"

THE CLINIC IS CLOSED.

It took close to half an hour to arrive, and I felt every one of those seconds like a piece of glass jabbing into my skin. Orion was no better or worse during the wait, but I couldn't stop myself from thinking that, the longer it takes to get to the clinic, the closer to death my baby is getting.

Part of the wait was because of Vin. Damien's cousin heard me and Genevieve panicking, stampeding around the house, searching for keys and the cat carrier. We woke him up, but before the grumpy giant could ask us what we were doing, Gen launched into an explanation that made the whole thing sound so much worse than it is.

She thinks it's all her fault. I try to tell her that, if a doctor gave me medicine and told me to pass it along to a patient, I'd do the same thing. Maybe not if it was *my* cat unless I did some research first, but there are a few people in this world you just think you can trust.

Doctors should be at the top of that list.

For Dr. Liz, it's probably the vet friend who gave her the injection to begin with.

To my surprise, instead of telling Gen to calm down, Vin waits until she's finished, then announces he'll be the one to take us to the clinic. That's how I found out that Damien told him he's responsible for watching me when the boss can't. And since Genevieve is Damien's beloved baby sister, that goes double for her.

I'll give him credit. He knew better than to insist on bringing Orion to see Dr. Liz himself. I have to go, and because Gen's still convinced she killed him, it would do more harm than good if we left her behind.

Explaining everything to Vin ate up time. So did the inevitable call to Damien.

Vin was right. If the three of us left the house and didn't tell him, my husband wouldn't like that one bit. Not like we could hide it from him, either. Me and Vin have the trackers, and despite proclaiming that

Genevieve doesn't, the overprotective Dragonfly I've come to know and love has some way of keeping an eye on her. I'd put money on it.

Damien didn't try to stop us, either. Instead, earning himself even more credit in my books, he says he'll be right there. He wants to be support for his sister and me—and Orion—and if Dr. Liz can't help or it's bad news, he doesn't want us to be alone, either.

Only one problem. We're standing in front of the clinic, the lights are off, the door's locked, and there's no sign of Dr. Liz *or* Damien.

Vin started calling him the moment we pulled up in front of the clinic. Too distracted by the dark windows, I didn't realize that he kept disconnecting and starting over until it's about the fourth time.

I swallow dryly. "Is... is he not answering?"

Vin stares at his phone as if he can make it put Damien on the line. "No. He should've been here already. He told me he'd be waiting for us. Damien doesn't lie."

No. He doesn't.

So where is he? Where's Liz? She knew we were on our way, and the clinic is open for a few more hours at least. Why did she shut down for the night before we got here?

What the hell is going on?

I don't know, but just as the panic starts to well up inside of me again, I remember the phone he gave me.

Like the stiletto on my hip, I decided to start

carrying the phone with me. After I got dressed this morning, I slipped it into the back pocket of my jeans in case my husband wanted to check in with me during the day.

I have one missed call from Damien. It puts it at twenty minutes ago, around the time he should've arrived here.

Was that him calling to tell me something came up? If so, why don't I have a text or a voicemail?

It doesn't matter. And I'm sure he never expected I would need to track him so soon as he gave me this phone, but I jab my finger on the blue app he pointed out last night, then select his name.

A green dot appears on the screen—and it's moving.

Vin looks over my shoulder at the phone. "Is that *Damien*?"

There's no time to explain. "Yes. And it looks like he's heading toward the West Side of Springfield." I don't understand. "Did he have to see Devil about something?"

The more Damien opened up to me about his life as a mafia leader, the more I couldn't stop referring to his truce with Lincoln Crewes as a 'deal with the devil'. Lincoln is the only one who has access to his location —well, apart from me now—and Damien prides himself on protecting his Family by keeping this relationship with the Sinners Syndicate solid.

Maybe that's what happened. Maybe Lincoln needed him, and he went.

The look on Vin's face says that's impossible. "No. And he wouldn't head onto Sinner territory without backup. *I'm* his backup. Something's not right. The boss is in trouble. I've gotta go after him."

He reaches for my phone. I hide it behind my back. "Savannah..."

"No. If you're going after Damien, I'm going, too. I have the tracker. You have to let me."

He so doesn't have to let me.

If he uses force, not even my self-defense lessons will keep Vin from snatching that phone from me if he wants it. But I think he knows that, if he does, Damien will have his ass for laying his hands on me.... And it's a lose-lose situation for the big guy.

Even worse because Genevieve pipes up with, "What about Orion?"

Shit. I didn't forget about my cat, but she's holding the cat carrier, lifting it up so she'll see any change in him.

"The clinic's closed," Vin begins.

"Obviously. But just because one vet is on vacation, that doesn't mean they all are. We've gotta find one and take Orion there."

"Genny—"

I've never seen Genevieve so serious. "I know you have to make sure Dame's okay. I want you to. But

Orion... this is my fault. I'll take care of him. You two go."

"And leave you alone?" asks Vin. "No. I can't—"

"You have to. Look, I have a friend, okay? He can help me."

"*He*?"

These Libellula men. "Can you call him?" I ask her. "Get him here?"

"I'm sure I can. It might take him twenty minutes or so to get here, but I'll be okay by myself until then."

"Is it Christopher?" demands Vin. "Why is Christopher twenty minutes away?"

She didn't say 'Christopher', did she? I noticed it. I know Gen did... but her cousin didn't.

"It doesn't matter. Gen, you know about the dragonfly decals on the windows, right?" I hurry over to the one on the clinic's locked door. "A safe space for members of your brother's Family. Find one. Hide out there with Orion until your friend comes. If you need us, call Vin. I'm sure you have his number. We're going to make sure Damien's okay."

She nods in determination. "And I'm going to make sure Orion is okay."

Because they better *both* be...

Revenge List

TWENTY-EIGHT
JIMMY WINTER

Damien

Fucking damn it.

I haven't had someone ring my bell so hard since I was a twenty-five-year-old idiot who teased Lincoln Crewes about being whipped by Ava Monroe. I'd forgotten for a moment that he was a brawler who idolized his girlfriend, and after he knocked me out, I made it a point to never talk down on St. Ava again.

The headache I had when I woke up from Lincoln's punch has only a slight edge on the one I have now. My head is splitting, my tongue too thick for my mouth, and my arms feel like they've been yanked from their sockets.

That's not all, either.

My whole left side radiates heat. My shoulder is in agony, bleeding through to my back, and there are parts of my lower body that have never hurt this bad before in my life.

With my eyes still closed—if only because it's too fucking painful to open them—I take stock of my injuries. I've obviously been beaten. I'm sitting now, and the way my arms are pulled, I'd wager that I'm tied to something. The pain in my shoulder? Gunshot wound, definitely.

And all of that makes sense since the last thing I remember was talking to Elizabeth outside of the clinic. She bumped into me after I parked my car. I had my phone out, already calling Savannah to let her know I arrived, when the doctor frowned.

She told me that she didn't know what I was talking about, that she hadn't heard from Savannah or Genevieve at all, and that since the clinic was so slow, she was shutting down early because she had an appointment she needed to go to.

My wife didn't answer, but before I could try to call her back, Elizabeth's face changed as she looked behind me.

She screamed one word—*shoulder*—before my body bucked as the gunshot hit me right in the back. The unexpected impact forced me to my knees. The doctor dropped right next to me, and just when I thought she was going to check my wound, he did the last thing I ever would've expected.

She jabbed me in the neck with a needle she'd had hidden in her hand.

After that, everything went black—until now. Until I'm slowly coming to, my surroundings still dark, though my ears prick, trying to listen to the sounds around me while I continue to fake being out.

Until someone slaps me upside the head, and I'm so stunned by the cowardly and cruel gesture, my eyes spring open just to catch sight of whoever would dare do that to me.

"Finally," comes a pleasant voice. "I was told that sedative was only supposed to last half an hour. It's almost been forty minutes. I was getting impatient."

I blink, trying to get a read on the man speaking.

The voice isn't familiar. Neither are my surroundings. At first glimpse, it looks like I'm in some sort of retail space. It's empty, though, with glass windows and a door in front of me.

Ballsy move. Now that I can kind of see, it's easy to notice the heavy rope keeping my hands tied to the wooden chair my battered body was tossed into. Anyone passing by could see what's going on in here.

Well, maybe. There aren't any lights on. The only illumination comes from the sun peeking around the skyscraper opposite where we are. The room is full of shadows and gloom, though maybe that's my hazy vision making it seem so much darker.

It's not so dark, though, that I can't make out the face of the man in front of me.

When Tanner prepared the folder all about Jimmy Winter, it had everything in it except for a photo.

Now I now exactly what he looks like. He's in his mid-thirties about, though his head of shocking white hair throws me off. His face is young so the hair ages him. No wrinkles, though, and his vivid green eyes are so cat-like, he reminds me of Orion.

Like me, he's wearing a suit, but his is—like his hair—a pristine white. The only spot of dark on him is the weapon in his hand.

He's not alone, either. He has three soldiers. A bald man in his fifties, a blond about a decade younger, and a Black man who's around the same age as Winter.

Because, yeah, there's no doubt in my mind that the white-haired freak is the one and only Jimmy Winter.

"He's awake?"

Now that voice? That I recognize.

Elizabeth Harper was hiding in one corner, arm wrapped around her white doctor's coat, the other hand lifted up to her mouth. My head swivels to look at her, and she flinches to see my face.

She swallows. "I should look him over. I patched up his bullet hole, but his eyes look swollen. And I want to make sure the sedative didn't do any danger."

She does, does she?

What the fuck is going on here.

Winter turns to look at her. "You stay where you are. When I want you to talk, I'll tell you. Until then, be quiet."

Elizabeth folds in on herself, nodding.

"Now. What was I saying? Ah, yes. I was blaming the doctor for giving too high of a dose. Doesn't she know we're working on a timetable here?"

The bald man clears his throat. "About that... We've got company, Jimmy."

"More distractions? Fucking wonderful. Alright." Winter uses his gun to gesture at the door. "See who it is."

He does, smirking when he obviously recognizes them. "Looks like the bodyguard is here."

Vin.

When I thought I caught sight of the familiar sleek and shiny black car passing by the window while Winter was talking to Elizabeth, I'd prayed to a God I'm not sure I even believe in that that the man with the buzz cut driving the car wasn't Vin. The woman next to him? That couldn't be Savannah. What would they be doing here? How could they find me?

And then I remembered how only last night I showed my wife how to use the tracker, and I purposely turned my attention to the quiet blond soldier so that none of these pricks got the idea to turn around and see the car turning around and heading back.

I'd hoped Vin would either get my wife to safety or at least call for backup. I could hold out 'til then—but I should've known better. If he saw me or guessed I was stuck with these idiots, nothing would stop him from coming to get me on his own.

Because he might be my cousin, but I'm the head of the Family first—and he'll do anything to rescue me—

"Really? Huh. I wasn't expecting that. More fun for us then." Winter jerks his chin at the bald man. "Kill him."

—even sacrifice himself.

I jerk against the bonds keeping me trapped to this fucking chair. They're too tight for me to do anything except rub my wrists raw, but I have to try.

I'm not the only one who doesn't like the idea of Vin getting tangled up in this, either. Because Elizabeth?

She gasps, drawing Winter's attention to her.

"Vincent? Why would you... no. He's not part of this. Can't we just lock the door?"

Winter snorts. Then, gesturing with his gun, the bald soldier pointedly heads for the front door and, on his boss's orders, props it open for a better shot. His gun is at chest level, and I can only hope like hell that Vin can fire off a shot before Winter's man does.

Elizabeth folds her hands in front of her. "Jimmy, please..."

"Do shut up," Winter says pleasantly. "Before I make you. You did what you were supposed to. You brought me the Dragonfly. If you don't want your precious little clinic to have an unfortunate accident, keep your fucking mouth shut."

Her mouth closes.

I smirk. "What's the matter, Liz?" My voice is rough.

Raspy. It's gotta be a side effect from whatever they shot me up with, but hell if I'm gonna ask the doc about that. Not when I'm seeing two of her as it is. "Did you forget that a big part of the life is death?"

"I doubt it," cuts in Winter. "Considering she was more than happy to set it up so that we'd take out your pretty little wife."

What?

"My wife?"

"Damien—"

"My *wife*?" I glare at her, trying to focus on her face so she can see the murder written in my eyes. "You were after my wife?"

"Sure was," Winter tells me. "So jealous of the new Mrs. Libellula, she was willing to do *anything* for one of my guys to take her out. And then, when the grieving husband needed a shoulder to cry on... well, the doctor would be right there for him. Only she didn't realize something. Rumors around this town say that the leader of the Dragonflies is an oxymoron. An honest criminal. Well, I'm not."

Yeah. No shit.

While his guy inches closer to the door, getting into position, Winter starts to saunter over toward Liz. "She got this idea that I'd kill your wife. Rough you up a bit, too, so she could be the heroic doctor who saves you. Everyone will think that Savannah Libellula was the target because she'll show up dead, but Damien won't. But, see, that doesn't suit my plan at all. I didn't come this far so that Damien could continue taking out my men.

"As it is, his should be roaches instead of Dragonflies. There's so fucking many of them. Kill one, two more take their place. Kill an enforcer? And the rest scatter around the city, searching for the one who disappeared him off the streets."

"Oliver," I hiss. "You're talking about Oliver?"

"Was that his name? Silly me. I got him to spill his guts about everything I wanted to know before he, well, spilled his guts. I guess it just never occurred to me to ask him his name."

Psycho. Jimmy Winter is a full-on psychopath.

And he knows about *Savannah*.

Worse, unless Vin brought a different woman with black hair across town, she's *here*.

I can never let this fucker know how close my wife is. Vin... he can take care of himself. Savannah, though... no amount of self-defense can prepare her for something like this.

"Anyway," he says, smug in the way he's monologuing like a stereotypical villain. "That means Damien has to die. Sorry. But he couldn't just *die*. It needed to look like the Devil of Springfield decided there won't be any more truce. So good ol' Link the brawler beats the shit out of him on Sinner territory, puts a bullet in his skull, and, whoops, a good citizen finds him in an empty store. Now the Dragonflies just have to retaliate for their leader, and next thing you know? No Sinners. No Dragonflies."

I spit on the ground, cutting him off. "Just Snowflakes? That it, Winter?"

He touches his belly, then bows his head. "And to think the great Damien Libellula knows how I am. I'm honored. Especially since I'll be the one to finish you off."

"He's coming, boss," says the bald man at the door.

"But I wasn't done revealing my plan. And, yes, I know that it's so terribly cliche, but since I rarely get to talk to someone who understands what it means to sacrifice *everything* for his family... you can't blame me, can you, Damien?"

I sure the fuck can.

"I know, boss. But he's a big guy—"

"Very well. Get in position," orders Winter.

The bald soldier nods, then backs up. His gun is steady. I hold my breath, the beginning of an oversized shadow falling in front of the door. The sun is setting, so that might throw me off, but the soldier has perfect aim.

He shoots. Fires. I hear a thud—Vin hitting the sidewalk—then one more shot. I dig my fingers in the wood of the chair, vowing that I'll destroy every last person in this room if my cousin is dead.

I can't tell. Winter waves his hand. The bald man holsters his gun, then darts outside. Another one of the three soldiers joins him. With each of them hefting a leg, they drag Vin in through the door, then close it behind his unmoving body.

From this angle, I can't tell what damage has been done. They didn't do a headshot—which gives me a tiny sliver of hope—but because I can't see the injuries, I refuse to react.

That's what Winter wants, after all. He wants to see me hurt before he takes me out, all so he can start a war between the Libellula Family and the Sinners Syndicate.

I don't react.

Liz does.

Pushing away from where she'd been hiding in her corner, she hurries for Vin's body.

Winter sighs. "No. Don't. Stop. Wait." It's a flat, emotionless voice, like he's doing his best impression of Willy fucking Wonka. But because he *is* a psycho, he doesn't really want her to stop.

The amusement playing in his green eyes makes that clear.

"Ah, well..." He raises his gun, aiming it at her back.

She keeps running.

"*Shoulder*," Winter says, an obvious mockery of Elizabeth's shrill shout earlier, before *bang*.

She crumples up on the floor.

Suddenly, I think I understand. She must've seen someone creeping up behind me, known from the gun that it was time for Winter's guys to work me over, and she tried to tell them where to aim for minimum damage.

Minimum, but from the way Liz grabs her shoulder, sobbing on the floor as she scoots away, seeking safety, it's probably far more than the good doctor ever expected.

Winter grins over at me. "Now, where were we?"

Revenge List

TWENTY-NINE
REVENGE

SAVANNAH

I shouldn't have let Vin go first.

That's all I'm thinking as I sit on the edge of the passenger seat, clutching the dash, about to climb through the fucking window if that'll somehow turn back time and stop Vin from walking up to the door.

He had his gun out. It should've been a protective measure.

It *wasn't.*

He knew Damien was in trouble. The moment the tracker finally stopped about twenty minutes ago, showing us that Damien's tracker put him along an abandoned stretch of empty and closed-down stores in the slums of Springfield, we both agreed that something was up. Technically, this is the West Side so it belongs to the Sinners Syndicate. But the area is usually reserved for junkies and prostitutes who are too much of a threat to join either of the two organized crime rings in the city.

According to Vin, there's absolutely no reason why Damien should be here. At first, we didn't think he *was*. There's no sign of his red car anywhere, but I'm not following any tracker that might've been installed in case it was stolen. I'm following the dot that correlates with the subdermal tracker in Damien.

Because someone stole my husband, and I want him back.

Once we arrived at the destination, Vin approached in a roundabout way. He didn't go on foot at first, either. He drove around in the car, searching the left side of the streets while I was looking at the right.

And that's how I saw a group of three or four people surrounding something in the middle inside of a store that looks like it's been available for rent for a long, long time.

They're not working on the inside or renovating it, either. After I point out what I saw inside of the suspiciously dark store, Vin agreed it might be something. We drove around again—and this time? I was almost positive I saw a man sitting in the chair where the other ones were gathered before.

The silhouette of that man looked like it might be Damien. The tracker lined up with it.

We had to check.

Or, considering Vin was in no mood to argue, he told me to stay in the car while he checked.

He parked about ten stores away so that he could sneak up on the store. If that *is* Damien, he's definitely not alone. He's probably in trouble.

Vin paused for a second, grabbing something from the trunk of the car. Once he was ready, he disengaged the safety on his gun before creeping down the street.

From where I was, I didn't see it when someone opened the door or stuck their gun out of it. I was too focused on watching Vin's back, and his bulk hid everything from me.

But when his body jerked, then fell backward on the sidewalk... I saw *that*. Even worse, I watched in abject horror as the door widened enough for two men to slip out, grab Vin by the legs, then drag his big body into the store before closing the door again.

The whole thing happened in a matter of minutes. One second Vin was up, then he wasn't, and all I could think is: if they'll kill Vin, what are they doing to Damien?

I don't have a gun. Vin had the only one. I have my stiletto, and I slap at my hip in panic, fingers unwilling to work right for a second before I'm unsnapping the top of the leather case, pulling the knife out.

But what now? If I try to stroll up the door, I'm dead meat, just like Vin. You don't bring a knife to a gunfight. The beauty of the stiletto is that it requires intimacy. It's an up-close kill.

What to do? What to *do*?

Okay. I can't leave Damien in there. I just... I *can't*. And maybe this is the worst moment in the world to realize just how much I've grown to care for him, to depend on him, to *love* him... but, suddenly, my revenge list has changed.

In my mind's eye, I cross off *Damien Libellula*, and then I add: *whoever the fuck thought they could take* my *husband*.

For months, I stalked him. I watched him. I studied him. I came up with a hundred plans for how I was going to kill him. In the end, I didn't use any of them. I took an opportune moment to touch him, to steal his knife, to *stab* him—and I failed.

I won't fail this time.

I got close, though. Even Damien will admit that. I got close, and all because I went with the first impulsive idea that popped into my brain.

And right now? I've got one even more impulsive than the last.

Clutching my stiletto, I climb up from the passenger seat. Flinging my body into the driver's side, I'm so glad that Vin left the engine running. He told me if things went south that I needed to be able to take off, get home, make sure Genny was safe. I lied and told him I would, knowing that nothing would stop me from getting to Damien.

Looks like I'm going to prove it.

The car's on. I pause only to throw on my seatbelt because God knows I'm gonna need it, then put the car into reverse. The street's empty, all the unhoused and down-on-their-luck people who flock to this neighborhood either hiding out until dark or tucked away in their hidey holes. Right now, it's just me and whoever is in that store... and I'm about to say 'hi'.

Once I've backed up enough to give me room, I lean forward in my seat as far as the seatbelt will allow. Then, staring unblinkingly at my newest target, I focus on the store. I won't take my eyes off of it. Even as I put the car back into drive, slam my foot down on the gas pedal, and *go*, I never once look away.

When I take a wide turn, crossing into the other lane before turning sharply, hopping the curb, and smashing through the glass windows of the shop?

Oh, yeah. I close my eyes then.

Not for long. Just upon the first impact because I'm not sure how the windshield on one of Damien's flashy cars will hold. At the speed I was going, I was hoping to smash the window and make a distraction, but I really didn't like the idea of the windshield cutting me to ribbons when I did.

Luckily, the windshield held. The glass windows of the store shatter, but they didn't really stop the car at all. I'm still pressing down on the gas pedal which means that, even after the windows break, the car keeps going.

At the first sound of gunfire, I duck—but I'm still going, baby. My hand is still on the wheel, my eyes opening just in time to jerk it so that I don't hit the chair that's holding my husband.

I do, however, send a bald man flying one way, see a Black man land on the windshield—and that *does* crack the glass, though it doesn't break—before he rolls off, hitting the floor hard. But, best of all, I keep going until I crash into a wall, pinning some freaky-looking dude all in white. White suit. White hair. White teeth bared as he howls in agony.

I'm still on survivor mode. The two guys I hit are down. Dead? Dunno. Maybe. I didn't roll over anything so I'd like to think I missed Vin, wherever he is; Damien is sitting in his chair, mouth open, beautiful face *destroyed.*

What did they do to my husband?

I don't think. My brain flew out the window when I thought it was a good idea to drive a car through a store full of bad guys, including Damien. I'm running on instinct, and one of the lessons Damein drilled into my head during our training sessions was: if you have a weapon, don't lose your weapon. If someone is dumb enough to lose their weapon, take it, and now you have two.

That was a memorable sparring session. That night, he got my knife from me and, instead of my panties being cut off, he sliced one of my favorite bras right off my chest, making my nipples hard when he lay the cool side of the knife on them before his hot mouth warmed them up.

Of course, I got a bag full of new panties, bras, and lingerie in his favorite style the next morning to make up for it, but I learned quite a few lessons *that* night.

Damien can be generous, I'm way more into knife play than I'd ever thought I'd be, and if someone loses their weapon, it's not gonna be me.

That's why, as the white-haired weirdo tries desperately to get out from where I pinned him, I throw open the car door and dive. I saw his gun fall out of his hand a second before impact. It had to have skittered among the glass that's everywhere, but I could give a shit if I get cut off now.

I need that gun.

Where's that gun?

Yes!

I don't even know if it's his. I'm sure the other two guys were armed, so it could be one of theirs. Doesn't matter. I grab the gun, hope like hell it's loaded, then start shooting wildly.

The Black man? Two bullets, and one of them gets him in the head. The bald guy? He's groaning, but I shoot two in his chest, and he stops. All that's left is the guy against the wall. He's cursing at me, but I'm not listening. I don't hear anything but the noise in my head, and it's saying: *Kill.*

And that's exactly what I do.

It's not pretty, but it's effective. I get him in the

cheek and the forehead, blood staining his white hair red, as his body stays up against the wall, thanks to the car.

I whirl around, looking for another target. It was hard to tell how many people were in here when we drove by before so maybe I got them all.

I better have gotten them all.

"Savannah... oh, sweet Savannah.... Ragna mia, cara mia, my love..."

It takes a second for the noise to quiet enough for me to realize that someone—that my *husband*—is talking to me.

His face is bloody and beaten, eyes so swollen I'm not sure he saw any of what just happened, but when he says my name, it's like a prayer on his lips. "Savannah... *my* Savannah."

To hear this man say that? I'm not Georgia. I wasn't sure I'd always be Savannah. But maybe... maybe I will.

He's alive. The realization that he is, that he survived, hits me a second later.

"Damien!"

I never dropped the stiletto. With the dead man's gun in my right hand, I held onto the knife in my left. I swap them back now, then, shaky and surprisingly exhilarated, I stumble over to where Damien is tied to the chair.

I have every intention of cutting him free from his bonds, but he stops me with a shake of his head.

"Vin," he rasps out now, nowhere near as musical as when he said my name. "Check on Vin first."

"Where is he?" I ask.

With his hands trapped to the armrests, he can't point. And though I'm sure it hurts his head, he nods toward the other wall, where the corner meets the glass door that is, surprisingly, still standing despite the rest of the windows being a glittery mess on the floor.

Vin is lying motionless on the floor. He's not bloody, though, and the glass only covers one side of him. I move toward him, still clutching my knife, and almost cry when I see his chest.

He has one shot in the shoulder. The other is lower, mid-chest. He got shot in the back, but his shirt looks like they managed to go clean through. Bloodstains blossom in his center, but he's breathing at least.

For now.

I start to get up, prepared to tell Damien what state his cousin is in. However, before I say a word, someone climbs out of the shadows in the corner opposite of where I am.

"Dr. Liz?"

She's clutching her own shoulder, blood leaking through the gaps of her fingers. Her hair is a mess, and when she shakes it, it glitters with glass.

"I'm a doctor. I can check him."

How did I miss her? I guess it makes sense. She was hiding in the corner, ducking low, nursing her shoulder. She must've been another victim, hoping for help, and now that I've provided it, she can use her training to check out Vin.

Only...

"Dr. Liz? What are you doing here?"

Damien looks over at the disheveled doctor. If looks could kill, she'd already be six feet under, but since I still haven't cut the rope tying him to the chair, staring at her is about all he can do.

"Don't you know, wife? She sold me out."

Sold him out?

"What?" I look at the three corpses I left in my wake. "These guys? What the fuck for? Why would you want Damien dead?"

"I didn't!" she explodes. "I wanted you dead!"

Oh. "*Why?*"

Damien snorts. Not because the injured doctor seems to have lost her mind, but because he's often pointed out how I ask many questions and rarely answer any myself.

But, seriously, *why?*

"Because I wanted to be Damien's wife!"

Oh. Well. That doesn't really explain things, but I guess it makes a little sense.

"For years I did whatever I could to make him happy!" she says, moving gingerly toward me. "I worked in that shitty clinic! I dealt with assholes and pervs and losers all day long! I didn't hire anyone else so that *I* could be the doctor, and just when I thought he might finally want to settle down, he marries *you*!"

"Well... if it makes you feel any better, he had to blackmail me into it."

Her eyes bulge. "You would be lucky to have a man like him!"

I shrug, fucking with her now. Whatever she did—and I'm sure Damien will tell me—she didn't accomplish what she set out to do. Like me, she failed. I'm not dead, and neither is my husband.

But Liz...

"Eh. He's alright."

Just like I figured, that was enough to push the doctor over the edge. Screaming at me, she runs right at me, dodging the bodies and the car until she's less than a foot away from me. Her hands are in front of her despite her injury, nails crooked as though she's going to claw my eyes out.

Bad move, Lizzie. You gave me something to latch on to.

Ducking my own shoulder, I grip her right arm, twist it, take a moment to revel in the renewed howl that tears out of her throat, then use her momentum against her. She flips over my head, landing on a pile of glass that jabs right into her back.

Once she's down, I straddle her, using my weight in a way that she's not getting up anytime soon.

Then, because I'm not done yet, I say, "One last question, Dr. Liz. When we got to the clinic, it was closed. You knew we were coming with my cat. Is this why you shut down? To threaten my husband? To threaten *me*? To betray the Dragonflies?"

Over my head, I heard Damien chuckle darkly.

After all, we both know what it means when you betray the Dragonflies.

Her eyes are still wild as she sneers at me. "Fuck your cat. I hope the sedative I sent home with that idiot ballerina was enough to put him to sleep forever, you bitch."

Wow. I'm such an idiot. I didn't even realize that she lied to Gen and gave her something to hurt Orion until right this very second. I guess, in my confusion, they were two different issues. My cat was unconscious and Damien was missing. Just two shitty circumstances...

But no. She used Genevieve. She risked my cat's life. I don't even know if he's made it, or if Gen was able to get to the vet or not... but it doesn't matter.

Her fate was sealed when she used my cat against me. Oh, and when she plotted against my husband...

Smiling down at Liz, I lift my hand—and the stiletto—up high before bringing it down in her side. Poetic justice and all that, I make sure it's just about the same spot as where this woman stitched up Damien months ago.

She howls, and I pull out the knife, making sure to twist it.

"That's for Damien," I tell her. "And this? This is for Orion. Say 'hi' to Ricky for me."

Her lips part, as though knowing exactly what to expect. She was at the dinner. She knows what's coming.

And I don't disappoint.

One fluid slice. The stiletto is even sharper than it was the night Damien cut Ricky's throat. With Liz on her back beneath me, in too much pain from her gunshot wound and the fresh stab, she does nothing to stop me from swinging the knife.

Only once I see the bloody smile in her throat do I get up, then kick her for good measure. Then, hoisting the red-slicked stiletto up, I make sure my husband can see it.

"Damien?"

"Yes, amore?"

I twist the blade, showing it off. "I love you."

His icy blue eyes seem to gleam through the shadows. "I know."

Revenge List

EPILOGUE

SAVANNAH

Orion is curled up on Damien's lap, purring like there's no tomorrow.

If that bitch doctor had it her way, there wouldn't have been. Not for my cat—and not for my husband, either.

The moment he had his family behind the gates that ward off our home, the first thing he did was take my chin between his hands and tell me that I have nothing to regret. I took my first life that night, followed by a few more, and he seemed so sure that I'd spiral when I realized that I'd finally done it. I'd finally killed someone.

I surprised him by patting his cheeks, telling my husband that he's adorable.

Killing Liz? I've never felt so fucking free. I spent so

long working toward revenge, and it turns out the thing that quieted those nagging whispers in my mind is *vengeance*.

I avenged Damien. He might've been sitting right there, bloody yet proud, but instead of letting Winter and his men hurt him anymore, I did what I had to. And then, when Liz came at me, I did what I wanted to.

For Orion. For Damien.

For *me*.

Georgia is dead. She's gone. The woman I was before Damien's men picked my shop to pass their bills through before he had an iron-tight hold on the cops, on the banks, on the judges... I don't even think I know how to be her.

But Savannah Montgomery— no. Savannah *Libellula*... that fateful evening in the alley, I was sure my new life was over. But then I agreed to marry this man —yeah, it was torture, convinced he could never love me—and some way, somehow, I've been born again.

I'm happy. And maybe I'm just as insane as I once accused Damien of being, but when he was so sure that I'd crumble with all that blood on my hands, I laughed—and he gave me that crooked half-smile of his that I couldn't stop myself from falling for.

That was two weeks ago. I expected him to be a little more gentle with me, but I should've known better. As soon as we got the all-clear from Springfield Med—since the clinic is obviously out of commission for now—that Vin was going to be in a sling for a while, but other than that just fine, Damien told Genevieve to watch over Orion, then led me right to the basement.

Why? Because even with one eye swollen shut and his body tied to a chair, he noted that the way I flipped Liz after she ran at me wasn't as clean as he would've liked. Doesn't matter that I got her down and slit her throat. Oh, no. If she'd managed to knock me over instead, maybe the doc could've taken me out, and that wouldn't have been acceptable to him.

I smile to remember that training session now, especially considering it ended with Damien on his back. So what if he was achy and bruised from being worked over by Winter and his guys. He managed to act like it didn't hurt after I stuck him with his knife. Enticing me to ride him... he'd ignore the pain for some pleasure any day.

That's my husband. God knows why I love this overprotective, controlling man, but fuck it, I totally *do*.

Maybe it's because he's stroking Orion's fur with one hand, playing with a lock of my hair with the other. My cat loves him, and though I was terrified that the sedative Liz tricked Genevieve into giving Orion would have hurt my baby, it didn't do any lasting damage to him. He's been spoiled with treats since we got him home from the vet, the same way Damien's cook has been serving Vin's favorite meals for the household since he was released from the hospital.

Damien insisted. When his staff tried to focus their

attention on him, he scoffed and said a shiner was nothing. Vin had a hole in his shoulder, plus one in his upper chest. He got lucky. He just barely missed his lung being hit, and I'm just glad I didn't accidentally run him over when I bashed into the window.

We have our own truce now, me and Vin. I don't know if he'll ever forgive me for stabbing his cousin, but he's magnanimously decided to overlook it since I did *save* Damien. He's also very pissed that Liz was the one who betrayed the Dragonflies, and if I hadn't already killed her, Vin would've made her pay no matter how much he wanted to bang her.

There's only one of us in the household who is struggling to get over what happened. Poor Gen's spent nearly all of her time on the third floor lately. We can always tell when she's dancing because the music filters down to our level, but like Damien, I've learned to tune it out when we're watching TV together.

Like now.

I don't draw my husband's attention to the fact that the music's been playing since we settled down in the den after we ate dinner. At first, I was concerned that his sister could spend hours upon hours in her studio, but Damien assured me that was usual for Genevieve. To be as good a dancer as she is, she needs to practice anywhere between four to five hours a day, especially when she has a performance she's preparing for.

Only... there's none on her schedule currently. She's not dancing because she's practicing, she's dancing because—like me—she needs to take her mind off of things. I used to do that by stalking Damien; now I distract myself *with* him. Having someone she trusted betray her... like her older brother, she isn't taking it so well.

She'll be okay. She's only twenty-five, and I remember how innocent and naive I was back then. Because Damien coddles her, she's even *worse* than I was. One day, he'll have to realize that his baby sister needs to grow up, and after her first taste of what it's like to really be involved with an organized crime syndicate, I wouldn't be surprised if that's what she's working through upstairs now.

I'll let her. And when the time comes that Damien will have to let her be an adult, I'll be there for him, too.

For the moment, I just enjoy this peaceful evening with my husband as he loops a stray curl of mine around his finger.

Last week, I decided to dye my hair again at his urging. I understand why he's so concerned. One of Winter's men got away. I thought I got them all, but I was wrong. So, depending on just what information Liz gave that crew, chances are he saw a woman behind the wheel and figured I was Damien's wife. If he didn't, the most he could've seen was my determined face and my head of black hair.

I can't do anything about my face except change the way I've been doing my make-up just like how I did when I went from Georgia to Savannah. My hair, though? It was a pain in the ass to strip out the black dye, but after Damien brought me to a local hairdresser to color my hair, I decided to go back to my old sandy-color shade again.

Damien loved the black hair that was so similar to his, but once he could see what I used to look like? I haven't been able to keep him away from my hair.

And that's not all...

When we're in a communal part of the house, Damien is careful to keep all of our touches G-rated out of respect for Genevieve and her promise that, if she catches either of us naked together again, she might have to wash her eyes out with bleach. I don't blame her. Damien's dick might be one of my new favorite things, but I can't imagine his sister getting an eyeful of it. But because of that, he's gotten used to stroking my hair or pulling me onto his lap so that she can't see the way that I affect my husband.

Over the last few days, though, he's found another part of me he can't keep his hands off of it...

"How are you healing?" he murmurs, freeing my curl before dropping his thumb to the back of my bicep.

I thought he was worried about the dragonfly inked on my forearm getting infected. That's nothing compared to his concern about the four leaves tattooed there.

I think it's because they're not as common among

his Family. Every member of the Dragonflies has a similar tattoo to the beautiful one that wraps around Damien's forearm, but only five living enforcers have the tell-tale leaf tattoo on the back of their bicep.

Well, six now that my husband hired me on...

"I'm fine, Damien. What about you?" Turning into him, I lay my hand on his heart—and the bruise that's a mottled shade of green, yellow, and purple instead of the deep purple-y red it was last week. "Feeling okay?"

Still stroking my most recent tattoos, he shifts in his seat, turning so he can nuzzle the point where my shoulder meets my neck. Orion yowls as the lap he was sitting on shrinks, but since that means my husband can sidle me closer so that he can kiss my throat, I don't mind half as much as our cat does.

"You tell me, cara mia. I was well enough to have you sitting on my face earlier, bracing yourself with your hand in that same spot."

"I checked with you then," I remind him.

"That you did. And with your pussy in my mouth, I'd let you stab me again before I'd give you any reason to stop me from eating out my wife."

I arch my neck, giving him better access to it. "If I stabbed you, you'd probably fuck me with the blade still inside of you."

"And you'd like it, too, wouldn't you, ragna mia?"

Know what? I would, but since I'd never risk this man again... "Sorry, but I'm out of the 'killing Damien Libellula' business."

"No, you're in the 'killing *for* him' business," he breathes against my neck. "And I *love* that. What better enforcer and protector than the woman who owns this body? Owns my soul? Ti amo, amore." He presses a kiss to my skin. "Sempre."

"I love you, too," I say, my voice shaky as I shiver. It didn't take long for my husband to realize that my neck is a big erogenous zone for me, and even before he starts to lift me up so that I'm sitting on his lap where Orion was before, I'm wondering how bad would it really be if I got caught fucking my husband in the den.

Vin's supposed to be resting. Genevieve's music is still playing.

And Damien's erection is pushing against my ass as I get cozy on his lap.

It wouldn't take much. I could wiggle down my pants, he could unzip his, I grab his cock, and I can have him inside of me in no time. A quickie might be enough to take the edge off, and since Damien is already dropping his hand to stroke my pussy through my leggings instead of paying attention to my enforcer leaves, I don't think I'll have to work hard to convince him it'll be worth it.

And that's when I hear someone clear their throat, and it's so careful, I know for sure it's not Vin.

One of the staff, maybe?

I look over Damien's head. At the same time, he turns just enough to see who's standing in the doorway.

It's Christopher.

I'm being cockblocked by Christopher.

Damn it.

The frustrated scowl on Damien's face echoes the way I feel right about now as I plop myself down on the seat next to him as if I wasn't two seconds away from riding him here out in the open.

I've only met Gen's friend and Damien's assistant a few times, but they've both spoken highly of him. Unlike Vin, he doesn't know the true way that his boss and I met so he's always been friendly enough to me— until he caught the first glimpse of my leaves and, suddenly, he's a lot more careful around me.

Damien warned me that that would happen. It's one of the reasons that Vin hides his leaves from anyone who's not part of Damien's inner circle. Dragonfly enforcers have a rep in Springfield, and if it's anything like the one that's followed Kieran Alfieri even after his death, I can only imagine what the other Dragonflies think of me.

Enforcers only get their leaves when they make a kill that benefits the Family. I went from being introduced as Damien's 'shy' wife to showing up with *four* leaves. Three for each of the rival gangsters I shot and killed, plus the fourth that represented the ruthless way I slit Liz's throat for betraying Damien.

And while my arm might not be as big as, say, Vin's, I've got two of them, plus an entire fucking spine now. The only one allowed to kill this man is me, and since

—surprise, surprise—I love him too much to see him dead now, I'll target any soul who thinks they can take him down.

Maybe he was right. Maybe I am his black widow. His *spider*.

But I'm *his*, and that's all that matters to me.

He likes Christopher. He's fond of his personal assistant, so though my stiletto is never out of *my* reach now, I leave it where it is as I give him a smile.

Damien's not feeling as forgiving when it comes to the interruption. "Christopher. What are you doing here?"

His Adam's apple bobs as he swallows nervously. "It's about Gen, boss."

"Genevieve?" Damien waves his hand flippantly toward the ceiling. "She's upstairs, dancing. If you want to see her, go on up. But I'd call her first if I were you. You know how angry she gets when anyone interrupts her practice."

The way Christopher pales tells me that he's probably had a run-in or two with Genevieve when she's been distracted. I haven't seen her lose her temper myself, though I've heard more than a few stories from Damien about her threatening to kick him out of her studio.

I've seen the muscles on her dancer's legs. She could do it easily, I'd bet.

But then his gaze flickers from Damien to me and back, chewing on his bottom lip, and I know that, whatever he's about to say to Damien, none of us is going to like it.

"She's, um, she's not up there, boss."

Damien's cheeks hollow. "What do you mean? I hear the music."

"I know. But, I promise you, she's not up there."

One look. He gives the younger man one look, then rises up to his feet. I expect him to gesture for me to stay where I am since this involves his sister—but then he holds out his hand to help me up.

I take it, and together we head for the stairs that lead to the third floor, Christopher trailing anxiously behind us.

The studio door's locked. That's not unusual. To keep others from distracting her during her rehearsals, Genevieve has a habit of locking the door.

Damien knocks. He waits a beat for her answer, then knocks again *louder* when he doesn't get one. When there's still no answer, he doesn't knock.

With his bare foot, he kicks in the door to her studio.

Like the gym, Gen's studio is covered in mirrors. These are wall-to-wall, and all we see reflected in their depths are the three of us.

The room is otherwise empty. Her music is playing from the speakers, but there is no Genevieve.

Damien's attention snaps to every corner of the studio. When he has to admit that she's not there, he storms to the next door. Her bathroom.

No.

Her bedroom.

Nothing.

Her walk-in closet.

Except for a pale pink leotard tossed haphazardly in the middle of the space, it looks untouched.

There's no sign of Genevieve *anywhere*.

He whirls on Christopher. The lanky man twitches, and I feel sorry for him. Damien made it clear from the beginning of our relationship that his sister would always come first. Something tells me that Christopher's unexpected arrival is his way of trying to protect Gen, and it's taking every last nerve he has to confront Damien to do so.

But if he goes from suave, sophisticated Damien to the brutal Dragonfly leader in front of Christopher, I'm sure he'll regret it.

So, instead of letting him, I lay my hand on his arm. I tell myself I won't be offended if he shakes me off, but the opposite happens.

Damien keeps the connection. His gaze slides my way, and though I can see the matching fury simmering in his normally icy blue eyes, he gives me a reassuring nod.

Then, blowing a calming breath out through his nose, he turns back to Christopher. "You're right. Gen's not here. So, tell me, Christopher. Where is she?"

Christopher gulps. "That's why I had to come here today. Why I had to tell you that she's been turning the music on and sneaking out through her window. Because Gen... she's *gone,* and I can't find her."

And it's a testament to how much Damien loves me that, when he goes eerily quiet upon hearing the news and I wrap my hands around his middle, he doesn't push me away. He lets me hug him—and my embrace might be the one thing that saves Christopher's life when he confesses that he's known about Genevieve sneaking out to see a guy this past month... and he never told Damien.

Because that guy? He belongs to the Sinners Syndicate—and he's missing, too.

DAMIEN
THE DRAGONFLY

Dragonfly

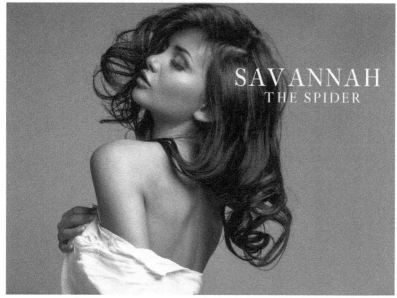

SAVANNAH
THE SPIDER

AUTHOR'S NOTE

Thanks for reading *Dragonfly*!

I had a lot of fun taking a trip over to the East End of Springfield, seeing how the other side lives. Ever since the debonair gangster walked into the room to talk to Ava after she was abducted by a Sinner turned Dragonfly, I've wanted to get into his head. I also loved the idea of a heroine who went through something traumatic, decided she would no longer give any fucks, and ended up with a new family, a new *purpose*, and a happily-ever-after that's just perfect for these two.

This won't be the last you see of them, though. Because the next book in this series? It gives Genevieve a chance to step out from beneath her brother's stifling shadow, and also brings readers back to the West End where we find out more about her artist friend...

If you purchase a physical copy of this book—paperback, discreet paperback, or hardcover—send me your name and mailing address via email (carin@carinhart.com) and I'll mail you a free bookmark and a signed bookplate!

Thanks again, and keep reading for more information about Cross and Genevieve's book!

xoxo,
Carin

PRE-ORDER NOW

IF SHE'LL BE HIS MUSE, HE'LL BE HER SAVIOR...

A modern day retelling of *West Side Story* and *Romeo & Juliet,* what happens when two members of rival syndicates have a chance meeting and sparks fly? Well, if you're tattoo artist Cross and his new muse, Genevieve, you try to stay away from each other — and when that doesn't work, you hope love will be enough to overcome tragedy... and betrayal.

---

*This is the fourth book in the **Deal with the Devil** series. It tells the story of Genevieve Libellula, the coddled mafia princess, and Carlos "Cross" da Silva, the Sinner artist who has spent his whole life searching for his muse...

KEEP IN TOUCH

Stay tuned for what's coming up next! Follow me at any of these places—or sign up for my newsletter—for news, promotions, upcoming releases, and more:

CarinHart.com
Carin's Newsletter
Carin's Signed Book Store

facebook.com/carinhartbooks
amazon.com/author/carinhart
instagram.com/carinhartbooks

ALSO BY CARIN HART